Why on Earth would someone like Tyra Grimes want to come here?

I'd gotten Paradise the attention it supposedly wanted. But now that it had it, the town didn't really like the price of fame.

So I slunk on back to my laundromat, kept on cleaning and washing, even cleaning up the stockroom.

Truth be told, I was waiting.

Tyra's announcement felt like a big, fat, dark storm about to break wide open and suck up all of us—my customers, me, and everyone else in town—spinning us around until we were dizzy and confused before spitting us out back to Earth.

I was waiting for the storm to hit. But there were no provisions to take in, no way to protect people I knew and loved. So I just waited, hoping I was wrong, hoping the storm wouldn't come at all.

But of course it would. It had to.

DEATH
OF A
DOMESTIC
DIVA

A TOADFERN MYSTERY

SHARON SHORT

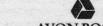

AVON BOOKS
An Imprint of HarperCollinsPublishers

This is a work of fiction. Names, characters, places, and incidents are products of the author's imagination or are used fictitiously and are not to be construed as real. Any resemblance to actual events, locales, organizations, or persons, living or dead, is entirely coincidental.

AVON BOOKS
An Imprint of HarperCollins*Publishers*
10 East 53rd Street
New York, New York 10022-5299

Copyright © 2003 by Sharon Short
ISBN: 0-06-053795-7
www.avonmystery.com

First Avon Books paperback printing: August 2003

Avon Trademark Reg. U.S. Pat. Off. and in Other Countries, Marca Registrada, Hecho en U.S.A.
HarperCollins® is a registered trademark of HarperCollins Publishers Inc.

Printed in the U.S.A.

10 9 8 7 6 5 4 3 2 1

To Gwenie, who likes to say,
"you gotta laugh sometimes, ma."

Acknowledgments

No book is ever created without the support of others, and I am particularly indebted to the following people. Any errors are mine alone.

- Judy DaPolito—friend and writer, who read nearly every draft, provided great feedback, and kept telling me: "you can do this."

- Joe Niehaus—writer and Kettering Police Department Sergeant, who provided guidance on the nuts and bolts of police procedure.

- Bittersweet Farms and its Executive Director, Charles R. Flowers, who so graciously hosted me on a visit to its residential program in northwest Ohio for persons with autism.

- William M. Klykylo, M.D., Wright State University School of Medicine, Professor, Department of Psychiatry.

- Authors and experts in stain removal whose web sites and books provided a wonderful education: Linda Cobb, Jean Cooper, Don Aslett, Heloise, and the Iowa State University Extension.

- David, Katherine and Gwendolyn—the family team of my dreams—and of my daily life. Thank you.

DEATH
OF A
DOMESTIC

Time moves differently in a laundromat.

How differently depends on the person.

For Becky Gettlehorn, who stood in the corner folding clothes for a family of seven, I suspected it moved slower. Sure, she had two of her little ones with her, but the older three were in school on this glorious April day in Paradise, Ohio. Four-year-old Haley was busily coloring under the folding table, while three-year-old Tommy was at the front of my laundromat getting his hair trimmed by my cousin Billy. Becky had a peaceful, almost dreamy look on her face, as if the rhythm of folding countless tiny T-shirts and towels and jeans and her husband's Masonville State Prison guard uniforms and just the occasional blouse was somehow soothing—a welcome change from, say, fixing macaroni and cheese for seven in the tiny kitchen of the Gettlehorn bungalow on Elm Street.

For my other Monday morning regular—the widow Beavy—time seemed to move frantically. Once upon a time, Mrs. Eugene Beavy had as many children as Becky, plus one, and I reckon that back then—when my laundromat was still owned by my aunt and uncle—she was a lot more like Becky. But time, besides moving differently in a laundromat, also has a way of taking its toll. Now, Mrs. Beavy had one load, maybe two, every week, but she always seemed overwhelmed by them, even though she did only her outer clothes, as she called them, at my laundromat. Once she confided to me that she did her undies at home in her kitchen sink, because, as she said, she didn't want the whole damned town of Paradise gawking at her panties and bras and extra-support stockings. I've long ago given up on pointing out to her that the whole damned town of Paradise, even with its tiny population of 2,617, could not fit in my laundromat, and even if it could, its citizens would hardly be interested in observing Mrs. Beavy launder her undies.

For me, laundromat time moves as normal time. I'm Josie Toadfern, owner of Toadfern's Laundromat, the only laundromat in Paradise, Ohio. I'm a stain expert—self-taught and proud of it. Best stain expert in all of Mason County. Maybe in all of Ohio. Maybe even in all of the United States.

And on that fine spring day about four weeks ago—before trouble came to Paradise—I was using that expertise to finish up the last of Lewis Rothchild's white dress shirts. By the clock that hangs on the wall behind my front counter, it was 1:45. Hazel Rothchild would be in at precisely 2:10 P.M. to pick up her husband's shirts. She was always on time and always fussy about the shirts. Lewis was the third-generation owner of Rothchild's Funeral Parlor. He was also heavy and sweated a lot, and I did what I could about his shirts (pretreating with a mix of equal parts water, cheap dishwashing soap, and ammonia usually worked). Still, Hazel always found something to complain about, saying that he had to look his best for his clients. And I always resisted pointing out that actually, he had to look his best for his clients' *fami-*

lies, his clients being, after all, dead. (A good business-woman must know when to bite her tongue.)

Hazel would command all my time once she arrived, so I decided to check on my other customers now. I trotted over to Mrs. Beavy, who was fiddling with the cap on her bottle of detergent.

I peered at her clothes whirring around in the washer. "You're on the spin cycle," I said, gently taking the bottle of detergent from her. I put the detergent on the folding table and picked up the bottle of softener.

"Oh. That means it's time for the cream rinse, right?"

"Fabric softener," I corrected kindly, although I could understand her confusion, given that my ever-down-on-his-luck cousin Billy was demonstrating his Cut-N-Suck haircutting vacuum attachment by the big window that fronts my laundromat. His hope was that Paradisites would come in for his free demos, and then buy their very own six-payments-of-$5.95-per-month Cut-N-Suck hair-clipping vacuum attachment, which was supposed to allow the user to clip hair while the trimmings got sucked into the vacuum.

"I'm not going to get hair in my blouses, am I?" Mrs. Beavy asked nervously, pointing toward Billy.

"No, no, not at all," I said, measuring fabric softener into the dispenser on top of the washer.

"Because Cherry warned me I would, and I don't want hairy blouses." She added in a whisper, "Makes me glad I do my undies at home. Because I surely don't want hairy panties."

I thumped the bottle of softener back down on the folding table. Mrs. Beavy jumped, and I immediately felt sorry. I smiled at her, glancing over at the TV, mounted on a rack just to the right of the entry door, positioned so that anyone in the laundromat could see it. "It's about time for your favorite show. You want me to turn it on for you?"

She smiled back at me, instantly soothed. Her favorite show was, of course, the Tyra Grimes Home Show. Everyone in America loved, or at least knew about, Tyra Grimes—a home decorating and lifestyle expert with a cable TV show filmed right in New York. She had books and videos, plus a company that made dishtowels and bath towels and sheets and other stuff for the home—all very stylish, of course.

On the way to the TV, I took a detour by Becky, chatted for a few seconds about how fast her kids were growing, and suggested she help herself to my supply shelf for a dab of plain glycerin to treat the mustard spot on Haley's new sun dress. Then I went on over to my cousin Billy.

"Mrs. Beavy is concerned about hairy panties," I said, loudly, over the whir of his canister vacuum.

Billy frowned at me as he shut off his vacuum. "Shush, Josie," he said in a hush-hush voice. Then he patted little Tommy Gettlehorn on the head.

"You look great, son!" he pronounced, switching to the booming voice he'd once used in the pulpit at the Second Reformed Church of the Holy Reformation—before he'd taken to drinking from depression over his wife running off with a quieter parishioner. Billy had lost his job after having been found one too many times with a bottle of wine in his desk in the office of a church that used sanctified grape juice at communion.

"Doesn't he look great, Josie?" Billy boomed.

I resisted a knee-jerk "Amen!" (I am a demure Methodist) and said instead, "Yes. You look great, Tommy." And in truth, his burr hair cut was nicer than I would have expected the Cut-N-Suck—or Billy—to be able to produce.

Tommy looked up at us and smiled the best he could, given that he was frantically rubbing little hair bits away from his nose. He sneezed, wiped his nose on his shirt sleeve—another laundry item for his poor mama—then ran off, zipping around washers and dryers and folding tables, hollering, "Mama, mama, look at me! Josie says I look great!"

Billy gave a little-boy grin, an expression at odds with his beefy, square-jawed face, his short, stocky build, and his new haircut—a black burr as thick as a bush, on account of his first Cut-N-Suck demo having been on himself. The style made him look like an escapee of some kind.

Billy leaned toward me and whispered, "I think Becky Gettlehorn is really interested in buying a Cut-N-Suck."

I frowned at Billy and whispered back, "Even at $5.95 a month, she can't afford it."

"But it comes with free electric tweezers—and a rotary-action nose-hair trimmer!"

I folded my arms. "Billy."

He sighed. "Demos and sales have really fallen off ever since last week when you-know-who started her little protest. She's at it again." He jerked a thumb at my front window.

I have, for advertising purposes, painted on my front windowpane a much-larger-than-life toad atop a lily pad with a cartoon-like bubble coming out of its mouth with the words, "Toadfern's Laundromat. Always a leap ahead of dirt!" (A good businesswoman must know when to use marketing.)

To see what Billy meant, I had to kneel down and gaze out below the bottom fringe of the lily pad. I then saw short stubby legs in stiletto heels trekking back and forth in front of my window. The legs belonged to Cherry Feinster, owner of Cherry's Chat and Curl, the only hair salon in Paradise, which happens to be next door to my laundromat. I stood up again.

Besides attending to customers, Cherry had been marching with a sign protesting Billy's demos. I'd complained to the chief of the Paradise Police, John Worthy, but he'd said that even though I was correct, ours was a free-market economy; Cherry also had her right to free speech. So long as she didn't physically stop anyone from coming into my laundromat, there wasn't much I could do about her protest—other than threatening to stop doing the towels from her shop . . . but I needed the business.

"Mrs. Beavy says Cherry's telling people they'll get hair in their laundry if they come in here, Billy," I whispered. "And I think she may be right." I stared pointedly down at the burst of telltale little black Gettlehorn hair clippings on my floor, a sight that did not please me. I keep my laundromat spotless. People do not like to wash their undies—or other garments—in a grimy laundry.

Billy shrugged, then whispered, "I had a little trouble with the attachment earlier. It's this doggoned old vacuum cleaner of mine. Not the Cut-N-Suck—that works great."

"Look, get this cleaned up. I need to turn on the ceiling fans because it's starting to get hot, and the last thing I need is hair blowing around the place to prove Cherry right. You can use my vacuum cleaner from the storeroom—but only through the end of the week. After Friday, you need to find a different way to give demos. Maybe door to door."

He nodded eagerly. "Yeah! I should have my car fixed by then. Thanks, Josie!"

He pulled me to him and gave me a big hug and kiss. I wiped my cheek off as soon as he released me. Billy's a wet kisser. "And lay off on demos for the next half hour," I added. "The *Tyra Grimes Home Show* is coming on and my customers want to watch it."

"Sure, Josie," Billy said. "You're the greatest." And he trotted off to the back room to get my vacuum cleaner.

The greatest? I wondered, looking at Billy's old canister vacuum. Or just a sucker? Besides letting him use my laundromat space to launch his new career as a Cut-N-Suck distributor, I'd been renting him the spare apartment next to mine on the second floor over my laundromat. In two months, I'd yet to collect any actual rent. Despite his zeal as a salesman, Cut-N-Suck sales were slow, Billy said.

I moved back to my counter, picked up the remote, pointed it at the TV, flicked it on, and found the right channel.

The background music to the *Tyra Grimes Home Show* cued—a soft, dreamy melody. Then there was Tyra Grimes herself, her smiling face filling the screen, beaming her enthusiasm for all things elegant and beautiful all over my laundromat.

And then time shifted again in my laundromat. It seemed to fold in on itself, then stop, as Mrs. Beavy and Becky and even her two little ones and I all stared up at Tyra. We were, like a lot of people across America, hooked on Tyra Grimes and her show. There was just something so seductive about the idea that your life would somehow get better, if only you could fluff your pillows just right, or maybe make cute window toppers out of old potato sacks, or whip up origami party favors to take to the next church carry-in. And Tyra Grimes— with her perky laugh, a self-sufficient competence that would make even a Marine wince, and her trademark signoff line— "Simply wonderful!"—sold that idea to us day after day, making the mundane minutes that marked our lives seem to stop, to give way to something more . . . well . . . simply wonderful.

Sometimes, I wish I could go back to that moment four weeks ago when the *Tyra Grimes Home Show* made life slow for a little while in my laundromat.

Maybe I'd do things differently. After all, some folks say it's because of me that trouble came to Paradise.

In the form of murder.

Two murders, to be exact.

But I think folks saying that everything that happened is all my fault is mighty unfair—not to mention ungrateful.

Because me—well, I was just trying to help.

* * *

Ten minutes later, time started moving again, because two things happened at once.

The Tyra Grimes Home Show went to a commercial break. And the bell over my front door chimed.

I startled, breaking from my Tyra-inspired reverie (today's topic being napkin folds) and automatically launched into the usual speech I give Hazel Rothchild every week: "I pretreated Lewis's collars with an emulsion perfect for ring-around-the-collar . . ." (Said "emulsion" was cheap shampoo—but it's what really works, and a good business-woman knows her customers' preferences. Hazel would prefer to hear I use an emulsion.)

And then I stopped, for Hazel was not in my laundromat. Instead, in had trooped Lewis Rothchild, followed by Elroy Magruder and Cherry Feinster.

I retreated behind my counter.

Lewis was a portly man who always wore suspenders and a tie, no matter the occasion or the weather. He always carried hankies, too (which, thankfully, Hazel chose to hand-wash for him) and he pulled one out now to mop his brow.

Elroy joined Lewis at the counter, standing to his left. Elroy was a skinny, nervous man with eyes too big for his narrow little face and too waif-child sad for a man in his sixties. He stared up at Lewis now. Cherry stood to Lewis's right, but she didn't seem to be paying attention to any of us. She was staring pointedly at Billy's Cut-N-Suck. Her head was turned so that all I could see of her face was her pointy nose and half of her downturned red-lipsticked lips—and lots and lots of her frothy hair. Cherry's do—which is dyed to match her name and accounts for at least three inches of her five-foot-three stature—makes Dolly Parton look like a big hair wanna-be.

This unlikely trio made me nervous. I decided to get to the

bottom of what was going on, one question at a time. I started with the most obvious.

"Lewis, where's Hazel?" I asked.

"She isn't feeling well—bronchitis," he said shortly. He wiped his brow again, stuffing the hanky back into his pants pocket. "I'm having to run her errands for her."

I was tempted to point out that actually, for once, he was running his errands for himself. But Elroy Magruder saved me from giving in to temptation. "Lewis, I can prove it," he hollered. "This is serious! This calls for an emergency meeting of the Chamber of Commerce . . . a conference with the Mayor . . . letter writing. Something!"

Cherry looked away from the Cut-N-Suck and fixed me with a hard stare. "Elroy's right, Lewis. He showed me the map. Business here is bad enough what with people in town trying to get into areas they don't know anything about. People you think are your friends."

"Look, Cherry," I said, "it's not like you can get a perm or hair coloring out of a vacuum cleaner attachment. Plus competition is good for business, and—"

"Being dropped off the Official State Map of Ohio definitely is not good for business!" Elroy hollered.

I looked at him, stunned.

I have to take a little break to explain that we have very few points of pride here in Paradise. One is our name. My junior high history teacher, Mrs. Oglevee, may she rest in peace, drilled it into our heads how our founding fathers, Northwest Territory settlers in the late 1790s, took a little rest break in the very spot that would become Paradise. Three families got down from the wagons, sat under a big, shady oak, and had a nice picnic lunch—pickled beef tongue on rye, Mrs. Oglevee told me when I pressed for details, although I have my doubts. Then everyone took a look around on that perfect spring day—birds singing, trees leafing out, nice little breeze—and said, let's stay! And they called it Paradise.

What I think is that they all got lost. I can't really explain how you get lost off what had to be one of the only trails going through Ohio at the time, with twelve horses and three wagons and ten kids whining, "Are we there yet?" but I think my theory makes more sense than taking a rest break in a forest about thirty miles south from the only settlement at the time (Masonville). Then I think they decided to make the best of a tough situation, and told the whiny kids and each other that they'd found Paradise, their new home, and everyone decided to believe it, since they happened to hit southern Ohio when the weather is absolutely perfect for three whole weeks.

What they didn't know at the time, of course, is that the perfect three weeks in spring are followed by tornado season. Then a dry spell. Then snowstorms. Then floods, from the melting snow. Then the perfect three weeks again. After a year like that, I think everyone was just too tired to move on—or to rename the little settlement of Paradise.

When I put forth my theory to Mrs. Oglevee, though, she made me stay after school and write one hundred times on the blackboard, "I am proud to be a Paradisite," all the while explaining how I should appreciate the fine name of our town—point of pride one.

Our only other bragging point is that ever since its incorporation back in 1810, Paradise has been on the official map of the State of Ohio.

So now, I stared at Elroy Magruder in dismay. "Did you just say we're no longer on the map?"

"It's true," Cherry said. "Elroy showed me. But he can't get Lewis to take him seriously."

"For pity's sake, what difference does it make?" Lewis hollered. "Josie, just give me my shirts."

I folded my arms. "Not until Elroy gets a chance to tell us what's going on."

Lewis sighed heavily, wiping his brow again. "Fine, fine. Go on, Elroy."

Elroy straightened himself up the best he could, given his lifelong habit of slumping his shoulders. "I got a new set of maps today, to put on display at my station." Elroy owns the only gas station and towing service in Paradise. In this town, with the exception of antique shops (of which we have six), we have just one business of every kind. Small towns are great for monopolies.

"I unfolded one to put up—you know, in case someone comes in asking directions. And that's when I saw it. No more Paradise in Ohio." With that, Elroy pulled a map from his hip pocket. Then he opened it out on my counter. "Look," he whispered, pointing to the general area of Mason County, in south central Ohio.

We looked. Truth be told, there's not much to look at in that part of a map of Ohio. Columbus is to the north, Cincinnati to the west, the Ohio River to the south, and the Appalachian foothills to the east. We aren't bisected by any major highways, so we're just a quiet region of rolling hills, cornfields, and the occasional horse farm.

But we looked to southern Ohio. Then we peered at Mason County. And then we—Cherry and I—gasped as we realized that Elroy was right—Paradise, where it should have been just southwest of the county seat of Masonville, wasn't on the map. Where our little dot had been for nearly 160 years . . . there was nothing. Just a tiny circle bearing the number 26—the state route that cuts through our town.

I looked back up at Lewis. He looked bored. "Fine," he said, "Paradise is not on the map. It's not like we dropped off the face of the earth. Or even of Ohio."

"Look, Lewis, it's fine for you not to care. It's not like there's much of a tourist trade in funerals," I said. "But Elroy, Cherry and I, the antique shops, Sandy's Restaurant—we all rely on some of our business coming from people who are visiting over at Licking Creek Lake." The nearby lake is called that on account of there used to be just Licking Creek, until it got dammed up to make a lake for a state park years ago. People go swimming and camping there. We're the nearest town to Licking Creek Lake. "So how are people supposed to find us if we're not on the map?" I asked.

"She's got a point," Cherry said, apparently forgetting for the moment that she was mad about the Cut-N-Suck. "Any ideas what we can do?"

"We should have an emergency meeting of the Chamber of Commerce! I'm going to personally launch a letter writing campaign—" Elroy started.

"To who? You think our state rep is really going to care? Why don't you leave well enough alone?" Lewis said. "Probably if we'd gotten that mall development, we wouldn't have to worry about silly things like this."

Cherry and I moaned. We knew his comment would rile poor Elroy. And that meant we'd have to hear—again—the story of how, twenty years ago, when some businessmen had come to town to consider buying up land to build a fancy antique mall and turn us into the Antique Capital of the Midwest, it wasn't really Elroy's fault that the project got canceled before it ever really got started. It was a story that might have been forgotten, except that Lewis took every chance to taunt Elroy about how he'd made the businessmen sick and caused Paradise to lose its shot at a bigtime mall. Since Lewis owned most of that still undeveloped land—inherited from his father—he'd probably never let Elroy forget it.

"The tuna salad was fresh that day," Elroy started now, in

this mournful singsong voice. He'd gone over this story so many times, always using the same words. He could have set it to music and called it "The Ballad of the Tainted Tuna."

The short version is that the businessmen, who were staying out at the Red Horse Motel (yes, the only motel in Paradise), decided to come in to town for lunch at Sandy's Restaurant, but Sandy's was closed that day on account of it being Sandy's birthday, for which she always closes, although she's open for Thanksgiving and Christmas. So they went down the street to Elroy's Filling Station and picked up a passel of tuna salad sandwiches and Big Fizz colas. Two days later, the businessmen left town—and the rumor that went around was that they'd been laid up sick from food poisoning before they left.

Poor Elroy Magruder. He'd become such a sad sack that even his wife had left him. Who knows how life would have turned out for the Magruders (or for Paradise) if Elroy hadn't fed those businessmen tainted tuna salad.

Now, I knew Elroy'd keep going on and we'd never get to figure out what to do about not being on the Ohio map, so I said, "Look, Elroy, maybe it wasn't the tuna salad."

That stopped him. He looked at me, his russet eyebrows pushed up near to his hairline. "What? What did you say?"

"Maybe it wasn't the tuna," I said again. I was making stuff up, hoping to get us off this topic and back to the map. "Probably something else altogether. Maybe something on the land they were surveying."

"Like, like what?"

"I don't know. Uh, maybe poison ivy. Or wild mushrooms. Maybe they had some for a snack and that made them sick."

Elroy started crying. "That's the nicest thing anyone's said to me in twenty years." I patted him on the shoulder.

"Can we please get back to the map?" Cherry said.

"Can I please have my shirts now?" Lewis said.

"Can you all please quiet down so I can watch the end of my show?" said Mrs. Beavy.

We all looked over at Mrs. Beavy, who was standing below the TV. I glanced around. Wendy Gettlehorn and her children had already left—and I hadn't even noticed. At that moment, Billy emerged from my storeroom, towing my vacuum cleaner.

But then Mrs. Beavy pointed up to the TV. "See? You all have been yapping so much, it's been hard to hear the show. But here's my favorite part."

We all—even Lewis and Billy—looked up at the television. A commercial for toilet paper ended, giving way to the end of the *Tyra Grimes Home Show*. Tyra appeared, her face, haloed in auburn hair, filling the screen.

"Today we've discussed the wonders of napkin folds— how with just a few minutes of extra effort you too can add a touch of grace to all your meals—whether a sit-down dinner for twenty or a breakfast buffet for one hundred—with how you present your table linens." Never mind that none of us would ever host such an event. We were still entranced with her. "Try these tips in your own home," Tyra beamed. "And let your daily living be . . . simply wonderful!"

Cherry sighed. "Isn't she great."

"The greatest," Mrs. Beavy agreed.

"I learned how to display my pop bottle collection for best decorative effect from her," Elroy said.

I stared at him. Elroy, a Tyra Grimes fan?

Then Billy said, "Hey, Josie, that reminds me, I've been meaning to show you this!"

He started unbuttoning his denim shirt—which made me a mite nervous, because truth be told, I wouldn't put it past him to shave some design into his chest hair to demonstrate the prowess of the Cut-N-Suck—but what he actually showed us was a red T-shirt, with the Tyra Grimes logo—her name in fancy script, with a swirly line below it—emblazoned on the chest.

"Uh, Billy, where'd you get that? Tyra Grimes doesn't put out clothing. Just stuff for the home."

"Ah, that's where you're behind the times," Billy said. "I was at the Red Horse Motel's lounge last night." Somehow, my cousin the Cut-N-Suck distributor and former preacher never minded admitting he liked going to one of Paradise's two bars (not every non-antique industry is a monopoly in Paradise)—and the only one that comes with motel rooms.

"Met a nice little lady, with a pretty little accent, says she's in the area on vacation. She told me how she had a supply of these T-shirts. So I got two. One for me. And one for you! I, uh, have yours up in my apartment."

"Ooh—a signature line of Tyra Grimes clothing," Cherry cooed. Then her eyes narrowed as she peered at Billy. "How is it this woman has Tyra Grimes T-shirts for sale?"

"Said she has special connections to Tyra Grimes's company and it's okay for her to sell them, kind of like a promo. They were expensive, coming out ahead and all, but since you're being so kind, Josie, as to let me stay rent-free, I dipped into my savings money."

What I should have done was get annoyed at Billy for spending money on T-shirts when he claimed he couldn't pay rent.

What I did instead was get an idea.

"I've got it!" I hollered. "We need something fast that'll make everyone else notice Paradise—make the world think of us as important, right? Help get us back on the map? Get people to come here, visit our antique shops, visit the lake, right?"

Everyone—except Lewis, who was staring at Billy—looked at me. I went on, "Well, I'm a stain expert, right? I could go on the *Tyra Grimes Home Show* and share all I know about getting out stains. People won't want stains on their new Tyra Grimes T-shirts, will they? Maybe she could even come here to do the show—an on-location kind of thing. She's done that before at restaurants and stores, so why not at a laundromat? And Tyra is so famous that her coming here to do a show would get Paradise a lot of attention. I'd mention Licking Creek Lake and the antique stores in town. What do you all think?"

There was a silence. A long silence.

And then Cherry started laughing. "Oh, you do beat all," she said, hooting and fanning herself with her hand. "Someone as wonderful and important as Tyra Grimes, wanting you on her show? Why, she probably knows a dozen other stain experts she could ask on. Your plan just won't work, Josie!"

Then she left.

Elroy shook his head sadly. "As wonderful as it would be to have her here, I think Cherry's right. No one important ever comes to Paradise. But maybe if I get a petition going to send to our state rep . . ." Then he left, too.

Mrs. Beavy looked at Billy. "Billy? Will you please help me get this basket out to my truck?"

"Sure, Mrs. Beavy," Billy said. He shot me a sympathetic look, then picked up her basket. They left, too.

Just Lewis and I were still in my laundromat. I sighed. "I'll get your shirts," I said. I didn't even want to know what Lewis thought of my plan.

But suddenly Lewis grabbed my arm, forcing me to turn back and face him. "Don't do it," he said, through clenched teeth. He was pale and shaking. His face was red, his mouth tight, his nostrils flaring—a 9-1-1 emergency waiting to happen. "Don't even think about getting that . . . that woman to come to our town. If she does, I'm warning you, Josie, blood will flow. It'll be on your hands. And that's a stain you'll never get out."

With that, he stormed out the front door, not even taking his shirts.

I rubbed my arm where Lewis had grabbed me. Everyone else was so sure Tyra'd never want to come to Paradise or have me on her show, but Lewis—who I'd never seen so worked up before—was all in a lather at the very thought of me trying to contact Tyra. Strange. Maybe Hazel had fed him one too many Tyra-inspired quiches. Lewis was definitely a steak-and-potatoes guy.

But I wasn't about to let go of my idea for getting on the *Tyra Grimes Home Show* . . . no matter what anyone else said . . . so I told myself to forget about Cherry and Elroy's naysaying and Lewis's weird temper tantrum.

But I wouldn't forget it for long. Not when his prediction of bad things happening if Tyra came to Paradise started coming true—and everyone started blaming me.

2

There are some things that are just plain true about living in a small town, population 2,617.

One is that wherever you go, you see someone you know. And the worse your appearance, the more people you see. Want a minireunion with the junior-high teacher on whom you had a crush? Or with your best customers, or your old flames? Just get real depressed, have an acne breakout, and run out to the Quick Mart for the only fast fix for depression: a mega-sized block of chocolate. You'll meet everyone from your past and present.

Another truth about small town life is that word gets out fast when something new happens. Such news falls into two general categories. If it is Shocking-News-About-a-Tragedy-That-Everyone's-Glad-Didn't-Happen-to-Them, small town folks will generally (after passing the word) pitch in to help to make things better for the tragedy's victim(s).

If the latest rumor instead falls in the category of Shocking-News-About-Someone-in-Town-Acting-Even-

More-Ridiculous-Than-Cousin-Billy-at-the-Red-Horse-on-Friday-Night, the news will spread even faster . . . and everyone will then want to confirm this news with you.

News about my plan to get on the *Tyra Grimes Home Show* fell into the second category. Soon Paradisites—some of whom even had their own washers and dryers—were coming into my laundromat and saying things like, "Hey, Josie, we hear you have some highfalutin idea of going onto the *Tyra Grimes Home Show* to tell how to get lipstick out of collars. Will this be an X-rated show? Ha-ha-ha."

So for the next two days, I hid.

At home, I didn't answer the phone. Or the doorbell. I even refused to go out with my boyfriend, Owen.

At my laundromat, I stayed back in my combo supply room–office. Sat at my desk and caught up on reading my back issues of *Laundromat Today*. Worked on the monthly column I do for the *Paradise Advertiser–Gazette*, "Josie's Stain Busters."

I admit, I was pouting. Because I'd given my all to the people of Paradise, laundrywise. Running a monthly Super Seniors Saturday where I went around to all the shut-ins and gathered up their laundry to do at half price. Building up my stain expertise, so I could give one-on-one laundry consulting to my customers. Writing the monthly column—for free.

I couldn't completely hide—sometimes the coin trays jam on the machines, and sometimes people need change. So I made up an answer for people who made jokes about the complete impossibility of someone like me getting on the *Tyra Grimes Home Show*.

I told them I had connections.

That shut people up, whether they believed me or not.

And it was kind of true, me having connections to Tyra Grimes. I'm best friends with Winnie Porter. She runs the

Mason County Public Library Bookmobile, which comes through Paradise on Wednesdays.

Not that Tyra and Winnie were old buddies, or even knew each other, or had even heard of each other—well, of course, Winnie'd heard of Tyra. Winnie adored Tyra.

But I wasn't exactly lying, either. I knew that if anyone could find a more direct connection to someone famous and popular and important like Tyra Grimes, it would be Winnie Porter. I've seen her find out everything for people, from "what to feed your pet hissing cockroach" to "paper towel crafts for young scouts."

Now, since I'd hatched my plan to get on the *Tyra Grimes Home Show* on a Monday, I had a couple of days to work on my letter to Tyra Grimes before seeing Winnie. By Wednesday morning at 2 A.M., I finally finished the letter.

I went to bed, and got up again at 7 A.M., so I could go meet Winnie at her first bookmobile stop in Paradise—out at Ed Crowley's place on Sweet Potato Ridge Road. She gets there at 8 A.M., which some folks might think is pretty early to have a big red-and-white bus pull into your driveway so you can look over books and magazines, but Ed's a farmer, and by the time Winnie gets to his place he's just finished up with the hogs and cows. Ed's an avid reader, too, so he's always glad to see Winnie.

Winnie's got a few other stops to shut-ins before she pulls up in front of my laundromat at 10 A.M., but I wasn't about to give her this letter and ask her help in a public place like a bookmobile—not after all the ribbing I'd been getting.

So my plan was to get out to Ed Crowley's place before Winnie, then get back to my laundromat in time to open up by 9 A.M. It was going to be tight.

I had a quick bowl of Cap'n Crunch, then pulled on my jeans and one of my business T-shirts with the logo "Toad-fern's Laundromat—always a leap ahead of dirt," and made a

to-go cup of instant coffee, then piled the books I had to return on the front seat of my car, then carefully put my letter to
Tyra Grimes on top of the stack of books. It looked so perfect
there, in its clean white envelope, with nice black letters on
the front: To—Tyra Grimes. I'd left space for Tyra's actual
address, once Winnie had found it for me.

I had to smile, just looking at it.

Then, after three or four tries, I got my ten-year-old Chevy
started, and I pulled out of town, going kind of slow and
looking around at Paradise, still quiet and asleep. I grinned to
myself, feeling a tickle of excitement. I grinned at the lovely
tree-lined streets—named, cleverly, after the trees themselves: Elm and Maple and Birch. I grinned at the pretty
houses—little two-stories, most all bearing porches with
swings.

All is forgiven, dear Paradise, I thought! I was determined to get Tyra Grimes to come here, to get Paradise
some attention, to get us back on the map. It would be a
fresh start for all Paradisites, young and old! And I, Josie
Toadfern, would make it happen! Soon, life in Paradise
would never be the same!

After all, it seemed like nothing could go wrong on such a
beautiful spring day. Bright blue, cloudless sky. Birds
singing. Trees leafing out. Nice little breeze, just right. Sun
shining. Just like the day Mrs. Oglevee had told us about,
when those founding fathers of ours had had a picnic lunch
here, decided to stay, and called it Paradise . . .

The likeness should have served as a warning.

I swear I wasn't really speeding.

At least, not as much as Chief John Worthy said later, although I couldn't be too sure, since the speed gauge on my
car doesn't work anymore. Still, it didn't *feel* like I was
speeding—more like I was just in a hurry.

But about two miles out from Ed Crowley's place, I heard the siren behind me. I looked in my rearview mirror and saw Chief John Worthy right behind me and gaining fast.

Well, what I actually saw was a blue-and-white Police car. And it could have been any of the four officers at the Paradise Police Department. But something in my gut—which was feeling all hollowed out and queasy—told me that with my luck, it was Chief John Worthy.

Now, on this one little spot on Sweet Potato Ridge, there are three quick rises and falls, right in a row.

Since I was looking in my rearview mirror, I didn't see I was about to hit them. My car went airborne on the first hump, bounced on the second one, and launched again on the third one. My books—and my letter to Tyra Grimes—slid into the floor. My coffee went flying and landed right on top of them.

I screamed, put on my brakes, and grabbed for my letter. I jerked to a stop right by a cornfield—freshly plowed but otherwise empty. I turned off the ignition and moaned, picking up the letter, my hands shaking.

My poor letter was ruined.

At least, that's what I thought at first. But I'm a natural born optimist, so other possibilities started rushing through my mind. Maybe Tyra Grimes would see the coffee stain on the envelope and think it was symbolic—what with me being a stain expert.

Or maybe if I dabbed at it a little, the envelope would dry without wrinkling, and Tyra would think I'd used some fancy marbleized stationery, instead of just plain old white paper.

Why sure, I thought, rubbing the envelope against my shirt (I could always use an all-fabric bleach on my shirt later)—Tyra Grimes would be mighty impressed with my fancy marbleized stationery. She couldn't help but say yes to my offer to go on her show as a stain expert, and everything would work out just fine. I was close to downright happy again.

Then I heard the tap at my window and saw John Worthy. I rolled down my window. He leaned in, his jaw so tense that his ears quivered.

"Do you realize," he said, his lips barely moving, "that I clocked you going 75 miles an hour?"

"Really?" I said, genuinely surprised.

Chief Worthy whipped out a pad of paper and pen and started writing. "Really. So I'll be citing you for speeding—violation of code 618.62." He flipped to the next sheet. "And reckless driving. Code 901.93."

I whimpered.

"Failing to stop for an officer in pursuit. Code 110.6l."

Now, that one irritated me. "I couldn't stop because I was flying through the air."

He stuck his head into my car, glared at my dash. "Plus you still haven't gotten the speedometer fixed since the last time I caught you for speeding, have you?"

"It's only been a week," I said, "And I've been real busy—"

"With this?" He snatched the envelope from my hand. "You planning on driving it up this morning to New York yourself?"

I snatched my envelope back from him. "It's a violation to take private property from a citizen without a search warrant," I said. "And that's not just a county code."

Chief Worthy's smile disappeared, along with his lips, which he sucked right back into that thin line of mouth.

"Josie Toadfern, I won't write you up on all those violations, if you'll just listen to me. Give up on this nonsense about getting on the *Tyra Grimes Home Show*."

For a second there, I thought he was going to predict a dire outcome if I persisted, like Lewis Rothchild had done.

But instead he added, "I was up in Masonville yesterday on business and word's already spread up there. They were all laughing about your plan up at the sheriff's department. You've got to give this up—this crazy dream of yours isn't going to come true anyway." Then he grinned. "You just can't resist thinking you can make things go your way, can you—Nosy Josie?"

Now, I've got to take a break here to explain a few things.

Back in high school, I was president of the Reading Club and worked on the school newspaper. I got a reputation for being nosy because I was ruthless about following up on any story I thought might interest more than two people.

For example . . . young John Worthy, second-string quarterback for Mason County High School South, suddenly in a starring role? That was a great story, I'd thought. Just what did him dating the coach's daughter have to do with that change? And, I thought, let's get opinions from all the kids who knew John pretty well . . . especially John's ex-girlfriend. Which was . . . me.

Yes, that story made for a sold-out issue of our little high school newspaper. It also got me thrown off the newspaper, because the advisor was the coach's cousin. Then John got back at me by telling everyone something that was totally untrue—that I liked working in the laundromat with Uncle Horace and Aunt Clara because of all the secrets I could learn from other people's laundry.

Well, actually, that's only partially untrue. I did (and do) like working in the laundromat. And you can learn a lot of secrets—or at least, pick up some mighty interesting clues—from other people's laundry. Lipstick on a collar is just the beginning, believe me.

Still, I'm not a gossip or rumormonger—unlike most of my fellow Paradisites. So it hurt when John started a rumor that I am, and gave me the nickname Nosy Josie. Not a fun taunt for a teenage girl. For a while there, that nickname even hurt my aunt and uncle's business. Fortunately, even though the nickname's stuck, everyone knows they can trust me not to gossip—which is why Paradisites tell me all kinds of things about themselves and each other. I admit I'm glad, because I have a deep and abiding curiosity in human affairs of all kinds. Which kind of does make me a nosy Josie, I guess. But I still hate that nickname.

Now, I looked at Chief Worthy and said, through gritted teeth, "I will get Tyra Grimes to come here. You'll see."

Chief Worthy ripped off the top ticket and handed it to me. "Speeding," he said. The next one. "Reckless driving." Then one more. "And failure to stop for a police officer."

He left then, and I sat there for a moment, still looking at the three tickets in my one hand and the coffee-stained letter to Tyra Grimes in my other hand.

Then I folded up the tickets and put them in my glove compartment. I put my letter to Tyra Grimes back on the passenger seat.

Fancy marbleized stationery, that's what she'd think, I told myself. I drove on—going fairly slow now—knowing that somehow my friend Winnie Porter'd make me feel better. She'd know how to get my letter to Tyra Grimes.

Then I rounded the curve and pulled up to Ed Crowley's place—just in time to see her big red-and-white bookmobile pulling away.

Two weeks, four days, and six hours later, on a Sunday afternoon at my apartment, my boyfriend Owen said softly, "Now Josie, you do understand that you're not going to hear from Tyra Grimes, don't you?"

I glared at him.

"I mean, not today," he went on hastily. "Not on a Sunday. There's no mail today and you can't expect a business call.

You even close the laundromat on Sundays, and . . . Josie? Aren't you ever going to cheer up?"

I closed my eyes and groaned.

You see, I did catch up with Winnie and the bookmobile right after she pulled away from Ed Crowley's place. I told her about the map and my plan and showed her my letter to Tyra Grimes, which she looked at for a while until she finally said, yes, if you squinted at it just so it really did look like fancy marbleized stationery, which she was sure someone of Ms. Grimes's grand taste would truly appreciate. Winnie adores Tyra Grimes. She has taped every one of Tyra's shows—and cataloged them.

Then she looked through some thick reference volumes she keeps just below the back desk (built in, so it won't slide around), and frowned and said, "Hmmm." Then she poked on the computer, up front behind the driver's seat, and frowned and said, "Hmmm." Then she called someone at the main library, and frowned and said, "Hmmm." Then she repeated the whole process, only this time through she frowned and said, "Uh huh, uh huh,"—a change in gutteralities I found encouraging. Sure enough, Winnie finally found it— the direct and specific address to Tyra Grimes's office, not just a general TV show address. Winnie is magical when it comes to research.

So I addressed the envelope and mailed it.

But now here it was, Sunday afternoon, two and a half weeks later. Paradisites elsewhere had moved on with their lives—so I could now run my laundromat without being teased—but I was stuck. Stuck with a book I didn't really want to read—*The Idiot's Guide to Home Decorating and Style in General*. Winnie'd made me check it out because she said I should have at least a basic parlance with such matters if I was going to be on the *Tyra Grimes Home Show*.

Which it didn't look like I was.

"How about we go see Guy?" Owen said gently.

I opened one eye and looked at Owen. My community college professor, book-loving boyfriend was cute, I decided, in a goofy way, with his goatee and mustache and long, thin blond hair pulled back in a ponytail.

"We haven't done that for three weeks. What do you say, Josie?"

I opened my other eye and grinned.

"Bless you," I said. I stood up, headed for my fridge. A six-pack of Big Fizz diet cola, and I was ready to go.

"You could even wear your new Tyra Grimes T-shirt!" he said.

I turned and gave him a look.

"Uh—I guess that wasn't such a great suggestion."

"No, it wasn't—but not for the reason you're thinking."

On the drive over to Stillwater, I'd explain to him why I couldn't wear my red Tyra Grimes T-shirt to see Guy—or any red T-shirt, for that matter. Of course, I had no way of knowing that later on he'd get a personal demonstration of the reason that he'd never forget.

An hour later, Owen and I were at Stillwater Farms, sitting in rockers on the back porch of the main building—an old farm house with lots of additions—with Guy between us. We rocked and whittled, not making anything in particular, not saying anything in particular, although every now and again Guy hummed.

Stillwater—named that on account of the nearby Stillwater River—is a home for autistic people, about 15 miles north of Paradise, where the residents are more or less as independent as they can be. Some of them come just for the day. They all have routines and jobs, working in the pumpkin patches or flower gardens for the annual fall and spring sales, or taking care of the Angora goats, whose wool is shorn and sold every year. Guy's about fifteen years older than I am, and he's been there since he was twenty. Uncle Horace and Aunt Clara saved every penny above and beyond basic needs in a trust fund for Guy, so he will be able to stay at Stillwater the rest of his days. Plus after they died, I sold their house—just as their will ordered—and put that money into his trust fund. I'm Guy's official guardian. I think leaving me the laundromat was their way of saying thanks, because they knew that of course I'd take on the role. Guy's more like my brother than a cousin.

Guy always likes it when I visit. I always enjoy stopping by, too, because I like Guy, and because visiting always reminds me that the truth is in how you look at things. Some folks think it's sad, Guy and the others having autism severe enough that they must live in this quiet place, unable to make choices about careers and mates and such that the rest of us do.

What I see is that each of them's found a way to work with the life fate's dealt them and to find a niche up at Stillwater, a way to do things that matter to them and to other people. The way I figure it, that's all any of us needs to do. Guy's specialty—growing pumpkins for the annual Stillwater Hayride and Pumpkin Picking Day—is closer than a lot of folks ever get to really making a difference in the world.

This day, Guy gave me a big hug and even gave Owen a long look, which was progress. Being a person with autism, Guy really likes routine and gets upset about anything that throws off his understanding of his world. Owen had only been coming with me off and on for the past three months—we'd been dating for the six months since I'd taken his class, "A Review of Popular Movements," up at the junior college.

Most of the younger students seemed to think the class was going to cover dance steps to go with pop songs and ended up being disappointed and dropping out, so the class ended up being me, a young man who slept a lot, and two elderly sisters who giggled a lot because they thought Owen was cute (which he is).

Owen was glad that I paid attention to his lectures on the Women's Rights Movement and socialism and so forth. At my suggestion, Owen changed his course name to "Influential Sociopolitical Movements of the Twentieth Century," (so he still gets only four students, but they at least all pay attention), and since then we've been dating, and Owen's come to meet Guy a few times. Owen quickly understood how important Guy is to me, a fact that makes me like Owen even more than the other fact that makes me like him—we can talk about anything.

Now, as we rocked and whittled, we mostly looked out at the pretty day and the fields that were being tilled for the gardens the residents would tend. Guy and some others would take care of the pumpkin fields, further out.

But every now and then I looked over at Guy. He's a big, hammy fellow, with overly meaty features, a full thicket of light brown hair that never quite seems neat, and green eyes—the image of Uncle Horace.

It always makes me feel good to see Guy at peace. As I rocked back and forth and whittled it started not to matter so much whether or not I ever heard from Tyra Grimes.

"Seeds started for the pumpkins?" I said to Guy. I knew that was one of his favorite things, putting the seeds in the peat pots, and seeing the little shoots pop up through the dirt.

Guy didn't say anything right off, just tottered back and forth in his rocking chair, rocking, whittling, rocking, whittling. But it didn't bother me—I knew he would answer sooner or later.

And sure enough, after a few minutes, Guy finally stopped

rocking, jumped up and whirled so he stood in front of me, and hollered, "Greenhouse! Starts!"

Then he sat back down and started rocking and whittling again.

This was very good for Guy. A few years ago, he would have kept shouting in his odd, punchy voice—"Greenhouse! Starts! Greenhouse! Starts!"—over and over and over. Now he didn't repeat things unless he was upset.

We rocked awhile, whittled awhile, then I asked, "Can we see the pumpkin starts in the greenhouse, Guy?"

More rocking and whittling. Me, waiting for Guy to answer, although I wasn't really waiting. I was just going along with the rhythm we'd fallen into, Guy's rhythm. Poor Owen, though, still wasn't used to the long waits before Guy replied to comments or questions, and he was practically turning purple with anticipation, looking like he was trying hard not to sneeze.

Then, all at once, Guy was up and standing before me again—it's always been his habit to make sure he's facing anyone he's talking to—hollering, "After! Dinner!"

Then he went back to the rocking and the whittling.

Suddenly, the quiet on the back deck was broken by the sounds of screaming and someone running. There was a blur of red as someone ran toward us—and I felt my heart start to race and pound, seeing it. Guy gets really upset at the color red—which is why I hadn't worn my Tyra Grimes T-shirt.

No one knows why red upsets him so. He's never been badly cut. Or seen anyone else bleed a lot. Or had any other encounters with red that were horrible—but there it is. Guy hates red. One red tulip poking up among, say, a hundred yellow ones might be okay, but a whole mass would set him off—and the more red, the worse it is. The saying "seeing red" could have been made for him.

Now here was not only someone wearing red, but running and screaming, too. Guy dropped his whittling, jumped up, put his hands over his ears, and started yelling, "No! No! No!"

Guy doesn't put his hands over his ears when he doesn't want to hear something. He does it whenever he sees a lot of red. Maybe, at some level, he can hear red, and to him it's a nasty sound.

Owen jumped up, bewildered.

And the person in red came to a stop in front of us, because the person chasing her grabbed her and began to hug her close.

The person in the red shirt was Verbenia Denlinger, who'd been here a lot longer than Guy and was one of his best friends. The person who'd grabbed her was her twin sister, Vivian Denlinger. They're not identical twins and Vivian doesn't have autism. They're forty and don't look a thing alike—Vivian is squat and plain and brown-haired, and Verbenia is tall and lovely and blond.

Now it was my turn to be confused, because Verbenia is always quiet. So I jumped up, and over Guy's hollering of "No, no, no," I said, "What's wrong?"

"It's this shirt," Vivian said. "I want to get it from her." Usually Vivian was really quiet too, almost too docile, and now she looked really mad. I couldn't see why she'd want to take a simple shirt away from her sister, especially if it was all that important to Verbenia. That's one thing families learned at Stillwater—don't fight battles just because you can't understand why it's important to the person with autism to do something, as long as whatever that something is won't hurt the person with autism or anyone else. If, say, the person with autism wants to take a toy bunny everywhere, let him. Taking a live bunny everywhere might be a problem—but there are other ways to deal with that. Vivian knew this as well as anyone.

By now, Guy was slapping his own ears, a sign he was truly distressed, and so I started to turn to him, to try to get him back inside the house, but then Vivian angrily pulled Verbenia around so she faced me.

And I saw the front of Verbenia's red shirt.

It was a Tyra Grimes T-shirt, just like the ones Billy'd gotten for him and me. And now Verbenia had one on and apparently was partial to it, because she was clinging to the hem of it, grabbing it with both hands, pulling it down tight over her hips, as if this would guarantee it wasn't taken off her.

Vivian's pale, chubby face quivered and she wailed, over Guy's screaming, "Where did she get this? *Where?*"

"I—I don't know," I said, feeling suddenly guilty. Somehow, these T-shirts kept popping up—which couldn't have anything to do with my failed plan to bring Tyra Grimes to Paradise—but still, I felt guilty. Looking back, I think it was just plain old-fashioned intuition that soon things were going to go wrong—very, very wrong.

Vivian went on, "I don't know where Verbenia got it, or why she wants it, but I'm getting it from her and burning it! It's evil, a sign, a terrible, terrible sign!"

She sounded, I thought, just like Lewis Rothchild had when he'd gotten upset about me trying to get Tyra Grimes to come to Paradise. Which was pretty strange. Vivian and Lewis didn't know each other. And I didn't think word would have spread all the way on up to Columbus—which is where Vivian lived—about my plan. Even if it had, why should Vivian care?

Then Vivian did something I'd never seen her do. She started crying. That startled Verbenia so much that she stopped whimpering, and turned back to her sister, and hugged her and started patting her on the back as if somehow, deep inside—although all the experts would say it wasn't possible for someone so deeply affected by autism—she understood Vivian's pain. As if, for a moment, their roles had been swapped.

We had dinner with Guy, stayed awhile longer, and left late. We had a good time, but Owen and I didn't talk much on our way home. I tried to tell myself it was because it was late and we were tired—but I knew it was because of the scene with Guy, Verbenia, and Vivian. Owen does not like scenes.

And once Owen got me to my laundromat and walked me up the metal stairs to my door, he just gave me a brief brush of a kiss—not even trying to wheedle his way in for some heavier necking, like he usually does. Truth be told, I usually let him in—but tonight, even if he'd tried to wheedle, I would have sent him on home.

I could understand that the whole scene with Guy and the Denlinger sisters had shaken up Owen. It had shaken me up, too. But the fact was that Guy was a permanent part of my life, and such scenes can't always be avoided. Guy couldn't discuss his feelings, or even identify them, like Owen could. And Owen would have to come to terms with that if he wanted to be part of my life, too.

I went on in—I always leave the exterior door unlocked—and stood in the tiny hallway that fronts the two apartments. Maybe, I thought, I could talk with Billy. I went to his door and knocked. No answer. Billy was out somewhere—probably wouldn't be back until the wee hours of the morning.

I went to my own apartment door and started to put my key in, but the door gave way. As I stepped into my apartment, I shook my head at myself—I have a bad habit of forgetting to lock my door. In a town like Paradise, it usually doesn't matter.

As it turned out, this time it did.

For there, perched on the edge of my couch, with my quilt spread over her knees, was Tyra Grimes herself.

3

For just a minute, I thought this was someone's idea of a joke . . . maybe Cherry, or Lewis, or even Billy . . . maybe one of them had found a life-sized cardboard cutout of Tyra and stuck it in my apartment. You see those cutouts every now and then, of Presidents and stars that folks like to get their pictures taken with. That's how still Tyra was.

Suddenly, she gave a start, followed by a snort/snore combo, and I realized that Tyra had just fallen asleep. My entrance had probably awakened her. But she didn't seem to notice me, because next she peered down at my quilt and began doing something to it with her hands. It took me a second to realize that she was picking it apart.

Now, my quilt is the one and only heirloom from my great-grandmother Maybelline Toadfern. (Actually, it's my one and only heirloom of any sort.) She made one for each of her grandchildren (18) and great-grandchildren (52)—for a grand total of 70. Mine's got flowers with yellow centers and purple petals and a green background, all made out of hexagons.

And now, Tyra Grimes was picking it apart.

So the first thing I said to Tyra Grimes—this very famous woman that I had so hoped would come to Paradise, that I had given up on ever coming to Paradise, that seconds before I would have begged to come to Paradise—the first thing I said—well, shouted—was, "What the hell do you think you are you doing? Stop!"

Tyra looked up at me. She seemed smaller in real life. She had beautiful aqua eyes, which didn't show to advantage on TV, and now she gave me a patient smile as if I were simply a child who needed instruction to understand her wiser ways. She kept working while she looked at me, expertly using a needle to unpick the orange thread that my great-grandmother Toadfern had used to sew my quilt. Tyra had undone almost an entire flower, so there was a long curly strand of orange thread. I had the feeling Tyra was one of these people who end up with one long, even strand of thin skin when they peel a potato.

"What," I said again, a little calmer, "are you doing to my great-grandmother's quilt?"

"I'm picking it apart," she said. Her voice, in person, was warmer than on TV. "You see, dear, how the orange thread clashes most unfortunately with the lovely fabrics used in the quilt? White thread would be much better. It would enhance the value of the quilt. There's no tradition for orange thread in quilting. Although, in some regions, blue thread was used when . . ."

She was off on a lecture about appropriate thread colors for quilts while her fingers still worked over my quilt. The purple petal hung forlornly on, by just a few stitches. If I didn't do something fast, it would meet the same fate as its friends, and other little petals would soon fall too.

So I did the only thing I could. I grabbed the quilt right out of Tyra's hands. While hugging my maimed quilt with my left arm, I reached out with my right hand and snagged the three dequilted purple petals from the end table.

Tyra looked stunned for a moment, then shrugged. "I suppose you're right, dear. It is getting on in the evening. I can finish resewing your quilt in the morning." She said this as if I was worried that she might not continue deflowering my quilt.

"I didn't say that I wanted . . ." I started. "I just . . ." I started again. Then, finally, I got out a complete question. "What—what are you doing here?"

"Well, your door was unlocked, and given the rather desperate tone of your letter—and I did just so love the marbleized stationery, by the way—you'll just have to tell me how you went about creating it—it was homemade, wasn't it?"

I just stared at her.

"Anyway," she went on, "I guessed from your letter that you wouldn't mind me staying here, and of course your doors were unlocked. A charming custom that just isn't done in the big city, I must say." Tyra laughed merrily.

I gulped and took a step back.

"We stopped at the Red Horse Motel on the edge of town, but the place was, I'm sorry to say, just overwhelming with the smell of mold, and if I stayed there with my allergies, the consequences would just be, well . . ." She stopped, shuddered, and fanned herself with her hands, as if the consequences were just too horrible to think about. "Anyway, unless there's a Hyatt in the environs that we somehow missed, we decided it was best that Paige Morrissey—she's my assistant . . . you'll meet her tomorrow . . . would stay at the Red Horse and make arrangements for our film crew, and that I would stay . . ." she paused, looked around, taking in my tiny living room and kitchenette with a single glance, and I could practically see her judgment imprinted in block letters in the air: CLEAN AND NEAT BUT DULL, DULL, DULL.

"Well," she finished, "here." She smiled, gesturing to a tiny, tiny black suitcase by the end of the couch. I hadn't noticed it before. It looked big enough to hold just a hanky, undies, and a toothbrush, at least, if *I* was packing. "Of course, we were hoping you'd be here, and Paige waited with me until I sent her on her way—she tires easily—so here I'd like to stay. Unless there *is* a Hyatt?" she added hopefully.

"N-no Hyatt," I said, taking another step back.

"A deli?"

"Uh, no. The A&P over in Masonville sells salami, but it's closed now. I have some garlic bologna, though and—" I stopped, shook my head again. This person couldn't really be Tyra Grimes, could she? Maybe this was a severely deranged Tyra Grimes wanna-be, escaped from some institution, who'd somehow heard about the letter I'd sent and managed to find her way here . . .

Tyra laughed. "Oh, don't be so nervous, dear! I'm just a regular person, really. Although," she added thoughtfully, "I have been given an incredible gift for design, far beyond the reach of most people . . . anyway." Her voice snapped back to what seemed to be its default tone—merriment. "Just relax and we'll get along fine. The crew for my show will be here in a few days and will be staying at the Red Horse. We'll have plenty of time to get to know each other over the next few days—I always like to really get to know my guests before I interview them, and I think your stain expertise will be just perfect for my show."

She stood up and flicked her delicate fingers through her short auburn curls. I took another step back. "You don't mind," she said, "if I make myself at home, do you?"

"Uh, no, not at all, feel free," I blithered as I walked backward to the door to my bedroom, still clutching the quilt.

Tyra Grimes gave me one of her famous, dazzling smiles—and said, "Simply wonderful!"

* * *

I shut my bedroom door and—never mind my usual habit of leaving doors unlocked—locked it. Then I put my quilt down on my bed, and the petals on my dresser. And finally, I took the spare kitchen chair I keep in a corner in my bedroom and rammed the back of it up under the doorknob.

Sound extreme?

Well, here I was, in my apartment, with a woman who claimed to be Tyra Grimes . . . who was now in my living room/kitchenette singing with gusto and only a little off-key, *"The hills are alive with the sound of music,"* while making lots of other loud noises. Banging sounds. Cabinets opening and shutting.

What to do, what to do? I could call the police—but if that really was Tyra Grimes, I'd be forever embarrassed. Of course, if it wasn't, I might be forever dead if this woman—who seemed a lot perkier and older and smaller than the Tyra on TV—turned out to be a deranged Tyra wanna-be and slipped into some dark side of her personality . . . maybe she was a Tyra devotee who'd tried unsuccessfully one too many times to whip up faux chiffon window toppers using just tissue paper and string, and she'd slipped over the edge, and any minute she'd break into my bedroom armed with a sharpened spatula . . .

There was a loud thump.

Something was being dragged across my floor, with a scraping sound. Tyra had launched into a throaty rendition of, *"O-O-O-Oklahoma where the wind . . ."* I guess Tyra was a domestic diva in more ways than one.

I ran into my closet, flipped on the light, and shut the door. One more shut door between me and Tyra/the Tyra wanna-be couldn't hurt. I pulled off my shoes, then peeled off my socks and tossed them down the laundry chute, which I have in my closet and which goes down to a basket in my office/storage area below (one of the perks of living above your own laundromat). I wiggled my toes—letting them enjoy a few seconds of airy freedom—then pulled on my Tweety Bird slippers. Somehow, putting them on made me feel calmer. I'd just go out, talk to this woman, maybe ask for some identification . . .

Thump. *Bang.* Tyra crooning, *"Don't cry for me, Ar-gen-ti-i-i-n-aaaa . . ."* I could hear it even inside my closet.

I opened the closet door, dashed out, grabbed the handset to my phone, and ran back into my closet, planning to call the Red Horse Motel and see if Tyra's assistant had really checked in. It wasn't as though so many guests deluged the motel that the owners—Luke and Greta Rhinegold—wouldn't remember her.

As I dialed the number from memory—I do the motel's linens once a week—I toed open the shiny metal door to my oversized laundry chute. I'd installed the super-deluxe model, big enough to let my bed's queen-sized comforter sluice down easily.

Greta answered on the third ring.

"What? We already have an ad in the Yellow Pages," she crowed, when I asked her if a Paige had checked in tonight. "Not that it does us any good, being out here in the boonies . . ."

Greta's a little hard of hearing.

I repeated my question, raising my voice, partly for Greta's sake and partly because Tyra's singing had gotten louder.

This time, Greta realized who was calling and what I was asking. "Oh, yes—Paige Morrissey. Yes, she checked in tonight. She said to tell you when you called not to worry and she'll meet you in the morning. This some long-lost friend?"

Greta kept her voice casual, doing her best to keep her curiosity in check, but I knew she was dying for an explanation.

Everyone knows I grew up my whole life in Paradise. And everyone knows everyone I know, because they all know each other. Another fact of small town life. A stranger claiming to know me would definitely raise curiosity.

"Something like that," I said to Greta, then thanked her, disconnected, and slid down to the floor.

Oh, God.

Apparently, I really did have Tyra Grimes in my living room.

Now, there's a funny thing about having what you want to happen actually happen, after so many times of having what you want mostly just rinse on down the drain like dirty wash water.

See, I'd waited and waited to hear from Tyra Grimes. And now here she was—in person. So it sure seemed like I was getting my wish to come true . . . like I might really be able to pull off getting some free, and positive, publicity for Paradise.

So on the one hand, my heart was aflutter with hope.

On the other hand, I didn't trust what was happening. It seemed just a little odd that Tyra would show up unannounced. It seemed even more odd that she would want to come two days before her crew arrived. At most, I'd be on for five minutes. I couldn't believe someone as famous and important and busy as Tyra Grimes would want to talk with me for two whole days about how to take care of mustard versus beer stains. This was wholly unlike what I'd imagined.

So, when Tyra knocked on my bedroom door and called, "Josie? Can we talk for a moment?" I followed my first instinct—escape.

I opened the laundry chute door, stuck my head in. Nope, that way wouldn't work. I lay down on my back, hooked my leg over the rim of the chute, and butt-scooted forward.

Nope, that way wasn't going to work, either.

For a minute, I just stayed there like that, trying to think.

No brilliant escape plans, after all. I was going to have to stay and deal with Tyra. I'd wanted her here, and now she *was* here and I didn't know what to do with her. She'd apparently moved away from my bedroom door because now I could only faintly hear her plaintive warbling of, *"Send in the clowns . . ."*

I punched in Winnie's number. No answer. The answering machine kicked in. I hung up, suddenly remembering that Sunday nights, Winnie and her husband go out square dancing up in Masonville. They'd probably be sashaying left and right till all hours of the night. How do you explain to an answering machine that a major media star has responded to your letter by showing up and basically moving in with you for a few days? You don't. So I hung up without leaving a message.

For a few minutes, I just lay on my closet floor. I squeezed my eyes shut, trying to figure out what to do. And then I realized that my apartment had gotten very, very quiet.

I tried to pull my feet out of the laundry chute so I could sit up properly. My right foot came out okay. My left foot was stuck, though, at an odd angle in the chute. I'd stuck my leg in too far.

I bucked my butt up and down in a frenzied effort to loosen my left foot. I'd never look at the little mousetraps I have back in the storeroom of my laundromat in quite the same way. In fact, maybe I'd replace them with something more humane—or more mouse-mane. Like little silk beds and pillows and little silver plates of cheese.

I rested for a second—then did a combo half-twist-and-lunge. And my woman-eating super-deluxe laundry chute finally spat me half way out of my closet.

A few minutes later, I had my ear to my bedroom door. Still just silence. I gulped, moved the chair away from the door, and slowly opened it.

I limped out—the woman-eating laundry chute had done a number on my ankle—then stared in shock at what was supposed to be my apartment.

The furniture—instead of being lined up against the walls—was at a jaunty angle beneath the window. The beige curtains that had hung limply on either side of the window had been taken down and rehung, now as a scarf swag, the two halves joined with an arty rosette knot. The curtain rod was gone. The swag hung over two metal scarf holders—except on closer examination, I saw they were serving forks, taken from my kitchenette, the tines stabbed into the drywall, the ends bent up to form the hooks.

Books had been artfully stacked under the lamps on the end tables. My pale yellow throw pillows—usually wadded into either end of the couch—were now prettily turned so they were diamonds rather than squares. And Tyra had found a black magic marker and quickly sketched orchids on them.

My magazines were now on the coffee table in two stacks, but twisted, to make twin spirals. And on top of and around each spiral were a menagerie of origami animals, created, I could see, from pages torn from the latest issue of *The Star Reporter*.

And, curled up on my couch—sleeping peacefully, snoring softly—was Tyra Grimes.

I stared at her for a long moment. And then I did the only thing that I could think to do. I went to my bedroom and retrieved my maimed quilt and spread it over her.

Remember Mrs. Oglevee—my eighth-grade history teacher? The one who made me write 100 times over, "I'm proud to be a Paradisite" when I shared my theory about the true history of Paradise? Who lectured me all the while about how that very pride should come from Paradise being on the Ohio map every single year since 1844?

If it hadn't been for me dreaming that night about old Mrs. Oglevee, maybe things would have turned out all right. Or at least, a little better. Maybe, if I hadn't dreamed about her, I wouldn't have made the phone call later, that led to Billy getting thrown out of his apartment and moving to the Red Horse, and we would have just one murder in Paradise later on, instead of two. Maybe. The saying "Hindsight is 20/20" isn't really true. Sometimes, it's just as hard to look back and see what you should have done as it is to look ahead and see what you should do.

Anyway, after tucking Tyra Grimes in, I found myself in my kitchen, staring at the super-large family-sized jar of peanut butter in the cabinet. Then I found myself carrying the jar and a spoon into my bedroom.

And then I started eating the peanut butter.

Oh, Lord—Tyra Grimes, really here? And me? On her show?

Now, don't get me wrong. I know my stains. I was nervous about the show, but not panicked. Not too panicked, anyway.

I ate some more peanut butter. I read once that longlasting protein counteracts panic. So I thought, if I just have a big helping of peanut butter, and kind of let it work overnight, I'll wake up in the morning unpanicked.

But even after two spoonfuls, I still had the nagging sense that something wasn't right. For one thing, Tyra wanting to come here two days before filming. What in the world would I do with her for two days?

I ate more peanut butter.

And what about this Paige Morrissey? I didn't know a thing about her.

A double-dip into the peanut butter . . .

I ate peanut butter until my jar was empty. Then I licked off the inside of the lid. I put the jar and lid and spoon on my nightstand, then tried to read *The Idiot's Guide to Home Dec-*

orating and Style in General. Somewhere in the middle of the chapter on "How To Accessorize With Candles Without Appearing Either Tacky or Ghoulish," I dozed off.

And then, Mrs. Oglevee showed up in my dreams.

There she was, at the foot of my bed, looking just like she always had. Tiny. In a frilly, prim pink blouse and a straight navy skirt, and brown orthopedic shoes. Except now she was carrying a large wooden spoon. And wearing a starched apron that was crisp and white, not a stain on it, so I couldn't even make cleaning recommendations to show how far I've progressed since junior high.

To make things even worse, Mrs. Oglevee—who's been dead six years now—was wearing a Tyra Grimes wig of auburn curls. The wig was askew, so one ear stuck out and one was hidden.

Risen-from-the-dead, Tyra-wigged Mrs. Oglevee shook her wooden spoon at me and squeaked, "Well, Miss Toadfern, I can see you haven't changed a bit."

"Yes, I have. I'm a business owner. And a stain expert. And—" I sat straight up in my bed, in my dream, at least—in real life, I reckon I was sweating and tossing and turning. "Why are you dressed like that, anyhow?"

Mrs. Oglevee snorted. "Don't you remember when I substituted in home ec? When Mrs. Mendenball was off on maternity leave? You were even more pathetic at home ec than you were in history. You sewed right through your thumb, trying to finish up the class project, what was it, a skirt, a muumuu, a—"

"Vest," I muttered. "It was a vest."

"Don't interrupt me! You always were an insolent child." She licked her lips. "You sewed right through your thumb and broke off the needle! Do you realize the expense of sewing machine needles? Of course not! You were always bad at economics, too. You only have the laundromat because your aunt and uncle had no one else to leave it to! If it weren't for that, you'd probably be broke, living in the streets, homeless in Paradise . . ."

"What do you know? You're only here because . . ." Well, why was she here? My tummy ached. "Because I ate too much peanut butter!"

At the words "peanut butter" she shrank back for a second. But she recovered and hollered, "I'm telling you, Josie Toadfern, you need to call this whole thing off with Tyra Grimes! Just send her home, or you'll end up regretting it!"

Now, this was too much. The ghost of Mrs. Oglevee, also against Tyra's visit?

I groaned. "Oh . . . my tummy hurts. I wish I hadn't eaten so much of that peanut butter . . ."

Mrs. Oglevee yelped before I could finish my moaning. What was her problem with peanut butter?

But she was starting in on me again. "Do you really think you can handle yourself on national TV? Quick—what's the proper presoak for grass stains on denim?"

I moaned.

"You've never been good at thinking on your feet." She cackled. "So before you embarrass yourself and Paradise, send Tyra home, tell her you're sorry, you just can't do it . . ."

I tuned her out, because my brain was starting to itch with the memory of Mrs. Oglevee substituting for home ec, and the annual home economics eighth grade tea, and how Mr. Humphries, the junior high principal, was the honored guest, and how Mrs. Oglevee had assigned me to make peanut butter cookies, because, she said, even Josie Toadfern couldn't mess those up—while all the other girls got to make fancy little cakes and fancy little sandwiches and fancy lime Jell-O salad.

Yet somehow, I used baking soda in the peanut butter cookies when I was supposed to use baking powder. Or maybe I used baking powder instead of baking soda? In any case, when Mr. Humphries took the first bite of peanut butter cookie—because he got to sample everything first at the eighth grade home economics tea—he started coughing and choking and wheezed out peanut butter cookie crumbs all over Mrs. Oglevee's face.

So now, in my dream, I looked right at Mrs. Oglevee, and smiled, and hollered, "Peanut butter!"

Mrs. Oglevee whimpered and threw her arms up to shield her face—and kind of faded. So, of course I just kept right on yelling, "Peanut butter" over and over again, until she disappeared all together.

And me, I woke up, sweating and thrashing and screaming, "Peanut butter!" So much for longlasting protein counteracting panic attacks. After a few seconds—when I realized with relief that I had not awakened Tyra Grimes—I made my next big mistake.

I called Winnie Porter again.

This time she answered, and I told her how Tyra was here, asleep on my couch, and how she'd redecorated my living room, and how her assistant Paige was staying at the Red Horse, and how I'd eaten too much peanut butter and then dreamed about Mrs. Oglevee.

Then Winnie said, "Don't you worry, sweetie. I'll take care of everything."

So I went back to sleep—this time, without dreaming.

And woke the next morning to the sound of all hell breaking loose.

4

Truth be told, I'm not sure what all hell breaking loose actually sounds like.

But when I woke up the next morning, my head was throbbing. I looked over at my clock. It was 9:30 A.M. on a Monday morning—an hour and a half after I was supposed to open up my laundromat. My first dim thought was that I'd forgotten to set my alarm. My second thought was that I had a peanut butter hangover.

Then I realized there's no such thing as a peanut butter hangover and that it wasn't my head throbbing, but music—loud jazz—in my laundromat, right below my apartment.

I moaned as I sat up. What was going on? Then I saw *The Idiot's Guide to Home Decorating and Style in General* where it had fallen to the floor—and it all came back to me. Tyra Grimes was here. In my apartment. Asleep on my couch.

At least, she'd been safely asleep on my couch last night . . .

I forced myself to stand, my stomach feeling as though it had reshaped itself into a giant peanut. I pulled my light blue robe on over my Tweety Bird nightshirt and shoved my feet into my matching Tweety Bird slippers. I waddled into my living room—it's not easy to move fast when you feel like a giant goober. No Tyra.

I blinked. Maybe I'd imagined the whole thing?

No . . . the tabloid origamis were still scattered artfully about, the forks-turned-window-scarf-holders still poking out of the wall, the tiny, tiny black suitcase still there, the jazz music cranked up a notch downstairs. Oh, Lord, what was the woman doing to my laundromat?

I lurched out of my apartment, down the tiny hall, and out the door to the metal stairs, galumphing down them to the front of my laundromat, where I came to an abrupt stop. My stomach roiled again, this time partly from shock at what I saw.

My laundromat's front window had been scrubbed clean of my store name and logo, the grinning toad amid ferns. Now, my plate glass window proclaimed—in fancy calligraphy and gussied up misspelling—Josephine Todeferne's Laundrette.

Plus, two big clay pots—filled with geraniums—had appeared on either side of my door. The sight of them made me nervous. I'm terrible with plants, as Rocky—my only houseplant, this poor viny thing with six leaves—would attest if it could talk. (I named it Rocky in one of my purest moments of optimism.)

But right then, I wasn't feeling the least bit optimistic. I was mad. Tabloid origamis were one thing . . . but Tyra Grimes didn't have any right to mess with my business. So I charged in, hollering—for the second time in less than twelve hours—"What in the hell do you think you are doing? *Stop!*"

* * *

But Tyra wasn't in my laundromat.

In a way, my laundromat wasn't in my laundromat, either.

In fact, if it weren't for the dozen washers and dryers—which are pretty hard to disguise—I wouldn't have recognized my own place. The jazz came from a small stereo on the folding table which had once held Billy's Cut-N-Suck demo machine, but which was now covered with a white tablecloth and held, besides the stereo, the weirdest looking coffeemaker I'd ever seen. Billy's Cut-N-Suck was nowhere in sight.

The metal utility shelf with small boxes of laundry soap and dryer towels had disappeared. In its place was an oak bookshelf.

Winnie was by the cash register, arranging a bouquet. Owen stood in front of the bookshelf, his arms full of books, his forehead glistening. Both grinned at me expectantly.

Winnie trotted over and hugged me, enveloping me in her favorite black shawl and the scent of patchouli. "Josie, I'm so glad you finally woke up!" she shouted over the music. "See, I told you not to worry! I told you I'd take care of everything!"

I wriggled free and went over to the boom box. I turned off the music. Suddenly the only sounds were just the weird coffeepot—hissing. And me—breathing hard.

"I couldn't help but wake up," I said. "I'm surprised the whole town isn't awake. What's going on here?" I stopped. "Where is Tyra?"

I looked around, panicked. Oh Lord. What if my friends had gone totally mad, maybe tied Tyra up in the storeroom while they wrought these bizarre changes? There'd be a lawsuit, I'd go out of business, I'd be drummed out of town . . .

"Tyra was down here earlier—excited about our changes. She said it would make a lovely backdrop for her show," Winnie said, her voice drained of excitement now. "Paige Morrissey—her assistant, quite a lovely woman—came by to pick her up. They're shopping in Masonville for tonight's entertaining."

I looked over at Owen. He stared pointedly at a book. I looked back at Winnie. "Entertaining? Tonight?"

"Yes," Winnie said. "They thought a little salon-style soirée would be nice, in the upper rooms over the laundrette. Just a few people. I provided a guest list of the upper echelon of Paradise society. The mayor, of course, and Lewis Rothchild since he's the wealthiest business owner in town, and—"

I glared at her. Winnie stopped talking. Her chin quivered. I was unmoved. Since when did Winnie use such hoity-toity language?

"What's next?" I asked. "Stenciling the washers and dryers? Maybe with lilies. I remember reading in the *Idiot's Guide to Decorating* that lilies are always a sophisticated choice."

Winnie's chin quivered hard enough now that her little bell earrings literally tinkled. Owen looked up from the book, and I could see the pain in his eyes. But I went on.

"Or maybe we could make washer-and-dryer cozies. Kind of like super-sized tea cozies. Embroider them little flowers. God forbid this place should actually look like a laundromat on TV, talking about how to get out stains . . . God forbid that . . ."

By now, Winnie and Owen looked positively hurt.

I staggered over to a folding chair and plopped down. At least they hadn't yet replaced my practical metal folding chairs with chaise lounges or whatever is considered refined seating.

"Josie, you were panicked last night and . . . well, what did you expect?" Now Winnie's voice was quivering, too. "I took the day off for this, and Owen doesn't have classes until afternoon."

I sighed. "All I wanted was a little moral support."

"Well," Winnie sniffed, "not all of this was my idea."

Owen smiled nervously. "I have to admit, after Winnie called me at two o'clock this morning, I came up with the cappuccino machine and the bookshelf and the books. And the music." He was warming to his subject now, forgetting that I was mad. "I wanted to create an intellectual waiting area for patrons to enjoy between loads. Winnie and I compared notes on our ideas and went to Big Jim's 24-hour Warehouse up in Masonville, got what we needed, and got to work." He beamed at me. "After all, you love reading. So isn't it a wonderful idea for you to encourage reading among your patrons, between loads? To lift the intellectual level of Paradise?"

I peered for a moment at the books on the shelf behind him. They were paperbacks, but classics. *Jane Eyre. War and Peace. Of Mice and Men.* I recognized them as paperback extras from Owen's house—he was on a mission to replace all the paperbacks he'd collected with hardcover volumes. That mission was one reason I found him endearing. Usually.

I turned to Winnie. "And where is Billy's Cut-N-Suck?"

"Well, he took it with him. When he left."

Now, this was alarming news, because I couldn't think of anywhere else Billy could go. His car still wasn't fixed.

"Why did Billy leave? And where did he go?"

"We explained the situation quite clearly to Billy right after we got back from Masonville—"

"You woke him up at, what, four in the morning?"

"No," Owen said. "He was just getting back from the Red Horse Motel—some woman in a white truck dropping him off." Owen frowned, shook his head. "He didn't look happy. He was upset by something—which is probably why he took our news so poorly."

"Your news?" I said.

"Now, Josie," Winnie said. "You know Billy can't be here while Tyra's here. He'll spoil the whole ambience. And wouldn't it be better if Tyra had her own suite, rather than you having to sleep on your couch?" I'd envisioned *Tyra* continuing to sleep on my couch, but I didn't bother to explain that. "So we told him he needed to move in with Owen, while we redecorated your spare apartment to get it ready for Tyra—as a Bed and Breakfast."

"Just what am I supposed to feed her? Pop-Tarts?"

Owen ignored my question. "Billy went into a rage, something about people with too much power hurting people with too little power. He said if Tyra Grimes came here, there'd be real trouble—which was pretty odd, considering he was wearing his Tyra Grimes T-shirt. Then he took his Cut-N-Suck and walked off, saying he was going back to the Red Horse Motel."

I groaned. Now the list of people predicting trouble if Tyra came to town was made up of Lewis Rothchild, Vivian Denlinger, the ghost of Mrs. Oglevee, and my nutty cousin Billy Toadfern. And Tyra was already here. Oh, Lord, was she ever here.

I groaned again.

"Maybe a nice cup of cappuccino will help you," Owen said.

He trotted over to the weird coffeemaker and in a few minutes came over to me with a mug filled with frothy stuff. I don't function well without coffee in the morning, and if I didn't take a sip I was liable to say something really, really hurtful to these two dear people who I loved very much and who were now making me crazy.

So, I took a sip. And right off, I started choking. All that white frothy milk on top was deceptive. The essence of the stuff was a thick liquid, riddled with coffee grounds.

I half swallowed, half chewed to get the mouthful down.

Owen grabbed the mug from me. "Must be the flubberguster," he said. Or something like that. He was muttering about mechanical parts. I stared at him, but he didn't notice.

This was Owen? My philosophical boyfriend? My society's-obsession-with-pretenses-will-undermine-us-all boyfriend, who was currently teaching the Art of Angst (or maybe it was the Angst of Art) at Masonville Community College? I didn't recognize him.

Then I stared over at Winnie. She was fussing with the books, trying to arrange them just so.

This was Winnie? My literary best friend? My all-individuals-are-equally-important-in-the-sight-of-God best friend, who knew the reading tastes of everyone on her book-mobile route, and who made sure her shut-ins got a fresh supply of their favorite books every week? I didn't recognize her.

I needed some real coffee. Around people I'd definitely recognize—across the street at Sandy's Restaurant. So I left. Owen and Winnie didn't notice.

I crossed the street to Sandy's. Just before I went in, I looked back at my laundromat.

Now that my window said, "Josephine Todeferne's Laundrette" in fancy script, it didn't look like my place at all.

Not at all.

At least things were normal over at Sandy's Restaurant.

The framed Norman Rockwell poster was still hanging in its spot on the knotty-pine paneling—the Rockwell of the police officer in blue uniform sitting at a diner stool next to a runaway boy. I just love that poster.

And then there was dear old Sandy herself. I took my usual spot at the counter and Sandy came right over to me, with a fresh mug of coffee. Just plain, black coffee. No froth.

As usual, Sandy had on her blue-and-white checked apron—which cleverly matches the place mats—right over her favorite NASCAR T-shirt and black leggings. As usual, her bluish-white hair was teased up so high that if she wanted to take a drive somewhere later on, she'd need an extra airbag just for the hairdo. And as usual, her voice was a gravely bass, made so from about 50 of her 60 years being spent smoking.

I could have hugged her, just for being her usual self.

Sandy said, "Lord, child, you're a sight. You okay?"

I grinned. Sandy, as usual, was blunt to the point of rude. What a relief. I'd have cried like a baby if she'd been nice.

"I'm tired—trouble sleeping. I just need my usual." Then I took a nice, long sip of my regular, plain, black coffee.

Sandy stared at me for a long moment, then shrugged. A few minutes later, she was back with my usual Monday morning breakfast: one biscuit, split open, smothered in sausage gravy. And a glass of cranberry juice. I applied ample salt and pepper to my biscuits-and-gravy, then happily set to eating. Away from Owen and Winnie, at least, life in Paradise was still normal.

I was about half way through my breakfast when the bell on the front door tinkled. Just one of the other regulars at Sandy's, I thought happily, coming in for breakfast—as usual.

But then Cherry sat down on the stool next to me and said, "Oh, Josie, I am just so thrilled to see you! Have I ever worked up an extra special treat for you!"

I jumped, sloshing some cranberry juice on the cloth placemat. I waved at Sandy—I needed some club soda to dab on the place mat or getting the stain out when I did the restaurant's laundry on Thursday was going to be difficult.

Then I looked over at Cherry. "What do you mean?" I asked.

"Josie, honey, I just walked by your laundromat. Winnie and Owen told me the good news about Tyra Grimes being here! So, you just finish up your breakfast, because it is time for your makeover! Hair cut, coloring, perm, a facial . . . ooh, it'll be so much fun! I've always wanted to do a celebrity!"

So much for life being normal. Tyra Grimes celebrity

fever—apparently more infectious than mad cow disease—
had already spread from Owen and Winnie to Cherry. The
rest of the town couldn't be far behind.

I said, "I don't want a makeover."

"You may not want one, but, honey, you sure need one.
You're going on national TV, remember?"

I remembered. My stomach clumped back into a peanut-
shaped—and now gravy-soaked—knot.

"No need for me to change how I look for one little TV
spot. All I have to do is share my stain expertise. No one will
care about how I look, because they'll just want to hear what
I know."

Sandy came over and I asked for the club soda. She
obliged, and I started dabbing it onto the place mat.

Meanwhile, Cherry was saying, "Please, Josie? You've got
to let me redo you. If Tyra Grimes sees what a wonder I've
wrought with you, then maybe she'll put me in touch with the
right people in Hollywood and I can go do hair there. That's
my big dream, you know." I knew. Everyone knew. She'd
been telling everyone about it since she was in third grade—
but she'd never traveled any farther west than Indianapolis.

I kept dabbing at the place mat, not quite able to bring myself to look at Cherry. "Now, Cherry—"

"And, honey, we've got to get you some new clothes. You
can't be running around in your jammies, for pity's sake."

Oh Lord—I still had on a robe and Tweety Bird nightshirt
and slippers. With all that was going on, I'd forgotten about
how I was dressed. No wonder Sandy had looked at me so
funny.

Cherry took my silence for interest. "Okay—we'll need
'before' and 'after' pictures . . ." she whipped out a camera
from her purse. The flash went off in my eyes. "You blinked!"

I couldn't see anything except the aftershock of the flash,
but I heard the tinkle of the bell again.

"Josie, I really need to talk to you." That was Chief John Worthy's voice. I swiveled in his direction, to the right, even though I couldn't see him—my eyes still hadn't cleared.

"I just saw Owen and Winnie," he said. "You should have told me about Tyra being here, because when filming starts, we'll need crowd control. Or will security be coming with her crew?"

"Turn this way, Josie." Cherry swiveled me to the left. "Stop grimacing!"

Flash! The bell tinkled again. Another flash.

"Josie, you little devil you, you really did it!" I recognized the voice of Cornelia Hintermeister, the mayor of Paradise and top seller of Joy Jean Cosmetics for all of Mason County. "Now, we'll need a parade—maybe we can use some of the floats from the Beet Festival Parade."

"We can't do anything of the kind!" hollered Chief Worthy. "We haven't gotten paperwork for the traffic control for a parade, and we need it at least two weeks in advance—"

Cherry swiveled me to her. Flash! Flash! "I think that does it for the 'before' pictures. Now, we'll have to find some makeup to keep you from looking so washed out on camera, and—"

"Josie, I need to talk to you! When can I interview Ms. Grimes—" that was Henry Romar, the editor, chief reporter, and president of advertising at the *Paradise Advertiser–Gazette*.

My vision, at last, cleared—and I was rewarded with the image of dear old Sandy, one hand on her hip, glaring at me, pot of coffee in her other hand.

"Get outta here," she growled at me, "before the whole town comes in here after you and breaks the place to bits."

I slipped off my stool, turned, and was blocked by the Mayor and Chief Worthy and three ladies from the church and the reporter and several other people who were hollering my name—and Cherry, who saw her opportunity and took it.

She grabbed my elbow and pulled me through the crowd. "Make way! Josie will get back to you on matters of crowd control and media and such. Right now, she's late for her makeover!"

I went along with her—anything to get away from the crowd.

It was late afternoon when I emerged from Cherry's a new woman. Well, at least a woman with new hair. Or changed hair, anyway—since, strictly speaking, it was still my hair.

Much to Cherry's disappointment, I refused the facial and manicure and pedicure she was sure I needed.

But here's the thing about my hair.

I hate it.

I've always hated my hair. Its color is dull—a bland shade somewhere between light brown and dark blond. It's fine and thin and gets split ends if I even sneeze.

And there's this one strand that insists on plopping right down in the middle of my forehead. I've tried hairspray and gel and mousse, but suddenly, this one strand'll start to quiver—I swear it will—and then plop down right over my left eye. I've even nicknamed it—the Forelock from Hell. And don't even mention bangs. Bangs make me look like a girl-version of Howdy Doody, except with dull-colored hair. Not pretty.

So I'd long given up on having any kind of style at all, and just went for clean and out of the way years ago. I shampoo it, and while it's still wet, just pull it back in a ponytail.

So when Cherry said she could do miracles for my hair, I thought, why not? I didn't want to go back into the laundromat and deal with Winnie and Owen. Or anywhere else in Paradise, where I was sure I'd just be greeted with more

Tyramania. Truth be told, I didn't want to deal with Tyra herself, either.

Besides, Cherry was doing my hair for free—on account of me now being a celebrity-stain-expert-to-the-stars.

And when Cherry turned me around, and at last I beheld myself in the mirror, I got very, very happy.

No, that's not quite putting it strongly enough. I was in a state of bliss because I had been transformed, all by one cut, perm, and dye job. Thanks to my new hair, I was popular and beautiful and smart and successful and hip and right on and cool and with it and all those great things I've never been and never knew I wanted to be until I saw how I looked in that moment.

The Forelock from Hell was no more. My hair was a soft strawberry blond, short and perky and wavy, curling around my ears. I even looked like I'd lost about half of the twenty extra pounds I've been carrying around for the ten years since my high school graduation.

I hugged Cherry. I floated in bliss out of the door—as if even my tattered robe and Tweety slippers had been transformed by a fairy godmother's wand into a power suit. I felt tall, thin and beautiful, and ready for the *Tyra Grimes Home Show*. No, I felt ready for more than that. Why stop at just being a guest on the Tyra Grimes show?

Why not have my own show? *The Josie Toadfern Stain Removal Hour of Power*—no, no, the *Josephine Todeferne Cleanliness-Is-Next-to-Godliness Show*. I could have sponsors. Spinoffs. My own production company, even. Yes, I was suddenly caught up in the very madness I'd tried to escape.

But then I stepped out into the brilliant bright light of that spring day in Paradise, and reality hit. Thanks to Billy Toadfern himself, who had reappeared in Paradise, right in front of my laundromat—with his very own effigy of Tyra Grimes.

5

Billy's big, hairy, naked belly bounced in keeping with his back and forth marching in front of my laundromat. Billy carried a homemade wooden cross on which he'd put his Tyra Grimes T-shirt—armpit sweat stains and all. At the very top of the cross, he'd put a Halloween monster mask—green face, warty nose.

A crowd had gathered around Billy, blocking the doors to several establishments besides mine—Tony's Pharmacy, the Antique Depot, Grunning's Watch and Shoe Repair. The gathering wasn't friendly. Everyone was shouting at Billy to shut up and go away.

Still, I could hear Billy over everyone else. "The devil has come to Paradise! You think you'll find fame and fortune with Tyra Grimes here, but mark my words, she brings trouble!"

I ran toward Billy and the crowd—never mind that I still had on my robe and Tweety Bird nightshirt and slippers—hoping to get Billy to go up to his apartment. I looked around for Winnie and Owen, but in my moment of need, they were nowhere in sight. Owen would be at the Masonville Community College by now. And Winnie was up in my apartment, I supposed, getting ready for Tyra's "soirée." Lord only knew where Tyra and Paige—who I still hadn't even met—might be. I looked around for someone who might help—and saw Lewis Rothchild.

He was the only one not shouting at Billy. His expression was a curious mix of satisfaction and grimness, his smile a half-grimace. I veered over to him.

"Did you put Billy up to this?" I demanded.

"No. Somehow he's figured out that Tyra is evil all on his own." I was about to ask what that was supposed to mean when a little girl, Haley Gettlehorn, started tugging on my robe and Lewis's pants.

"We came out of the laundromat to see what the ruckus was," Haley was wailing, "and somehow I got lost from Mama, and—"

Before I could say anything, Lewis knelt down next to her. His smile changed, all at once, to one of genuine gentleness— a most amazing transformation. Then he said, "I bet if I put you up on my shoulders, you can spot her. How about it?"

Haley nodded. Lewis hoisted her up onto his shoulders, stood, and in a second Haley clapped and pointed. "There she is! I see her! Mama! She's coming!"

A few seconds later, Becky was by us, gathering Haley into her arms. As they disappeared into the crowd again—which was growing angrier and more restless—Lewis looked back at me. "You would do well to listen to Billy. We all would."

Just what was Lewis's problem with Tyra? I was about to ask him, when a hush came over the crowd as an SUV—bigger, newer, and shinier than anything usually seen in Paradise—pulled up and parked in front of my laundromat. The passenger door opened, and Tyra Grimes herself stepped out.

She stared at Billy—a bemused look on her face—when suddenly, as if pulled by some magnet, she looked over to us.

She stared past me to Lewis, looking at him as if she was taking him in, bit by bit. Her face was expressionless and pale.

And Lewis stared back, equally riveted, equally expressionless—but beneath the surface was anger. Cold, hard anger.

Tyra looked away first.

By now, a slender, young black woman had gotten out on the driver's side and stood beside Tyra. Paige, I thought.

Mayor Cornelia Hintermeister stepped forward from the crowd. "On behalf of Paradise, I'd like to apologize for this buffoon—"

That miffed me. Billy could be an idiot, that was true, but he'd served Paradise long and well as a preacher, and now he was trying to make an honest living as a Cut-N-Suck salesman.

"No apology needed. I'm used to encountering a few people who aren't exactly fans. Hard to believe, but perhaps they're just so decorating-impaired they feel intimidated by little old me?" With that she gave a twittering laugh. The crowd twittered along with her.

Maybe Lewis was just one of Tyra's decorating-impaired un-fans—although his funeral home chairs did have nice upholstery. I turned to look at him, but he had disappeared. No, there was something more about why he didn't like Tyra . . .

I didn't have time to finish the thought. My attention was drawn back to the crowd by hollers of, "Stop! Somebody stop him!"

Billy had surged forward and was now facing Tyra, who looked totally unworried and just smiled up at him.

"Why," she asked, "are you protesting me, my dear man?"

"Look at this T-shirt," Billy shouted, shaking his T-shirt-on-a-stick. "What if these people knew how it was made?"

"Why, it was sewn together, of course," Tyra said, laughing.

Again, the crowd laughed along with her.

Poor Billy turned as red as the shirt. That was all the Billy-taunting I could stand. I put my head down and like a little bull—I was feeling mighty empowered by my new hair—I pushed my way through the crowd to Billy.

"Make him stop, Josie," someone near me hollered.

"Yeah," someone else shouted. "He's your cousin, Josie, do something about this."

But Billy hadn't even noticed me. Or the fact that angry Paradisites were closing in around us, no doubt ready to drag us away from Tyra and sacrifice us for her, if she should so choose. For the moment she simply looked bemused.

I saw Chief John Worthy moving toward us.

I grabbed Billy's arm, but he shook me off. So I grabbed him by the chest hairs and yanked, but he barely flinched. He started shouting, crazy loud, "Tyra Grimes is evil!"

Chief Worthy was moving fast and glaring at Billy—and I knew if Billy didn't shut up, he'd end up in jail. I also knew Billy wouldn't shut up. So I did the only thing I could.

I jerked Billy's cross-effigy of Tyra Grimes away from him, and whacked him over the head with it. Billy went down with a moan, into a heap between Tyra and myself.

The grotesque Halloween mask went flying off the top of the cross, and landed right on Tyra's head. The crowd went quiet.

Chief Worthy had made his way over to us, and now looked at Tyra with grave concern. "Are you all right, ma'am?"

"I am fine," Tyra said, putting a little space between each word. She plucked the monster mask off the top of her head, mussing her usually perfect hair.

"Would you mind returning this to your cousin," she said, holding the mask out to me.

I took it. "I'm sorry for the ruckus Billy's caused . . ."

Tyra held up her hand to silence me—a gesture which, I'm sorry to report, worked perfectly. "We have much to do before this evening's gathering," Tyra said. "Assuming, of course, your apartment is still available."

Tell her to go, a voice inside urged. Billy's figured out the truth about Tyra, I could hear Lewis saying. She's evil, I could hear Billy shouting . . .

"Assuming," Tyra added, "that you still wish to have your expertise—and your charming town—featured on my show."

The crowd gave a gasp, all at once.

Now, here's the thing I'll always wonder. If I'd told her no, I didn't want to be on her show anymore, would she have gone away? Would the murders that soon followed have been avoided? Maybe not. Maybe we Paradisites were just bit players, and Paradise just a backdrop, for a drama fated to be played out somehow, somewhere, with or without us. Or maybe I just want to see it that way to make myself feel better about what came later.

In any case, at that moment, all I really knew was that the fate of Paradise suddenly seemed to rest with me . . . that the best chance for the recognition our town needed lay with Tyra . . . and that she—and the people of my town—were waiting for my answer.

I smiled at her. "Of course you're welcome to have your party at my apartment."

She lifted an eyebrow—just the left one—wanting to hear the rest of the words.

"And of course I—we—want to be on your show."

She smiled. The crowd around me sighed in relief. She gestured at Paige and they headed toward my laundromat, Chief Worthy trotting along behind them, hollering at the people who followed them to back off and give them room. The rest of the crowd wandered off. Billy started stirring.

An old, half-rusted white pickup truck pulled up behind

Tyra and Paige's SUV. A dark-haired woman was driving the truck, and she blared the horn. At that, Billy stirred some more, then stood up unsteadily.

"Billy—are you okay? I'm sorry I whopped you, but—"

He rubbed his head. "I'm fine. I'll have a hell of a headache soon, but I'm fine."

"Billy, what's going on? What is all this about?"

He glared at me. "You wouldn't believe me if I told you."

The truck horn blared again. Billy grabbed the Tyra T-shirted cross from me, tottered unevenly off to the pickup, tossed the cross into the back, then clambered in the passenger side. The truck took off, muffler rumbling loudly.

Why, I thought, did Billy hate Tyra so? He'd never even met her until the confrontation a moment ago. And while he'd never been a devotee of her show, he'd never minded when it was on in my laundromat.

My laundromat . . . I felt a protective surge toward my business and started toward my laundromat. A line of people trailed out the door. I trotted over, glanced in the window, and saw that Tyra was in there, signing autographs. At least Chief Worthy was making everyone stay in a nice line. No one was doing laundry. Suddenly, I felt a strong need to get away somewhere where I could think.

I walked over to my tiny laundromat parking lot, jumped into my old Chevy, tossed Billy's mask into the passenger seat, pulled up the passenger side floor mat, and got my spare key. I fired up my car and pulled out, taking the only main road out of town.

Once I got out a little ways out of town, two things occurred to me.

One was that no one had commented on my hair. I mean, I know everyone was upset about Billy and excited about Tyra, but my hair was such a dramatic change, I couldn't help but be disappointed that someone hadn't noticed.

The second was that this was the very road I'd taken out of town a few weeks ago, but then, I'd left calmly, with my letter to Tyra Grimes in the seat next to me. I'd made the next to impossible happen—Tyra Grimes had come to my town. But now I barely recognized the town or its people.

I drove for a while, trying to sort out my thoughts and feelings—until I saw up ahead the old, rusty white pickup. The one driven by the mysterious woman and carrying my cousin Billy.

So I decided to trail them. They must not have noticed me because they didn't speed up. Instead, they slowed down and turned left onto an abandoned lane, now overgrown with shrubbery and wild blackberry bushes.

I knew where that lane led. The old orphanage. Mason County Children's Home. Why in the world would they go there? I intended to find out.

A dirt road leads off the lane to storage and work barns. They'd been off limits, but I'd snuck out to them anyway. They'd been good places to hide and think and read and sometimes cry.

I pulled down the dirt road and parked my Chevy out of view. Then I took a path I knew that led up to the top of a hill. From there I could look down on the Home.

I'd lived at the Mason County Children's Home for six months, when I was nine, after my mama ran off. None of the Toadferns—my mama's people—could afford another mouth to feed. None of the Foersthoefels—my papa's people—wanted a Toadfern child to tend to. The Foersthoefels always hated the Toadferns, called them white trash. The Toadferns always hated the Foersthoefels, called them uppity. There I was, abandoned by both families, until finally

Horace and Clara Foersthoefel took me in, and turned out to be good people.

I got to the hill top in time to see Billy and the mystery woman get out of the white truck, which was parked by the two-story main building. I watched them climb through a break in the wire fence, now half pulled down by overgrown shrubs and small trees. They disappeared into a door in the back of the building.

I watched, never taking my eyes off that door. Memories started welling up in my mind, but I pushed them back down for now. Now was not the time for dwelling on personal stuff. I wanted to know why Billy hated Tyra Grimes. He could be overzealous and stubborn, but he always had a reason—and if he wasn't going to tell me why he had decided to protest Tyra, I was going to have to find out some other way.

So, I watched and waited and finally Billy and the dark-haired woman came out of the back door, carrying boxes, which they put into the back of the pickup, then drove off.

I counted to one thousand. Since they hadn't come back in that time, I reckoned they wouldn't for a while. I walked down the hill and climbed over the fence—ripping my bathrobe—then worked my way through the grass and shrubs to the back door.

There was a new lock on the door. And the windows were boarded up from the outside. So I went back to my Chevy, got the tire iron out of the trunk, returned to the building, and pried off one of the boards from the window.

The windows had been boarded up from the inside too. But one of those boards had swung loose, so I could peek through.

And that peek revealed a whole lot.

A lot more boxes like the ones Billy and the mystery woman had been carrying out. New cardboard boxes. Probably twenty of them. And out of the corner of one was sticking the top of a Tyra Grimes T-shirt.

I drove around for quite a while after I left the Home, my head spinning with questions like, why did Billy—along with other unlikely candidates such as Lewis and Vivian— hate Tyra? Where had all those T-shirts come from, and who was the dark-haired woman and how had he gotten involved with her? Would Owen and Winnie and Paradise ever return to their normal states that I hadn't—until now—realized I so adored? Would Owen like my new hairdo—or even notice it?

Mostly, I have to admit, I didn't really want to face what-ever madness was going on in Paradise.

Finally, though, my gas tank was running low, it was nearly seven o'clock (according to my dashboard clock), and I was hungry. I didn't relish the idea of running out of gas and walking back into town in my bathrobe—now filthy and ripped beyond repair—even if my hair was lovely.

So I drove back to Paradise, hoping I could finally change into some real clothes and maybe grab a bite over at Sandy's, hoping things had quieted down a little.

They'd quieted down too much. My laundromat's tiny parking lot was full, so was the lot for Sandy's Restaurant across the street, and so were the curb parking spaces. I had to park all the way up by the Paradise Theatre (closed for ren-ovations for the past two years). But there wasn't another soul in sight. The shops were all closed. Someone had even locked up my laundromat. The only place that was open was Sandy's Restaurant. Sandy herself leaned in the doorframe, smoking a cigarette. She gave me a wave as I hurried back to my laundromat.

I swallowed, hard. Oh Lord. Tyra's soiree. What was go-ing on in my apartment now?

I rushed up the exterior metal stairs and jerked open the door—and saw where all the Paradisites had gone.

People were crammed in my hallway. Some of them stood in the doorway to my apartment, craning to see in. Some of them held cups and little plates and murmured things like "Have you tried the salmon canapés? They're simply delicious."

Paradise is not a salmon canapé kind of town. It's the kind of town where people buy canned salmon and mix it (flesh and skin and all) with bread crumbs and mustard, and make deep-fried salmon patties, serving them with tartar sauce.

So if Paradisites were murmuring delicately about salmon canapés, then Tyra, I thought, had hypnotized everyone. Or maybe zombified them. I groaned as I pushed my way through the crowd to get into my apartment, beset by un-pretty images of the night of the living Paradisites roaming southern Ohio . . .

Tyra, by herself, sat on my couch. Everyone else—except Mayor Cornelia, who was in my easy chair—sat on the floor, gathered around Tyra's feet. Teachers. Preachers. Shopkeep-ers. Even Winnie and Cherry, cross-legged at Tyra's feet. No one noticed me. They all stared raptly at Tyra.

Every last person was equipped with a bowl and a nut-cracker and walnuts and pecans.

"Most people," Tyra was saying, "don't consider the aes-thetic value of seasonal mulch."

Seasonal mulch? I thought, distractedly, as I looked around my apartment. I was disappointed not to see the one person I really wanted to see—Owen. Lewis and Elroy were the only other prominent Paradisites besides Owen who weren't here.

"Walnut and pecan shells make the best fall mulch," Tyra continued.

"But this is the springtime," Purdy Whitlock (the Baptist pastor's wife) said.

Tyra favored her with a patronizing glance, as if she were a dear but rather slow child. "One needs to think six months out—always. It takes time to crack enough walnut and pecan shells to create autumn mulch to replace the shredded cypress you'll use in the spring and summer. That's why we're starting now."

There was a collective "ah" of understanding.

"And what will we do with the walnuts and pecans themselves?" Mayor Cornelia piped up.

Tyra looked horrified. "Why, we throw them away. Pecan or walnut pies are just not seasonal for spring and these nuts certainly won't keep until the fall."

Another collective "ah."

I shook my head. This was just too much. I had to change my clothes and go find Owen, Billy, someone, to help me figure out what I should do. Or at least, find someone who still made sense to me.

I went to my bedroom. I checked the closet, even under the bed, and was finally satisfied that at least my bedroom was still private . . . except that on the end of the bed, I found my quilt, neatly restitched with the orange thread, and a note—written in fancy calligraphy: "Josie dear, Please do reconsider the white thread. Simply wonderful!—Tyra."

I indulged in extreme eye rolling at that while I shut my door and pressed the button lock. Then I went into the tiny bathroom off my bedroom, changed into jeans and a T-shirt, and attended to grooming basics: teeth brushing, face washing, and dotting on lip gloss and mascara, the only makeup I bother with.

When I stepped out of my bathroom, I found a visitor sitting primly on the edge of my bed, waiting for me.

She was a tall, slender black woman, with wire-rimmed

glasses and close-cropped hair, wearing a burgundy pantsuit. She was the woman who'd been with Tyra in the crowd earlier.

"Ms. Toadfern, I'm sorry to intrude, but I really must speak with you about Ms. Grimes's quarters—"

"How did you get in here? I know I locked the door . . ."

She looked at me blandly. "Hmmm. You must be mistaken, Ms. Toadfern."

And you must be lying, I thought. Somehow, she's picked my bedroom door lock. My heart was pounding at that realization, but I said evenly, "Just call me Josie. And you are?"

"I'm Paige Morrissey, Ms. Grimes's assistant. Pleased to meet you." Her voice was brisk and efficient.

"Great," I said. "Then you can tell me when Tyra plans to wrap up her soirée and get these people out of my apartment."

"You said you didn't mind if Tyra used your apartment. Have we harmed anything? If so, we can repay you—"

"Look, those people out there are the most practical people I know. Tyra has them out there shelling nuts for seasonal mulch! Seasonal mulch! Why, every Paradisite I know has been drilled since birth on understanding the sin of throwing away perfectly good food. Every Christmas party at Sunday School, we had to eat Miss Mulhern's fruitcake—which always smelled of mothballs—because, for God's sake, children were starving elsewhere, and somehow we were convinced that if we didn't eat our mothbally fruitcake we would make them starve even more. And now, your boss has people I've known all my life casting aside perfectly good pecans and walnuts so the shells can be seasonal mulch! She's turning this town upside down and I'm not even sure what she's doing here!"

Paige was not moved by my passionate concern over the mental condition of my fellow Paradisites. "She is here," she said flatly, "because you asked to be on her show."

I sighed. "Yes. But I didn't expect her to show up without warning and turn the whole town upside down."

"What did you expect?"

"Maybe a phone call or letter that she was coming. Some discussion about the show. She's been here twenty-four hours and hasn't brought the show up once. Where's the film crew? When are we doing the show? When do we talk about that?"

Paige shrugged. "I've booked rooms at the Red Horse for the crew, which will be here in a few days. Meanwhile, Tyra has other things to take care of, so you'll have to be patient."

"What could she possibly need to take care of here in Ohio? Does this have anything to do with Tyra's red designer T-shirts?"

Paige stared at me. Something told me not to bring up the T-shirts I'd seen at the old orphanage. "I mean—Billy, my cousin, had one. And I've seen some others . . . around town." No need either, I thought, to tell her about Verbenia's T-shirt.

"I don't know what you're talking about," she said. I didn't believe her. "But I do need to talk to you about Tyra's quarters."

I frowned. "My friends Winnie and Owen said they were cleaning up Billy's apartment—"

Paige shook her head impatiently. "It's clean enough. Your friend showed it to us earlier. But Tyra told me later that the decorating is, well, frankly, too banal. I'll have to do something about it before Tyra can stay there tonight."

"If she was able to sleep on my couch last night, then—"

Paige looked at her watch. "I don't have time for this. Now, if you'll just give me a spare key to the apartment. I don't want to bother your friend—"

"It's no trouble." That was Winnie. We hadn't noticed that she was in the doorway. She stepped into my bedroom and held out a key to Paige. Her chin quivered. "Here's Billy's spare key."

Paige stared at her a moment, taking in the hurt look on Winnie's face. Then she shrugged, grabbed the key from Winnie, and stepped out of my bedroom, shutting the door behind her.

Winnie collapsed on my bed, pulling my great-grandmother Toadfern's quilt over her. "Banal," Winnie moaned. "I got everything in the Tyra Grimes line at Big Sam's Warehouse! Yellow and blue window toppers, and kitchen and bath towels, and tablecloth, and bedspread, and pillows . . ."

I sighed. "Where's Owen?" I asked.

"He went home after we finished Billy's apartment. He didn't want to stay for the party, for some reason . . ."

I grinned at that. I was going to go see Owen. Sooner or later, Winnie'd stop crying and go home. Hopefully, eventually everyone else would, too.

I went out to the living room. Tyra's groupies were still gathered around her. "Now," she was saying, "for a festive touch at the holidays, you can thoroughly clean your pecan and walnut shell mulch, then spray paint it silver or gold . . ."

No one noticed me go to the door. And no one, but me, seemed to think the real nuts in my apartment weren't the pecans and walnuts.

Owen's house is a little two-bedroom box with a row of four garages, added on by the previous owner (who collected cars), growing out of one side, as if the house had sprung an appendage and was reaching for something.

An odd little house—but it is out in the country, on an acre filled with maple and oak and sycamore trees, which was what Owen loved about it. This time of year, the trees had just started leafing out.

When Owen answered the door, his long, blond hair was loosed from his ponytail, and his eyelids were droopy. He had on the Tweety Bird slippers (a match for mine) that I'd gotten him for his birthday and a blessedly plain green T-shirt and jeans. Anyone else would think he'd been sleeping.

But I knew better. He'd been reading, probably bouncing among at least three books.

He blinked at me a second, then said, "Josie!" He sounded surprised, but happy. Then his eyes went wide. "Josie! Your hair! It's—it's beautiful!"

Half an hour later, I was settled in the living room. Every wall has bookshelves up to the ceiling, overflowing with books. Plus books stacked on the floor. And on the shabby gray-brown couch, the striped red chair and the checked blue chair. And on the coffee table. The mismatched shabbiness of the furnishings would be Tyra Grimes's worst nightmare. I loved it. Owen had to move a stack of books from the couch so there'd be room for both of us. Still, we sat cozied up, which I didn't mind a bit.

Owen made me a sandwich and bowl of soup and as I ate, I told Owen everything—about the boxes of red Tyra Grimes T-shirts I'd seen at the old orphanage, and about how right now half the town was cracking nuts to make seasonal mulch as if this was perfectly sane, and about how Winnie was feeling over Tyra's assessment of her decorating efforts in Billy's apartment.

"Everyone's caught up in the fact that a celebrity is in town," Owen said. "I got caught up in it too. With the cappuccino machine. And all that." He paused. "Um, did I mention you look really great, with your hair and all?"

"About five times," I said, grinning—but then my grin

quickly turned to a frown. "I guess I did it because I also got caught up in the nuttiness about Tyra being here. But now . . ."

"The only one who isn't caught up in all this is Billy," Owen said. "He talked to me before the crowd started going nuts about his cross with the Tyra T-shirt. I saw him when I was leaving to go teach. He told me that he'd learned that the T-shirts that are popping up around town—they're illegal."

"Stolen?" I asked.

"Probably that, too. But Billy said they were made illegally. "I got the feeling he knew something very specific—but I couldn't get anything more out of him. He started marching up and down, hollering about Tyra, and then the crowd just grew."

Owen put his hand over mine. "Then I saw you—but you didn't see me. After class, I came home to think. I'm worried that Billy's mixed up in something that'll get him in trouble."

I was too. Before going home, I'd drive out to the Red Horse Motel and see if Billy was still there. But for the moment, I didn't want to leave Owen and his room full of books. He started telling me again how great my hair looked and then we started smooching—just nice, gentle, smooching.

Still, when he suggested that—what with Tyra and all—I should stay with him, I said no, because as much fun as smooching was, I wasn't ready for spending the night. But we smooched some more. After a while, Owen walked me out to my car.

As I pulled away, I thought I saw movement by the fourth garage over. Probably just a deer, I told myself, and headed over to the Red Horse Motel.

I was tired, so I took Licking Creek Lake Road, a short cut to the Red Horse from Owen's. It goes right by the Rothchild wooded land once considered for the antique mall development.

And right by that stretch of land, I saw two vehicles parked alongside the road. I recognized them both, one being Elroy's (because he has the only tow truck in town) and the other being Lewis's (because he has the only newer black Cadillac in town).

I pulled up behind Lewis's Cadillac. It's real dark in southern Ohio countryside at night, so I got my flashlight out of my glove compartment, turned on the flashlight and then shut off my car's engine and my headlights. Then I got out of my car.

The tow truck and Caddy were both empty. There was nothing weird in either of them—just chip bags and soda cans in Elroy's tow truck. The tan leather interior of the Caddy was spotless.

I checked all around the Caddy—no flat tires, no skid marks—plus the tow truck was not hooked up to the Caddy, so my first guess—that something had happened to Lewis and Elroy was out here to tow him—didn't seem likely.

So I went back up to the tow truck itself. Maybe, in a weird role reversal, Elroy had needed help and Lewis had stopped to help him. But there were no signs of that, either.

Maybe, I thought, Lewis and Elroy had come out here to meet and talk—but that didn't seem right, either. They weren't exactly friends.

On the other hand, it was hard to imagine they'd both ended up here by coincidence. And they were the only two Paradise business owners missing from Tyra's "soirée" at my apartment.

Then, I heard singing. I tensed, thinking of Tyra and her show tunes. But it was a man, off key, warbling "Amazing Grace."

Elroy came crashing out of the woods. At first, I had the shocking thought that always-somber-and-sober Elroy was drunk.

"Elroy," I hollered. "Over here, by your tow truck." He was now skipping up and down in the middle of the road.

He stopped. "Who's there?" he called out in a singsong voice.

I trotted over to him, calling, "Elroy, it's Josie. What are you doing out here?" Then I stopped shy of him when my flashlight picked out the handgun tucked in his waistband.

"Josie," he said slowly, as if trying to remember who I was. Then, all at once, he brightened. "Josie! This—this is a miracle! This is a sign! That you would show up, right now—"

"Elroy," I said, eyeing the gun nervously, "What are you talking about?"

"You said there might be some reason other than the tuna sandwiches, why the businessmen went away and didn't ever buy this land for the antique mall. So, I came out to look, and sure enough, you were right! There was something! It wasn't my tuna sandwiches at all!"

I sighed. "Elroy, let's get you home—"

Elroy giggled. "It was the mushrooms! Mushrooms, Josie!"

He ran off into the woods. I was, I realized, expected to follow him. So, I did.

I stumbled along after Elroy, keeping my flashlight trained on his back so I didn't lose him, while he hollered, "they must've eaten the mushrooms . . . ooh, watch out for that big white rabbit!" Elroy dodged to the left, then to the right. ". . . They were too mad to come back, maybe . . . or something . . . but it's as good a reason as the tuna . . . ooh, another big white rabbit!"

I groaned, realizing that Elroy had taken me seriously when I carelessly threw out the idea that something at this site might have been why the businessmen left. He actually found rare spring mushrooms and figured that mushrooms had made them sick, not his tuna, then tested the theory by eating the mushrooms. God only knew how many he'd eaten, but obviously they were poisonous and making him hallucinate—or else I was blind to the wild huge white rabbits of southern Ohio.

Elroy had gotten ahead of me, out of sight. I needed to catch up with him, get him up to the hospital in Masonville. I could find out later about why Lewis's caddy was here too and about Billy at the Red Horse.

I caught up with Elroy, all right. He stopped and I ran right into him. As we fell, I feared his gun would go off when we hit ground. But either the gun was unloaded, or we got lucky, because the only sounds as we landed were the thuds of Elroy hitting the ground, then me, landing on his back.

Elroy grunted, with me still on his back, and I pushed a bit of brush out of my face. I looked around with my flashlight—we had landed in a tiny clearing, which sure enough had mushrooms. Hundreds of tiny white ones, all over the place. And there was something else, too, in the clearing.

Two bodies—one was Lewis Rothchild, and he'd been shot in the chest. He was slumped against a tree. And lying on the ground, maybe 20 feet from him, was Tyra Grimes, not moving.

Elroy groaned. "They weren't here before . . . just the mushrooms . . ."

And with that, he passed out, right underneath me.

6

Now, it's times like those—not that I often find myself late at night in the woods surrounded by poisonous mushrooms and three bodies—that I really wish I had a cell phone.

But I just had a flashlight. I scrambled up off of Elroy, turned my light on him. His face was an unhealthy, pasty, shiny white, sweat beaded up all over his forehead. He was quivering, his breathing ragged and raspy.

Then I went over to Tyra. Except for a nasty lump on her forehead, she looked, well . . . artful. Like an actress playing the part of someone who's passed out. Unlike Elroy's, her breathing was smooth and even. She had a nice rosy color to her cheeks and her auburn locks were spread delicately on the ground, fanned out around her head. Even the way her arms and legs were spread out was prettily posed.

And then there was Lewis. His chest was a gaping open wound. There was no doubt—he was dead. I thought worriedly of the gun Elroy had. I've seen dead people before, but always fixed up, in caskets, laid out at Lewis's funeral home. This was the first time I'd seen death in its natural state, not all prettied up, and what surprised me was, it didn't seem horrible. No awful expression of fear was frozen on Lewis's face. But it didn't seem peaceful either—no beatific expression. Lewis just looked—dead. Empty. It wasn't like looking at Lewis at all.

The whole thing—checking the three bodies, checking the area—took me maybe a minute, give or take. I was out of ideas about what to do.

So I sat down and cried.

I'd like to say I cried because of Lewis—especially Lewis—and Tyra and Elroy. But the truth is I was crying because I felt really sorry for myself.

Now, I know that sounds terrible. But I've noticed that the maw of self-pity tends to open up and slurp you down at the worst of times—like when you're out with three bodies and poison mushrooms in the middle of the night in the middle of nowhere. It whispers, "of course you don't know what to do, you idiot! And if you hadn't gotten all high and mighty, thinking you could get Paradise back on the map just because you know a thing or two about stains, this wouldn't have happened. You think you're so smart because you're a stain expert? Why, a truly smart person would only need a paperclip and, say, a ketchup packet and maybe some dryer lint to rig up a radio device to fetch help . . ."

And so on, like that. But fortunately, my self-pitying despair lasted only a minute or so. It just felt like forever, as these terrible moments do. Then it struck me that someone like Tyra probably had a cell phone in her purse.

I trotted over to Tyra's big black purse and began emptying its contents into a pile on the ground. There was the usual stuff, like what I carry in my purse—a wallet, only leather; a comb, only sterling silver; pen, only the fancy gold kind you have to twist so the tip comes up through a hole. And a used, wadded up tissue. Nothing fancy about that. I guess some things you can't dress up. And a cell phone.

I held the flashlight with one hand, shining it on the cell phone, figured out I had to press the "Power" button first, then tapped in 9-1-1. Then I began talking to someone—well, I kind of shouted into the phone to explain the situation, since the mouthpiece seemed so far away from my mouth. I was reassured that help would soon be here, and I should just stay put.

So I turned off the cell phone and started to put everything back into Tyra's purse. I saw something I hadn't noticed before, a silver compact. It had popped open and revealed two pictures—on one side, a faded, old, black and white picture of a young, wistful looking girl between what I guessed were parents—a sour-looking man and a sad-looking woman. The other picture was of two young girls—but it wasn't really a picture. It was a magazine clipping, no words to identify who the girls were. I closed the compact and put it back in Tyra's purse, wondering about those pictures. They didn't seem to fit with Tyra at all.

A retching sound—half gasp, half cough—snagged my attention. Elroy. He sounded like he was choking.

I don't know what I thought I would do, but I wanted to get over to him, try to help somehow, so I quickly dropped the cell phone into Tyra's purse and started to stand up. But suddenly Tyra grabbed my arm, and I went back down on my knees.

I twisted around with the flashlight and pointed it at her. Tyra was sitting upright, looking scared and confused.

"What," she rasped, "are you doing in my purse?"

"I used your cell phone to call for help . . . I was putting everything back in your purse . . ." I stammered to a stop, feeling guilty, somehow, for the peek I'd had at her pictures.

Then I shook my head. This was ridiculous. This woman had just come to, in the middle of the woods in Ohio, between a dead man and a retching man, and her first question was about what I was doing with her purse. "Look," I said, wrenching my arm free of her grasp, "just what are you doing out here? And with Lewis Rothchild and Elroy Magruder, of all people? I thought you were back at my place, at your party?"

She stared past me, lost in her own world. Then she pressed her eyes shut for a second, opened them again, and looked around like she was just now opening her eyes.

"Where—where am I?"

"You're okay," I said, although I wasn't sure I believed that. "Do you know what happened?"

"I was at the party at your apartment, having a lovely time, and it ended, so I—I decided to take a walk, and . . . and . . ."

Elroy let out with another long, retching gasp. Tyra grabbed my arm again, only this time she was shrieking, "That man! That man! He attacked us!!"

She shook me and pointed at Elroy. "Him! That man there! He attacked us—oh, it's coming back to me now—he knocked me down, started arguing with poor Lewis, and the last thing I heard as I was passing out was a shot, and Lewis moaning, and that terrible, evil man laughing! Josie, keep him from me . . ."

I stared at poor Elroy, who—gagging and writhing about in his bright yellow windbreaker—looked like a ridiculously large goldfish out of its bowl. I said, "What? Elroy? Evil?"

That's when it started to drizzle. The three good weeks of spring weather—for which Paradise was named by its settlers—had come to an end.

"Oh, it was just awful. I was just taking a walk after the party at Josie Toadfern's humble abode, because I was so overwhelmed by the simple, homey sweetness of the good people of Paradise who had come to meet me and learn from the stores of my knowledge of elegant living—really, their adoration was touching, and I do so wish you could have been there, John—I may call you John, mayn't I?"

Tyra stared up at Chief John Worthy, her eyes big and wide. Chief Worthy nodded solemnly. I was hopping up and down, trying to get Chief Worthy's attention.

We—that is, Chief Worthy, Tyra, and myself, although Chief Worthy and Tyra didn't seem to realize I was right there—were all on the edge of the clearing, just yards away from where the county coroner and other officials were taking stock of Lewis and the area around him. Big lights were set up, so we could see each other, in a shadowy kind of way. Elroy had already been taken away by ambulance, the gun he carried bagged as evidence. I wished I could go over and watch the investigation—I'd never seen a murder investigation before, except on TV—but I figured that'd get me thrown out, and I needed to talk to Chief Worthy.

But all his attention was on Tyra. I swear, he was so entranced, he was practically purring.

Tyra went on. "I was taking a nice evening walk when Lewis Rothchild stopped to check on me—he was such a nice man, so kind to stop and check on me, and I was grateful, since I'd gotten lost and wandered far from the town. Then out of nowhere came that—that evil man—" Tyra shuddered and pointed toward where poor Elroy had been just ten minutes before, moaning and groaning, while the paramedics hoisted him up on a stretcher to take him up to Mason County General Hospital.

At least they'd listened to me—and taken me seriously—when I explained that Elroy had most likely eaten quite a few of the mushrooms in the clearing. One of the paramedics had even bagged a few mushroom samples to take up to the hospital. Elroy, she'd told me, would most likely be okay after getting his stomach pumped—but he was lucky I'd come along when I had, or he'd probably have died from mushroom poisoning.

It seemed that that was where his luck was going to end, because now Chief Worthy was saying, "Don't worry, Ms. Grimes—"

"Oh, John, please just call me Tyra, won't you?"

I swear, the man blushed. "Uh, well, Tyra, I was just going to say you shouldn't worry—we'll keep an eye on him at the hospital and as soon as he's released, question him down at HQ." His chest puffed out a bit when he said "HQ."

"Oh, you're so brave," Tyra gasped. "I mean, that man just came charging at us, knocked me in the head, and as I was going down, I saw him . . . saw him start to hit poor, dear Lewis—who put up a brave fight, but that man was just like a raging bull. He pulled out a gun from somewhere and shot poor old Lewis, right in the chest. I—I wanted to help—" Tyra paused long enough to hiccup out another sob—"but I just passed right on out."

Just then, another ambulance pulled up. "Here's the ambulance—let's get you up to the hospital, just to make sure you didn't get a concussion." John guided Tyra around the crime scene and toward the ambulance. I walked right behind them.

"Oh dear, do you think I'll have to stay the night?"

"That's up to the doctors, but it's likely. I assure you, Ms. Grimes—uh, Tyra—you'll get the finest medical care."

"I'd better call Paige and let her know what's happened." Tyra whipped out her cell phone and started punching numbers as the paramedics helped her into the ambulance.

"Thank you for your statement," Chief Worthy called, with a little wave, as a paramedic shut the doors. Our last view that night of Tyra was of her kicking off her high-heeled pumps.

Statement? Chief Worthy had written nary a note of Tyra's comments—and he certainly hadn't questioned a single thing.

But I had a lot of questions.

First of all, who wears high-heeled pumps to take a walk at night on a country road?

And second of all, even if Tyra had been taking a walk, why would Lewis stop to help her? He'd made it clear he hated her.

Third, how could anyone believe Elroy would shoot anyone?

I thought these questions needed asking, so I tapped Chief Worthy on the shoulder.

He turned, looked at me, and sighed. "What do you want?"

"To give you my statement, just like Tyra Grimes."

He stepped away from me, at the same time shaking his head dismissively. "You gave your statement to Officer Niehaus."

I'd barely gotten to tell Joe Niehaus how I'd seen both Lewis's and Elroy's vehicles by the road, got out to investigate, and what had happened next, before Chief Worthy had told him to go see if anyone needed extra flashlights or coffee or something. Then he'd told me to go home, but I'd stayed around, even though he kept ignoring me.

But I wasn't going to be ignored now.

I jumped right in front of him. "Look, there's a lot that Tyra's leaving out. Like, how could Elroy just sneak up on Lewis and Tyra with a tow truck, for pity's sake? And if Lewis was just checking on Tyra, how'd they end up back here? I mean, why would they take a walk in the woods together? And if Elroy's this mad killer, why didn't he kill Tyra too, since she allegedly," I paused, licked my lips, repeated the word since it seemed so powerful, with all its lawyerly innuendo, "*Allegedly* witnessed him killing Lewis?"

Chief Worthy stepped around. "Probably because Elroy

was confused by the opiate effect of the mushrooms he'd eaten."

I trotted after him. "C'mon, now, you know Elroy couldn't have killed Lewis—Elroy's a big old softy."

"Lewis was always making fun of Elroy for those tuna sandwiches. Murders have been committed over lesser motives than that. Maybe Elroy'd had enough. And Elroy had a gun. Look, Josie, just leave the investigation to the professionals, okay?"

I had to admit, it certainly looked like Elroy had killed Lewis. And he did have years of resentment built up against him. Maybe the effect of the mushrooms had pushed him over the edge? Still, I felt I ought to stick up for Elroy.

So I said, "Well, what about what Elroy has to say?"

"He'll be questioned after he's better and ready to talk."

"And he'll have a lawyer present?"

"No one will abuse his rights."

Poor Elroy, I thought. Even with a lawyer present, he'd stutter and stammer and cry the minute he was questioned.

"Elroy said, 'They weren't here before' when we found Lewis and Tyra, before he passed out," I said, even though Chief Worthy had moved past me—again. I followed him—again. "That must mean he was out here first, and then Lewis and Tyra came here."

Chief Worthy picked up his pace. He didn't say anything. I trotted after him, hollering so he'd be sure to hear. "And I know Lewis didn't like Tyra—although I don't know why. So it's hard to believe that he'd stop to check on her, so I think you ought to ask Tyra about that, and—"

Chief Worthy whirled to face me. That made me stop short—but not before running right into him, and scratching my nose on his jacket zipper. "Josie—thanks for your help. You've done enough, really—far above and beyond the call of a citizen." He put an awful lot of emphasis on that last word.

"But, I really think you ought to consider—"

"Go home, Josie. Stay out of this and go home now—or I'll arrest you for tampering with the scene of a crime. I don't want to—but I will if I have to."

He stared down at me, waiting for me to go. I didn't want to go. But I knew I couldn't do any of the investigating I was thinking I was going to have to do from the confines of the town jail. And it had started to rain again, hard this time. So I bit my lip, turned, and dashed back to my car.

By the time I got home, it was nearly 11 P.M., and I was pooped. But I could see my wish for a simple end to a very weird day wasn't going to come true, at least not right away.

Paige Morrissey was in my living room, sitting on the edge of my couch, sipping from a mug. She must have worked hard cleaning up, because everything was back as it had been before the party—still in the post-Tyra-redecorating-frenzy style, not the way I liked it, but clean and neat. You couldn't tell a party had been held here.

She put the mug down on my coffee table, then leaned forward so far that the room was filled with a certain tension—would she or would she not end up thudding her butt to the floor?

Now, Ms. Morrissey didn't exactly strike me as someone prone to watching late-night television, so I admit I crept forward a little more quietly than strictly necessary to see what boob-tube fare she was taking in . . . Leno? A movie classic?

Neither. It took me a minute to sort out what the men in suits were debating around a cherry table that, frankly, looked fake and needed dusting. It was a cable news chat show that was focusing on cheap labor as a practice for making clothing that's then sold at high designer prices here in the United States.

One of the pundits said, "All right, Paul, you make a good

case for how this helps commerce here, but what about the appalling labor practices some allege go on—use of children, low pay, long hours? We all know about the allegations against sports shoe giant Achilles—"

"Which were never proven, Tom—"

Paige shivered and wrapped her white sweater tighter around her, as if seeking comfort from the gesture.

"Maybe not, Paul, but I have some very good insider information that the government will soon file charges for using forced labor against Tyra Grimes . . ."

Paige moaned—just a tiny moan—but it was enough to send her butt off the end of my couch, down with a thud to my floor.

"You okay?" I hollered, moving toward her, which startled her enough—I'd forgotten she didn't know I was in the room—that she brought her head up too fast and whopped it on the corner of my coffee table.

Twenty minutes later, she was sitting across from me at my kitchen table, holding a cold, damp cloth to her temple. She was going to have one big knot.

"Sorry," I said, for about the seventh time.

Paige shook her head, managing to look weary and great all at the same time.

Of course, now that I was sporting a new hairdo, I looked pretty good too. Except my scalp tingled, so I scratched it—and then I thought that probably wasn't very sophisticated, so I stopped. I didn't want to ruin the fact that we were clicking—which was pretty amazing. Paige was cheese soufflé at the Ritz; I was Cheeze Whiz on a Ritz cracker.

Why do I always think in food analogies? I put that question out of my head and spooned up another mouthful of Cap'n Crunch. Paige had already finished hers. I think the head wound had made her a little dizzy, and that was why Paige—who was so slender she looked like she must interview every calorie before letting it pass her lips—agreed to a bowl of Cap'n Crunch. It was a kind of bonding experience, eating Cap'n Crunch together, while Paige filled me in on how the rest of the evening went before, she said, Tyra had left to take a walk. Paige had stayed to clean up, she said.

Now, to my apology, Paige said very kindly, with a smile, "Don't worry, Josie. It's not your fault. This is your home, after all. And you're a sweetie to fuss over me so."

Now, one of the problems I have with people is that I push the wrong things at the wrong time. Just like this one time in biology class, my sophomore year of high school. This very pretty and very popular girl—Tamara Sheehan—and I were paired up to dissect a pig. Somewhere between the liver and the kidney, Tamara—who'd been pretty upset to be paired up with the likes of unpopular, gawky me—said, 'You know, you're okay after all.' I think it was because she kept trying to pass out and I kept telling her she'd be okay. But her compliment made me goofy. I started cracking jokes about pork entrails, and the next thing I knew, Tamara's eyes were rolling to the back of her head—with disgust at me, not at the pig.

That was pretty much how I gummed things up with Paige and me now. I finished off my Cap'n Crunch, licked my lips, and decided I'd take our newfound friendliness as a chance to pry a little. Nosy Josie strikes again.

"That show you were watching when I came in—the government's going to press charges against Tyra?"

What a dud of a move. Paige went stiff on me—fast. "Those were just some talking heads trying to create trouble where there is none."

A look came over her eyes that reminded me of the Paige that had somehow picked the lock to my bedroom door. I suddenly felt uneasy about her, just as I had earlier. But I pressed on, anyway. What if this had something to do with Lewis's murder? It seemed unlikely—but everything was so topsy turvy now, I figured I couldn't discount any possibilities.

"You were pretty intent on listening to what they had to say," I said.

"I was just channel surfing, taking a rest after cleaning up from the party. Is that okay?"

"Of course," I said. "Thanks for doing such a great job cleaning up."

"I used your carpet shampooer, too. I found it in your bedroom closet when I was looking for a vaccuum. I'm afraid I used up the last of the shampoo, though."

"That's okay," I said. "So you were channel surfing . . ." I urged her back to the topic of the TV show on Tyra.

"Right. I stopped at that channel while they were talking about something else, and they started into the story on Tyra just before you walked in." She shrugged, as if the story were of no consequence. "I was about to click to the next channel when you walked in."

That's not what it had looked like to me, I thought. I stared into my bowl, empty except for the Cap'n Crunch sweetened leftover milk. Probably drinking it right from the bowl wouldn't help my fizzling relationship with Paige.

I looked up at Paige. "Why did Tyra really come here?"

Paige stared at me a minute. Then she said, "We went over this earlier tonight, before you left the party. She came to interview you as a stain expert—because you wrote her a letter suggesting she should."

I shook my head. "That's what I wanted to believe at first. But she hasn't asked me word one about stains."

"I'm sure she will sometime tomorrow." Paige said. "After she's back from the hospital." She sure didn't seem at all upset by her boss's experience . . . or about Lewis's murder. While we ate our Cap'n Crunch, I'd told her about how I'd found them, and she hadn't really reacted at all—just accepted the news with an occasional "hmmm" or "mmm hmmm." That seemed mighty odd to me.

Now, she switched from her left hand to her right to hold the cold compress to her bumped forehead. And that's when I saw the big, brown streak on the back of the right sleeve of her white sweater.

"What happened there?" I said, pointing to the smear.

Paige tilted her head to get a look at the sleeve. "Oh, that. Cocoa. I spilled some earlier and cleaned it up with a sponge. I didn't realize I'd dragged my sleeve through it."

"Well," I said. "That's a protein stain on a cotton-acrylic blend sweater—and believe me, if we don't get that in a cold water presoak, it'll be next to impossible to get out later."

Paige smiled. "You really do know your stains."

I looked at her. "I'm a stain expert. The least I can do is help you get your sweater clean."

She put the cold, moist cloth down on the table, shrugged out of her sweater, and handed it to me. I took the sweater from her and went over to the sink. I got a pail out from beneath the kitchen sink and put the pail under the cold water tap. As I waited for the bucket to fill, I examined the stain. It did have the coloring of cocoa. But it hadn't dried the way cocoa would. And how could she not have noticed she'd gotten cocoa on her sweater? Was she that wrapped up in the TV show? But no, she'd had the presence of mind to clean up the spill from the coffee table. But why would she lie about something like that?

More questions. I turned off the tap, set the pail on the counter, put the sweater in the pail, and returned to the table.

"Thanks," Paige said.

"No problem. Do you want to borrow a jacket of mine later? It's still raining."

"That's real sweet, Josie, but I'll be fine." She smiled again—but this time her smile was sad. "No one ever asks me things like that."

That comment inspired another question. "Why do you work for Tyra, Paige? You're smart—talented—and as sweet as she acts, I'd think she'd be tiring to work for. And demanding."

"She pays me very well." Paige's smile turned tight, thin . . . and scary. "I would do anything for her. Anything."

I shivered. Just how far did "anything" extend?

Paige shook her head as if to clear it. "Now, I ought to get back to the Red Horse Motel—"

"There's an example of just what I'm trying to say. You have to stay there, where Tyra won't even set foot, and she gets this whole apartment, not that it's a palace or anything, but—"

"Josie, do you want to be on the *Tyra Grimes Home Show*?" Paige asked, clipping off the ends of her words, as she stood up and went for her purse in the living room.

"Of course! It's just that—what with all that's gone on, and the fact Tyra hasn't expressed any interest at all in my stain expertise—"

"If you want to be on Tyra's show, stop asking questions."

But I've always been a question-asker. It's a natural gift, one that comes in handy, at least when it's not getting me in trouble. So when Paige was almost to my door, I stopped her with one more question. "Paige, why are there people around town wearing Tyra Grimes T-shirts—red with her signature on them?"

She stopped, then slowly turned, fixing me with her dark, probing eyes. "Tyra is not involved in clothing manufacturing at this time. If you've seen such T-shirts, it's because someone is trying to make an unlawful profit using her name."

Her statement sounded like it came straight from some speech made up especially for a news conference. And it was, also, I knew, a lie.

But I didn't say anything more—just watched Paige—ever elegant, even with a head wound—let herself out my door.

I went over to my living room table. Sure enough, her mug had the residue of cocoa in it. I took the mug to the sink and washed it out.

Then I peered in the pail at Paige's sweater.

The cocoa stain wasn't lifting at all.

You see, cocoa stains fall into the protein category. Which means you should soak them in cold water before laundering. If you try to wash them in hot water, you basically cook the stain into the fabric.

On the other hand . . . cold water doesn't do a thing for clothes with mud stains. But hot water will get them out, if you wash them soon enough.

And this stain, which Paige said was cocoa, was acting suspiciously like a mud stain.

Only one way to find out, for sure. If I washed the sweater in hot water, and it came out, it was mud . . . and for some reason Paige had been lying. But if the stain set, it was cocoa after all, and Paige was telling the truth. I shuddered at the thought of purposefully setting a stain into cloth to decipher what it really was.

I had to know. Because if Paige's stain was mud, that could mean she was out at the site where I'd found Tyra, Lewis, and Elroy. At the very least, it meant she hadn't been in my apartment all night as she'd claimed.

But why would she lie? Just how far would she go to do "anything" for her boss? And . . . would Tyra lie to protect her?

I was going to take that sweater down to my laundromat and wash it in hot water to see if I could discover a clue to help me find out the answers to all those questions.

But first, I picked up my Cap'n Crunch bowl, and slurped down all of the sweet milk.

An hour later, I pulled Paige's sweater from the hot water wash to see that sure enough, the stain had washed right out, proving my theory that it was mud and not cocoa. I was so tired. I'd have to figure out what I wanted to do about this knowledge in the morning. Chief Worthy sure wouldn't care. And I didn't like the idea of confronting Paige.

I threw the sweater into a dryer, then went back up to my apartment—making sure to lock the door. Then I had a glass of warm milk before getting ready for bed and finally crawling under the covers. That helped me get to sleep—but it didn't deliver me to a restful sleep, because it seemed I'd only just put my head on my pillow when there was tiny, old Mrs. Oglevee again, at the foot of my bed.

"Peanut butter," I muttered.

Mrs. Oglevee just smiled gleefully, and waved her supersized wooden spoon at me. "Won't work, little missy," she gloated. "I've had counseling."

I sat up. "You get counseling in—in wherever you are?"

Mrs. Oglevee smoothed her white apron, waggled her eyebrows at me, and said, "You'd be amazed at the benefits package that's offered here."

I yawned. "What do you want? I'd like to go back to sleep."

Mrs. Oglevee rolled her eyes. "You are asleep."

I glared at her.

"All right," she sighed. "You're busy, I'm busy, everyone's busy these days, so I'll get on with it. You're going to blow it if you're not careful."

"Okay, so I asked Paige a few questions, but I'll get on Tyra's show. I care about Paradise, you know."

"Forget about the show! You've got bigger fish to fry!"

"No show?" I squeaked.

"With all that's happened, Paradise is definitely going to get media attention now. But it's not going to be the good kind. The only way you're going to turn this around is to find out what happened to Lewis."

"You don't think Elroy killed him?"

Mrs. Oglevee shrugged. "Maybe yes, maybe no. From where I sit, I've observed that just about anyone is capable of anything. But Tyra showing up seems to have triggered his murder, wouldn't you say?"

"Not if Elroy killed Lewis over the tuna sandwiches . . ."

"But why now? Did Tyra say or do something to push Elroy over the edge at the party?"

Hmmm. I hadn't seen Elroy at the party, but maybe I could somehow ask Paige about that, and sneak in a few questions about the sweater's mud stain . . .

Then Mrs. Oglevee threw me a curve. "Besides," she went on, "You ought to be digging into why Tyra really came here."

I'd asked Paige about that—suspicious about Tyra's real motives. But now I stuck out my chin. "To interview me about stain removal tips. You're just jealous and—"

"Josie Toadfern, use your brain for once. Why does anyone ever come to Paradise in the first place? You've got three chances to name the one that correctly applies to Ms. Grimes. Think of this as *Truth or Consequences*."

Great. An afterlife version of an old game show—with Mrs. Oglevee as the host. I didn't want to think about what the consequences would be if I didn't figure out the truth.

But her question was one we'd discussed a lot at Chamber of Commerce meetings, while trying to figure out a way to get more people to come. "Camping over at Licking Creek Lake."

"Bzzz." Mrs. Oglevee made a sound like a buzzer.

"Antique shops!"

"Bzzz."

I suddenly thought of the pictures I'd found in Tyra's purse. "The lake and antiques are the reasons people who aren't from here to begin with come here. Otherwise, sometimes, people who used to live here come back to Paradise for a visit . . ."

Mrs. Oglevee grinned. "Bingo," she said, apparently not caring she'd mixed up her game metaphors.

Then she vanished.

7

The next morning—8:30 A.M. sharp—I deputized Owen and Winnie over chocolate chip pancakes and a to-do list.

We were gathered around the table in my kitchenette. With the bottle of maple syrup (the real stuff, imported from Vermont, because I'll cut corners on lots of things, but not on syrup) and the platter of pancakes, and the plates and forks and mugs of coffee, and the paper and pencils for note taking, my table was pretty crowded.

But as I'd explained when I'd called Owen and Winnie right away this morning, this was a working meeting. Fortunately, Winnie was able to take another day off and Owen didn't have any Tuesday classes. I'd asked Chip Beavy (widow Beavy's grandson) to watch my laundromat for me in exchange for fifty bucks and a month's free use of the laundromat for him and his grandma. I'd realized, with a pang, how used I'd gotten to having Billy around to keep an eye on my laundromat when I wanted to run out.

Now, Owen didn't seem to mind the table being crowded. He was on his third stack of chocolate chip pancakes.

Winnie was grouchy, though, which I did chalk up to the table's condition. Winnie likes things neat, orderly, and with space in between them, if possible. So now, Winnie was poking a finger on the to-do list in the middle of the table. Owen had dripped syrup on the paper, so Winnie's finger stuck for a few seconds each time she poked it, pulling up the paper. Then she'd shake her finger and the paper would fall away with a little "tick" as it unstuck.

"I don't like number three," Winnie said, poking in a little ticking rhythm. "After all, 'Interview widow about Lewis's possible connection to Tyra Grimes seems a little ghoulish just one day after he's murdered, don't you think?"

"I wasn't expecting you to take a tape recorder and stick it in Hazel's face, Winnie," I said. "You just need to nose around a bit. Hazel trusts you to handpick the romance books she reads every week. Maybe you could run a few books over to her—sort of as a service to the bereaved to help distract her from her woes."

"And slide in a few questions while I'm checking out her books? Let's see—'So Hazel, did your dear dead husband have a liaison going with Tyra Grimes? Maybe he just ran up to New York so he could ask her a few questions about funeral etiquette and they became friends? Ooh—look—I got you the latest romance with that hunky model on the cover, Jason Afire!' "

I scratched a tingly spot on my scalp with the erasure end of my pencil. "Winnie, what has gotten into you? This is research. You love research."

"You're not giving Winnie time to mourn," Owen said, around a mouthful of chocolate chip pancake.

Now, I'd never considered that Winnie might be mourning Lewis's loss. It was hard, in fact, to imagine that anyone— besides maybe Hazel—would mourn Lewis. He'd had a monopoly on funerals that kept him in business, but he was too outspoken for most people. Too likely to tease people when he shouldn't—people like poor Elroy.

Still . . . the image came back to me of Lewis just yesterday morning, outside my laundromat, comforting a lost little girl, helping her find her mother, while everyone else was too busy protesting my cousin Billy's anti-Tyra demonstration to even notice the little girl. It was a tender side to Lewis's character that surprised me, because I'd never seen it before. I figured hardly anyone had ever seen it before. And it bothered me that I—and no one else, either—would ever see it again.

So I put a hand on Winnie's arm. "You're right. We need to mourn Lewis. But one of the best things we can do for him is to try to figure out . . ."

I stopped. Both Owen and Winnie were staring at me, bewildered.

"She's not mourning Lewis," Owen said. "She's mourning Tyra—or at least the image she had of Tyra."

Winnie burst out crying, snatched up a paper napkin, and blew her nose. "I idolized Tyra Grimes, you know! And then you . . . you . . . had to bring her here . . . and I had to hear her assistant say Tyra thought the redecorating I did in Billy's apartment was banal. I did it just for her, and with her-her-her prod-d-ducts too . . ."

I looked over to Owen for help.

"It is a human tendency," he said, "to idolize people like Tyra, people who seem to have all the answers, no problems, and the consummate knowledge of how we can best run our homes and lives. Tyra taps into a fundamental need in all of us—the primal need to feather our nests, so to speak, as well as the need to be accepted by the group—by our tribe, if you will. Furthermore—"

I put a hand up. "Owen, please. I get it. Someone like Tyra comes along, tells us how to decorate and be tasteful and homey and all that. Then we turn around and idolize Tyra, who turns out to be—"

"A pig! She's an ungrateful pig!" Winnie wailed.

I thought that was a little extreme. Tyra was tireless in her efforts, which in my book made her tiresome, although no one else in Paradise seemed to mind. Even Winnie wasn't annoyed by Tyra's desire to make over everything, just hurt by the criticism of her decorating. And who knows, I might not have found Tyra's efforts tiring if I hadn't been so upset by her picking out the orange stitching on my quilt.

"Look, wouldn't figuring out what Tyra's up to make you feel a little better?" I said. "I mean, it probably won't help you go back to seeing Tyra as perfect again, but at least you'd be helping get at the truth. Like a research project." Winnie's big on research projects, especially genealogy. She's helped any number of Paradisites trace their roots.

Winnie perked up. "Well, ma-maybe."

"Okay, then. You know Hazel Rothchild better than any of us. Maybe start by asking her where Lewis went last night—anything you can get out of her about his activities. Then work into asking Hazel if she knows of any past connection between Lewis and Tyra that might explain why Lewis didn't want her to come here in the first place—maybe even why Tyra came. My theory is that Tyra really came here for some reason other than putting me on her show—my letter just gave her an excuse to come to Paradise."

"A cover?" Owen suggested.

"Yeah, a cover, for whatever else she's up to here. Winnie, you'll also need to see what you can find out about Tyra Grimes's past."

"You mean, like her childhood?" Winnie was frowning, but she was also calm again. I could tell she was already working this out like a research problem.

I grinned. "Exactly. Now, I've got a job, too."

I told them about the red T-shirts I'd seen in the old orphanage building and about the report on Tyra possibly being indicted on forced labor charges.

"So I figure Tyra being here might have something to do with that."

"Yeah," Winnie said. "Maybe she had someone hide the T-shirts here—the terrible pig! Exploiting workers!"

I sighed. Winnie was starting to sound like Billy. "We don't know that that's true. But I think Billy might know something about it, maybe from the lady he got the T-shirt from to begin with. So I'm going out to the Red Horse, track him down, see what I can find out from him.

"While I'm there, I need to talk to Paige. I hate to say it, but I have to wonder if she knew about some connection between Lewis and Tyra, and was afraid Lewis was going to reveal something that would hurt Tyra. She did say she'd do anything to help her boss, and her sweater had a mud stain on it, which could mean she'd been out at the site where I found Lewis, Tyra, and Elroy." I shook my head. "I don't like to suspect her of murder, but . . ."

"Well, she certainly didn't seem to care that my feelings got murdered," Winnie said.

I ignored her, looked at Owen. "I'll need your help, too."

"Whatever you want, my dearest."

I was tempted to suggest he clean up the sticky dishes on the table. Instead, I said, "While I'm off tracking down Billy and Paige, I need you to go up to Masonville General Hospital and talk with Elroy. You're a good listener, so at first just listen to what he has to say. He'll probably want to repeat the whole spoiled tuna fish story to you. But after that, you can start asking about what happened last night. Hopefully he's feeling better enough to give a little more information."

"Shouldn't he be telling all that to the police?"

I sighed again. For a bright man, Owen can sometimes be

awfully dim. "Of course. And he probably is. But the problem is that the police are already convinced that Elroy killed Lewis because they want to believe Tyra's story. That's why we need to do this digging. We all know Elroy couldn't kill a fly. So we need to figure out what really happened. What Tyra or Paige, or both of them, didn't tell us . . ."

"Yeah, the pigs!" Winnie said. "It's up to us to find the truth! To reveal the truth—"

My telephone rang, and I jumped up to answer it, so I didn't get to hear the rest of Winnie's rant. But after the brief call, my ears were ringing anyhow. I returned to the table and sat back down between Winnie and Owen, feeling worn out even though it was only 9 A.M. This deputizing and investigating work was a lot harder than I'd expected—and I hadn't even left my apartment yet.

Winnie and Owen were discussing research methods Winnie might be able to use to dig into Tyra's past, but they stopped when I sat down, looking at me expectantly.

"That," I said, "was Tyra Grimes. Seems Paige is missing."

"Missing?" Owen and Winnie chorused.

"Missing," I confirmed. "As in not at the Red Horse Motel. Not answering her cell phone. Nowhere to be seen. And not picking Tyra up at Masonville General. Tyra's been released, and she's anxious to get out of there."

"I can pick up Tyra and interview Elroy while I'm up at the hospital," Owen said.

I considered. Tyra had asked for me to pick her up. There'd been no question in her mind that I'd just come get her—and somehow, there'd been none in mine. Tyra had that affect on people. I shook my head to clear it. Maybe it would be a good idea to break Tyra of assuming that whatever she wanted to happen should happen. Maybe without Paige, she'd be more vulnerable . . .

Paige. Where was Paige? Last I knew she was on her way

back to her room at the Red Horse—the very place where
Billy was staying. My scalp suddenly felt itchy again. I
scratched it—hard—while I said, "Okay, Owen, you talk to
Elroy, then get Tyra. I'll take care of two things at once also.
I'll go to the Red Horse—try and track down Billy, and see if
anyone there knows where Paige might have gone off to."

The Red Horse Motel, out on Route 26, was a hot spot back
when travelers used state routes more often, before interstate
highways drew all the traffic. It still had the original sign outside that said "RED HORSE MOTEL," with a little picture of a
red horse, and "ALL UNITS HEATED!," and "VACANCY," with a
"NO" to the left that was never lit. But now the Red Horse
Motel was just a run-down stopping spot on a strip of country road.

Luke and Greta Rhinegold, who'd been very young newlyweds when they'd built the place in 1948, still ran it, still
lived in a small apartment over the office. Twenty years ago,
they'd added a small sign, right below the original one: "ALL
UNITS AIR CONDITIONED!" Ten years ago, when they
couldn't find any help for the family-style restaurant, and
Greta's failing eyesight made it too hard for her to cook, they
converted it to a bar with pool tables and game machines and
a few tables and chairs, a bar where Luke serves drinks and
sandwiches.

I go out twice a week to get their linens. They're a nice
couple, no kids, always together. And they always insist on
paying me when I pick up the laundry, and tipping me when
I drop it off. I always put the tip (two quarters, without fail) in
the "Save the Children Federation" can they keep on the bar.

I parked my Chevy in the lot in front of the office. The center of the building was two stories, the first for the motel office, the second for the Rhinegolds' apartment.

Sticking out from each side of the two-story center was a

single-story row of units, like blocky wings that had somehow landed this strange brick bird, and left it grounded there.
The doors—once a bright red—were faded, the brick weath-
ered, making the whole structure look like it was molting.

My car brought the lot's total to three. No sign of the truck
that Billy had hopped into with the mysterious woman. I
knew I didn't have to check behind the Red Horse for the
truck—all scruffy woods back there.

I had Paige's now perfectly clean sweater in my backseat.
I decided to leave the sweater in the car for now.

I always go to the back entrance to the bar, because that's
where Luke and Greta usually are even in the middle of the
day, watching their favorite soaps on a big-screen TV or talking or playing cards. But today I was here on a different kind
of business.

So, I went into the lobby, furnished with a pamphlet display rack, a couch, a fake tree in the corner, and a TV tray
holding a coffeepot, and about enough space left over for two
people to stand, assuming they liked each other a lot. I hated
to admit to myself that Tyra was right—the front lobby
smelled moldy, with an overtone of chlorine, even though
Luke had rented a backhoe and filled in the outdoor pool
with dirt about twelve years ago. (Greta plants petunias out
there every year, sticks out some plastic patio chairs, and ad-
vertises it in the *Paradise Advertiser–Gazette* as a "romantic
English garden, suitable for teas and wedding receptions.")

Maybe, I thought, I should research some tips on removing mold and see if I could use them on the Rhinegolds'
carpet and curtains. I knew they couldn't afford replace-
ments.

I gave the bell on the counter a good rap, then stepped over
to the display rack and counted my Toadfern's Laundromat
flyers—12, same as a month ago. I noted the Antique Depot
supply had gone down by two flyers, and Cherry's Chat and

Curl's were completely gone. The Dairy Dreeme's, like mine, hadn't changed.

Then I sat down on the red vinyl couch—the side without the crack down the middle of the seat, although that meant having a leaf of the dusty plastic ficus tree resting on my head. I looked out the window, thinking I'd watch for the white truck and Billy, but there were dead flies—six of them—all right beside each other in the windowsill, as if they'd had a little fly accident—a six fly pile-up. That was a bad sign. Greta and Luke always pride themselves on being extra clean. I didn't like the sight, or the thought that soon the Red Horse Motel would be too much for them, and another Paradise business would close.

Luke came into the lobby, with Greta right behind him, staring at me through her thick glasses with her pale blue eyes.

"It's not our laundry pick-up day," Greta said.

"And you didn't come to the bar door," Luke added.

"We did give you the right amount of pay last time, didn't we?" Greta asked.

I gave them a little smile, then stood up. "I'm here on a different kind of business. I need to talk with you about my cousin Billy, and another guest of yours, Paige Morrissey."

At that, Luke's eyebrows went up. "I think," he said, "we'd better talk in the bar."

"Yep, Billy left late last night," said Luke. "Although he didn't really check out."

We were sitting around a table, the only people in the bar at this early hour on a Sunday morning, drinking freshly brewed coffee. I added plenty of sugar and milk to mine and took a sip—ah. Now that was much better than the cappuccino my laundromat was offering.

Then I considered what Luke had just said about Billy, trying to recall my checkbook balance. "So when Billy left . . .

did he, uh, settle up with you?" I took another sip, trying to look casual.

"Well, he didn't leave with his bill unpaid. But he didn't pay for it, either. A lady paid for him. And for herself, too,"

"Pretty lady, Hispanic looking?"

Luke shook his head. "No—although he'd been hanging out with her and her husband. This was a different pretty lady. A black woman."

Luke tapped Greta on her shoulder. She had the remote aimed at the big screen, her bony arm sticking straight ahead, so the loose wattle of flesh of her upper arm, revealed by the short sleeves of her cotton housecoat, swayed each time she gave a click. She used the remote like she was doing target practice, flicking from station to station.

"What was that pretty black woman's name, Greta dear?" Luke said.

"Paige Morrissey," Greta said. "Billy's room was number 212. Paige's was 213. Paid two hundred and twelve fifty-seven, including sales tax."

"For two rooms?" I asked, amazed at the amount. They'd each only been here two nights. But maybe, I thought, Paige was also paying for the rooms of the television show crew that would be coming in a few days. My stomach flip-flopped at the thought of that. With all that was going on, how were we ever going to have a decent filming of the *Tyra Grimes Home Show*?

"She was also paying up for the couple who'd been here for about the past two weeks," Luke said. "They'd kept putting me off, so I was real glad to get it." He gave Greta another gentle pat on the arm. "What were their names again, Greta dear?"

"Jeff and Jane Smith. Room 219." Greta was squinting with great concentration as she clicked at the big screen with the remote, as if she was trying to improve her aim.

"The Hispanic couple?" I said. "They said their names were Jeff and Jane Smith?"

"If that's what Greta says their names were," said Luke, "then that's what their names were. You know Greta. Gets something in her mind, mind springs shut over it like a steel trap." Luke put the base of his hands together, then formed half fists and rapped his knuckles together smartly.

"It's not Greta's memory I'm questioning, just that a Hispanic couple would be named Jeff and Jane Smith," I said.

"I never question the guest's names," Luke said. "If they say they're Jeff and Jane Smith, then they are."

"Right. Do you know why Paige would pay Billy's and the, um, the Smith's bill?"

Luke shook his head. "Can't say for sure. But I will say, they all were getting mighty cozy last night in here."

I lifted my eyebrows at that. "Cozy, how?"

"Sitting at that table over there—" Luke poked a finger at a table in the farthest corner. "Huddled over their beers. They weren't talking loud, but they were mighty intense about something. Hushed up right fast whenever I came by."

"Was this the first time you'd seen them together?"

Luke thought for a moment. "First time all four of them were together. Billy'd spent a lot of time a few nights ago just with Jane Smith. I hadn't seen her husband since they'd checked in, and I thought maybe he'd taken off. Thought maybe Billy and Jane were getting a little close, a little fast, if you know what I mean. Then night before last, the fella, um . . ."

"Jeff Smith," offered Greta, without turning around.

"Jeff Smith, right. Well, he came in, saw Billy and Jane together. Sat down, started talking, all excited, kind of loud."

"What was he saying? Was he upset about Billy talking with his wife?"

"Can't say for sure—he was talking in Spanish. Jane

seemed to be translating for Billy, and listening to Billy and translating back to Jeff, but she and Billy kept their voices low. He seemed real upset about something, but it didn't look like he was upset at Billy."

"I don't understand how Paige fits into all of this."

Luke shrugged. "All I can tell you is, she came in here late last night, came up to the bar, asked me for a beer, which kind of surprised me, because she didn't seem the beer type. Up until then, she'd been asking for drinks made a particular way—like a martini, but made with a particular brand of gin, what was it, Greta?"

"Bombay Sapphire. And some fancy brand of olives I've never heard of." Greta laughed. "Like we'd have anything other than the pimento kind."

"Right," said Luke. "Anyway, Paige seemed really down, asked for a beer without even telling me what brand she had to have. Billy wandered in after that. Sat down, struck up a general conversation with her. Another couple who's staying here came in, wanted some grilled cheese sandwiches. I went into the back to cook them up. When I came back, Billy and Paige were over there with the Smiths in that corner table. About 1 A.M. I went over, told them I was closing up the bar. Billy and the Smiths were real quiet, but Paige said that was okay, they were all leaving, and she'd pay the room bill for all of them."

Why would Paige Morrissey—the devoted employee of Tyra Grimes—want to take off with Billy and the "Smiths"? Why, for that matter, would someone as elegant and sophisticated as Paige want to hang out with Billy? And why would someone as responsible as Paige take off when she knew a film crew would be here in a few days to do the Tyra Grimes show?

"What about the rooms she reserved for the film crew?" I asked.

"Film crew? Rooms?" Luke looked confused. "She just had the one room for herself. She never asked about other rooms."

"Just the one room, room 213," said Greta.

My armpits and forehead went all sticky and tingly. Tyra had never, I realized, meant to do a show here with me at all. She'd put me off when I'd tried to talk with her when she first came . . . and Paige had clearly told me she was going to block rooms for the crew at the Red Horse . . . but she hadn't asked about rooms at all.

"Oh look, here's the show, the *Tyra Grimes Home Show*," chirped Greta. "When will your show be on, Josie?"

I looked at Greta, who was gazing at me with her milky blue eyes, squinting as she tried to focus on my face, her own expression all lit up like she was real excited for me . . . the local girl, about to make good.

I grinned, so she could at least see a shadow of a smile. I was thankful she couldn't see that my eyes were welling up. And I crossed my toes, since what I was about to say was only a half truth, and said just a little too brightly, "No exact dates yet, Greta. That's show biz."

8

Luke and Greta let me go through the rooms where Paige, Billy, and the "Smiths" had been staying. They just said, "okay" when I asked to see the rooms and gave me the keys, which was just a little disappointing since I had a whole speech worked out to convince them.

The good thing was that Rosa Miguelaro—the Rhinegold's one and only maid—hadn't cleaned out the rooms yet, so I stood a chance of finding something in the rooms to help me figure out where the whole bunch had disappeared to—and why they'd want to leave together. The bad thing was that Rosa seemed to think that I was there early that week to pick up the laundry. She kept following me around with her cart and thrusting sheets and towels at me. She finally gave up, muttering something in Spanish as she walked off, even though she speaks English.

Billy's room was a pigsty—no surprise there. The bed linens were all over the floor, along with damp towels, already smelling mildewy. The bathroom mirror was speckled with toothpaste and shaving cream. The trash can was spilling over with beer cans and pop cans and chip bags and candy wrappers . . . and one *Playboy* magazine.

The "Smiths' " room was not too messy and not too neat, kind of the baby bear version of a used motel room. Nothing in there of interest, either.

Paige's room was as neat as if Rosa had already been there—the bed made perfectly, the countertop and mirror gleaming. Even the stuff in the trash can was neat—one newspaper, two cough drop wrappers and five tissues all folded into careful, exact squares, with three cotton balls right in the middle, like a trash can sundae.

But poking out of the newspaper folds were some ripped up papers. That intrigued me. The newspaper, cough drop wrappers and tissues were all folded—yet these papers were ripped up. Paige didn't seem to be the kind who'd rip up something.

I pulled out the scraps of paper. They were just ordinary sheets of paper with neat handwriting on them—Paige's handwriting, I was guessing. I spread them out, stared at the pieces as if I was studying a jigsaw puzzle, feeling only mildly guilty at snooping into someone else's private trash. After all, my town was going nuts, my cousin was acting even stranger than usual, one Paradisite was in jail for murdering another Paradisite—all of which was related to Tyra's showing up in town in response to a letter I'd sent her. If something in her assistant's trash could help me figure out what was going on and set it back right, then fine. I'd have to just snoop.

Some of the paper pieces had gotten wet and were all smeary so I couldn't read them. I threw those scraps back into the trash can. What was left didn't quite add up to enough scraps to create a full page, but I studied them anyway.

One piece, from the top left corner of a sheet of paper,

clearly said, "Dear Tyra:" while the remaining scraps had phrases like "I've been loyal; however . . ." and "can no longer support . . ." and "salmon, deboned," and "illegal . . ." and "when this comes out . . ." and "walnuts" and "this action not justified . . ." and "regretfully, I must . . ." and "popcorn."

I decided the food words must have been from a shopping list and the rest from a letter Paige had started to Tyra. But what could she no longer support? What action was unjustified . . . and illegal? Something she had done? Or something Tyra had done . . . or was about to do? The scraps hinted that she wasn't feeling totally loyal to her boss, and yet, last night she'd said she'd do anything for Tyra. And what about the lie about the stain being cocoa instead of mud?

I picked up all the scraps, even the ones with food words on them, and wrapped them up in a page of the newspaper. By the time I did that, Rosa was in the room, revving her vacuum. I stood, carrying the packet of scraps carefully, and squeezed past Rosa at the door. She held a towel out to me, as if there might be some hope I'd take at least a little laundry with me.

But I just smiled at her and trotted back to my car.

Now, I wish I could say that on the drive home, the whole of my mind was puzzling over what all I'd just learned.

But the truth is, the minute I was by myself, in my car, driving back toward Paradise, not having to smile at Rosa or talk more to the Rhinegolds, I found myself stewing over just one thing I had learned: Tyra had only used me as a cover to come to Paradise. She'd never planned to bring a film crew to Paradise, to do a show here. I wasn't going to be on the *Tyra Grimes Home Show*. I wasn't going to share my stain expertise with the world. I wasn't going to be a celebrity—complete with my new, puffy, strawberry blond do—for even five minutes.

And the truth is, I found myself crying, just a little, just a tear or two. I thought I'd achieved something for myself, for Paradise, but my dream had turned out to be just a fantasy. I was a failure, a fool, a wishful thinker, a chump. I knew just how Winnie felt about Tyra Grimes. She was, just like Winnie had said, a terrible person who'd come to our quiet little town, and then terrible things had started happening.

I caught my breath at that. Those were pretty much the words Lewis had used to describe Tyra when I'd first brought up the whole idea of getting on the Tyra Grimes show as a way to get Paradise on the map. As it turned out, all in all Tyra was pretty likable, if a bit fussy for my taste. Yet, Lewis had also said that if Tyra Grimes came to town, blood would flow. And it had. It had been his. And now Elroy Magruder was in jail for Lewis's death . . . although I suspected Paige.

That brought me around to living up to my duties in this investigation. I frowned with concentration, trying to think as I drove on the narrow country roads.

Who were the "Smiths," really, and why were they in Paradise? Why had Billy suddenly decided to protest Tyra—with the same hatred that Lewis Rothchild had seemed to have for her? It couldn't be just over losing his apartment. Why had Billy hooked up with the Smiths . . . and why would they want to hook up with him? More baffling, how was Paige connected with any of them . . . and why did she apparently leave with them and abandon Tyra, the employer she'd just hours before seemed so dedicated to?

Most baffling of all was why Paige and Tyra had come to Paradise in the first place, since it was now clear that it hadn't been to do a show with me. Somehow, I'd managed to write Tyra at the right time with a show idea that gave her an excuse to come here. But why had she needed an excuse to come here at all? After all, a celebrity coming to Paradise might be unheard of—even a little weird—but it wasn't illegal.

I got so caught up in my thinking, I didn't realize I'd missed a turn and was just a mile from the old, abandoned county orphanage. The T-shirts . . . maybe a closer look at them would reveal some clues.

I pulled up the dirt lane and saw the old white truck the "Smith" couple had been driving, pointing opposite to me, parked on the side of the lane.

I stopped my car, got out, and went up to the truck slowly, just in case someone was crouched down in the truck, hiding. But no one was in or near the truck. Then I saw the rear of the truck was tilted down nearly to the ground. Looked like the suspension was shot.

I guessed that the truck had been abandoned here, but I drove up the rest of the lane slowly and looked around warily. I parked in the shrubby area where I'd parked the last time I was here—that seemed like forever ago, now—and hiked up to the crest overlooking the orphanage. At least this time I was wearing jeans and a shirt instead of a bathrobe.

I took a long look around. I didn't see any activity but it was possible the Smiths were in the orphanage. I doubted it though. It was pretty obvious they'd been here, but had to abandon their truck.

I knew I should go on to the orphanage, check out those T-shirts right away. But I had a little more thinking to do. Maybe because of the mood I was in after my big let down. Maybe because I'd pushed aside the memories on my last visit here, memories I hadn't taken out and examined in a long, long time, even though I come out here every now and again, just because it's peaceful, just to think. I even bring Guy here sometimes because it's one of the few places he likes to go on outings away from Stillwater.

So instead of heading straight to the orphanage, I stared down at the old building. In my mind I was watching something else, too.

Me, age nine. Sitting at the kitchen table after school in the home of the then Chief of Paradise Police. Hearing Mrs. Hilbrink tell me how Chief Bernie Hilbrink had had a heart attack.

Me, sipping milk and eating chocolate chip cookies and taking in the news—not sure what heart attack meant, but sure that it was bad, because Mrs. Hilbrink's face was slick with tears.

Me, not wanting it to be bad, because I'd grown happy with the Hilbrinks. I called them Chief and Mrs. Hilbrink even though I'd been living with them ten whole months by then—after my mama ran off when our trailer burned down and everyone suspected her of arson and she left me and a letter I never got a chance to read on the Hilbrink doorstep. But in my heart I dared to think of them as . . . Dad. And Mom.

And since the Hilbrinks didn't have any kids and had started talking about adopting me, it seemed safe to dream that maybe I could stay with them and be part of a proper family. After all, it was always nice and warm at their house, and Mrs. Hilbrink baked the best chocolate chip cookies, and started making me cute little dresses, and helped me catch up on my reading, so I could go to school for the first time in my life. I loved school. And I loved how Chief and Mrs. Hilbrink were always extra nice to me, like I was someone fine.

But it turned out that "heart attack" was very bad, because a few days later, Chief Hilbrink died. There was a huge funeral at Rothchild's Funeral Home. All of Paradise turned out for it, because everyone loved Chief Hilbrink. And then, the next day, Mrs. Hilbrink said she was sorry, but she just couldn't stay in Paradise without the Chief, and she didn't think she could raise a child by herself, so she was moving on out to California, where she was going to live awhile with her sister.

So I came to the Mason County Children's Home and

stayed for six months until Uncle Horace and Aunt Clara took me in.

What makes me sad every time I thought about those six months in my life wasn't that the home was such a bad place to be. No one was mean to me. I had some chores, but none of them were hard. I had plenty of food. I had clothes. I even had some toys. There was a big library, where I discovered my love of reading and read most everything, and lots of things twice, like *Black Beauty* and *Little Women* and the *Chronicles of Narnia*. It's just that I was very, very lonely there. And alone. Two separate things, alone and lonely. And I was both. Alone can be okay, if it's for a time, and if it's what you want. But I had thought being alone—and feeling lonely—would never end.

Some of that feeling came back now, as I stared at the orphanage. A big old hungry maw of loneliness, wanting to swallow me whole again.

Then I thought of Elroy, and poor Lewis, and Tyra, and a mix of worry and sadness and anger filled the hole, kept me from tumbling into a pit of self-pity, moved me into action. I walked down the hill, being careful not to slip on the grass that was still wet from the previous night's rain. I climbed over the fence, trying to figure out how I could get in and take a closer look at those T-shirts.

But I didn't need to be clever about how to get in. As soon as I looked up after my climb over the fence and focused on the building, I saw the back door was hanging open.

I stepped in, to the smell and grit of dust and dirt, pulled out my flashlight, and shone it around. And found nothing there except the dust and dirt. The red Tyra Grimes T-shirts were all gone.

9

They were there when I got back to my apartment, waiting for me.

Not the T-shirts, of course.

But—them. A man and a woman, who would end up adding even more trouble to an already stirred-up pot of it.

He was tall, dark-haired, cute. She was petite, blond, cute. They were both in their mid-thirties, and they looked professional even though they just had on jeans and knit shirts and rain jackets. I think it was their shoes. They had on tan leather shoes and white socks—but not chunky athletic socks. Smooth knit socks. Professional people—people of a certain suburban middle class nature—always wear socks and shoes like that with jeans.

I didn't recognize the man or the woman, which meant they weren't from Paradise. (Of course, the shoes were proof of that anyway. Paradisites wear sneakers with their jeans, unless they're going hunting, in which case they wear hunting boots.)

They stood in front of my door, grinning at me with grins

that were big and eager and a little surprised, like the grins the scientists in khaki-colored clothes and funny bowl-shaped hats have when they sneak up on cheetahs or orangutans or other wild creatures on those public TV nature shows.

The woman stepped forward, holding her hand out, and said in this tone that was hushed with great reverence and awe, "Are you . . ." she paused to gulp—"are you Josie Toadfern? *The* Josie Toadfern? The stain expert?"

Now, I have to admit that her saying that, in just that way—especially after all the teasing I'd gotten when I first declared my plan to get on the *Tyra Grimes Home Show*, and after all that had happened since Tyra had come just yesterday, and after learning today that she wasn't really going to have me on her show—I have to admit that the woman talking to me like that, all reverent and awed and impressed, got to me.

So when the man stepped forward and said they really, really, *really* needed to talk to me, I said okay. And then I did something really, really, *really* stupid. I invited them into my apartment. After all, I told myself, maybe they were newlyweds and they'd found me because they knew only I, in all of the world, could help them with something important, like maybe how to get a pesky coffee stain out of the heirloom quilt they'd gotten from her aunt.

As it turned out, they were really Steve and Linda Crooks, former investigative reporters, now freelance writers working on a book, one of those tell-all, no-holds-barred, unauthorized biography–type books, about Tyra Grimes.

We were drinking glasses of iced tea at my table when they told me this.

"We'd like your help with the book," Steve said. "Your insight into Tyra's character, your observations about her, that kind of thing."

Linda leaned toward me, practically quivering with excitement. "You could really add a whole new dimension to our book. The depth we're looking for. Of course, we're hoping we can quote you . . ."

"Now, Linda," Steve said. "Don't be too pushy. Maybe Josie would rather be quoted anonymously."

"Oh no, you can use my name," I said hastily, then stopped. What was I saying? I was agreeing to something without really thinking it through . . . but me, Josie Toadfern, in a book? Maybe *that* would be important enough to help get Paradise back on the map, since I obviously wasn't going to get Paradise any attention by going on the *Tyra Grimes Home Show*.

Plus I have to admit that the thought of being in a book made me feel important. Special. *Somebody*. I'd loved books all my life.

And there was another thing, too, which I'm not proud of. A little bit of me wanted to get back at Tyra, for not really planning to have me on her show. And for stirring up the town so much. Not to mention my lingering snit over her wanting to transplant the orange thread in my heirloom quilt with white thread. "Simply wonderful . . ." Hmmph.

"We wanted to get to you first, before the others," Steve added.

"The—others?" I asked.

"Oh yes," Linda said. "Journalists. From newspapers. Magazines. TV stations. With what's happened here, this town is going to be swarming with reporters from all over the country by tomorrow morning. We were really, um, really hoping that you'd give us an exclusive."

I didn't say anything for a moment, while I turned this proposition over in my mind, and Steve added, "She means not talk to any other reporters, just us."

Now, all this big talk about a book and exclusives, as exciting as it was, hadn't turned my head from the fact I needed any information I could get to help me figure out why Tyra was really in Paradise . . . who had killed Lewis, and why. These two might just have information that would lead me to the answers.

"I know what you mean by exclusive," I said. "But I'm thinking . . . if I'm going to give you something, you ought to give me something, too."

They both looked alarmed and glanced at each other, exchanging one of those looks that somehow gets across a secret message. Then they gave each other a tiny nod.

"What do you want?" Steve said. "We can't offer any percentage of the royalties we'll get from our book—"

"I'm not interested in that. I want information. If you've been researching Tyra Grimes for your book, you must already know a lot about her. There are some things I'd like to know."

"Like what," Linda said.

I had to think about that for a moment. There were lots of things I wanted to know. What Tyra's connection with Lewis Rothchild had really been. Why her assistant had apparently run off with my cousin Billy and two strangers who spoke Spanish. Nah, they couldn't tell me any of that. What else?

How about—a little voice whispered from the corner of my mind, a voice that I swear sounded like Mrs. Oglevee's— how about what's up with those red Tyra Grimes T-shirts? And what about the TV news report that Tyra was going to be investigated for having illegal aliens working for her? These two, especially as former investigative reporters, should know something about that.

I took a deep breath, then told Steve and Linda about the TV news report I'd heard. Then I told them about the red T-shirts that had popped up around town. I left out how upset Vivian Denlinger had gotten over them, since that didn't seem anything except just weird, and I left out the part about Billy and his two new friends who were strangers to town and their comings and goings at the old orphanage where there had been boxes and boxes of the T-shirts, until they were moved. Or stolen. Something just told me—maybe the way both Linda's and Steve's eyes got all narrow and intense and drilling at me when I just mentioned those red T-shirts—that I'd be better off not mentioning all those details just yet.

When I finished, Steve said, "Here's what we've heard, from, er, some unnamed but reliable sources. Tyra Grimes has a labor camp out in California—"

"A labor camp?" I jumped in. "You mean like a prison?" It was hard to imagine what a Tyra Grimes prison would look like. Maybe lace valances over the jail cell doors. Or cute handcuff stencils on the bars. Toilet paper roll crafts out in the yard, right after basketball . . .

Steve smiled. "Not a prison like you're thinking of. But, yeah, kind of like a prison. A forced labor camp where the employer uses illegal immigrants, who are terrified of being sent home. The camps are illegal, and the conditions are bad. Long hours. Little pay. Unsanitary conditions. Poor nutrition."

I could hear the outrage in Steve's voice . . . felt the outrage rising in me, too.

Linda shot Steve a look like she thought he was saying too much. She leaned forward to me and said in a near whisper, "Anyway, that's what we've heard—from, um, someone who knows someone who used to work there. A Mexican fellow. But he and his wife broke out, stole a truck, took off—apparently with several boxes of T-shirts that are just like the ones you've described."

I felt a sudden pressure on my arm. It was Steve, his hand grasping my arm just a little too tightly. His grin was just a little too tight, too, as he said, "You sure you just saw only the two T-shirts being worn around town?"

I surprised him by doing a pretzel-y move that quickly got my arm free and left his hand flopping around on my dining table like a fish having an out-of-water experience. My grin was also a little tight as I said, "Yes, I'm sure." Technically, I was not lying. I had told him I'd seen two T-shirts being worn by people in town. The ones I'd seen in the boxes weren't being worn by anyone.

"The couple," said Linda softly, "is armed and dangerous."

"Oh, yes," Steve said. "They were seen at a convenience store not long after they took off from California. Somewhere around Phoenix. Robbed the store, beat up the manager really badly. Was he expected to live, Linda?"

"Last I heard, his prognosis wasn't so good."

Now this scared me, sent my stomach folding itself into a panic origami. This couple sounded like they could be the same two Billy, and now Paige, had taken off with. Maybe I'd been all wrong to suspect Paige. Maybe this couple had attacked Lewis and Tyra . . . and poor Lewis had gotten unlucky.

"Should we tell Josie the rest?" Steve was saying.

"I think we'd better," Linda said. "After all with Tyra Grimes staying in the apartment next door . . ."

"Tell me," I snapped.

"Well, word is that this couple is after Tyra. They have it in for her," Steve said.

I gulped. My tummy origami got tighter.

"So, if you see them, you must contact us right away—"

Now that comment worked like a pan of cold water dumped on my head. Something suddenly didn't seem right to me. I wasn't sure who these two really were, or what they were up to, but I didn't think it had anything to do with being writers.

"Why would I contact you, if this couple is so dangerous? I should call the Paradise Police Department."

They exchanged looks again. "Oh, no, you don't want to call the local police," Linda said. "No offense, but I'm sure you're aware how incompetent small town police departments can be when dealing with a problem of this nature." She chuckled, as if to emphasize the humor in the idea of small town cops capturing such dangerous outlaws.

I, for one, was not amused. As much as Chief John Worthy might annoy me at times, I have nothing but total pride and trust in the officers of the Paradise Police Department. They do a top-notch job of carrying on the proud heritage of Chief Hilbrink. So I just glared at her.

"We, um, want an exclusive interview with them first," Steve said. "We've interviewed criminal types before, so we'll be okay. Plus we've got contacts with the, um, FBI, INS, um . . ."

"CIA," Linda added helpfully.

I lifted my eyebrows. "Interpol, too? Look, I don't see why this couple would follow Tyra if they just escaped from this labor camp of hers, and I'm not sure who you are, really—"

"Like we said, writers—"

"Uh huh."

Steve gave me his thin grin again. "Now, Josie, you said you'd help us out if we gave you information about Tyra for our book. So why don't we get back to that. Maybe you could just describe what it's been like having her around, maybe let us just take a look around the apartment she's staying in—"

I hooted at that. "So you can snoop through her stuff? I don't think so."

They exchanged looks, this time telegraphing to each other their frustration and mutual desire to whop me upside the head. Clearly, I wasn't the pushover they'd expected Ms. Josie Toadfern, laundromat owner and stain expert, to be.

"At least," I went on, "I don't think so unless you can give me just one more bit of information."

Steve closed his eyes and put his head in his hands.

Linda just sighed. "What's that?"

"The names of the couple who are after Tyra."

Linda frowned, not speaking. I pulled my keys out, dangled them. For a minute she looked like she was going to lunge.

"You can force them from me, or break into the apartment," I said, "but then I would have to call the police, and your story would get out. Whoever you are, your cover would be blown."

Steve moaned. Linda tightened her lips. "We give you the names, you let us in the apartment?"

It didn't seem quite right, letting these two go through whatever personal stuff Tyra might have left in Billy's old apartment, but then, I didn't see as I had much choice. The T-shirts and this couple seemed to be at the center of the mess that had developed since Tyra's arrival, a mess that had left Lewis dead and Elroy accused of his murder. So I just nodded.

"Aguila and Ramon Cruez," she said.

I ran to my kitchen, grabbed the notepad I have for grocery lists, and a pencil. "Spell the names," I said.

She did. I wrote them down, right below "eggs."

Then I pulled the next door apartment's key off my ring and tossed it to Linda. She caught it smoothly. "Leave it under my door when you're done, and don't mess anything up or think you can just keep the key. I know where to find you."

Steve looked up. He looked a little scared. "You do?"

I gave a half laugh, half snort. "Sure. There's only one place to stay, unless you're camping. The Red Horse Motel."

"C'mon," Linda said to Steve. "Let's go."

They let themselves out, Linda slamming the door just a little harder than she had to. I locked the door after they left. Then, I went to take a shower. I thought maybe a fresh shampoo would help relieve my itching scalp, a condition that kept getting worse and was starting to worry me.

By the time I'd finished my shower and changed into fresh jeans and a T-shirt, my scalp felt better. The key for Billy's old apartment next door had been slid just under my door, and that relieved me. At least the Crookses had returned it. I put it in my junk drawer in the kitchen, and while I was in there, I got out a fresh package of vanilla wafers and poured myself a glass of milk. I needed to think, and a little snack to give my brain some extra fuel seemed in order.

I sat down at the table with my vanilla wafers, milk, and the spiral notebook in which I'd been jotting notes since this morning. I munched, made a few notes, flipped back through my notebook, made a few more notes, then tried to look at the whole story logically.

It was impossible. There were too many angles, all jutting out from the fact I'd gotten this crazy notion about being on the Tyra Grimes show to help get Paradise on the map . . .

Except Tyra hadn't come here to have me on her show. She'd come here for some other reason. And Lewis had been murdered.

And this couple—Aguila and Ramon Cruez—had come here, too. I shivered, thinking about how Steve and Linda Crooks had suggested that the Cruez couple was after Tyra. Could Lewis have been an innocent bystander who just got in the couple's way?

But then why would Tyra want to protect them and accuse Elroy of murdering Lewis? I could almost see her protecting Paige if she were the murderer, but why protect this couple?

Then I thought maybe I should stop trying to see this from Tyra's point of view. Maybe I should look at this whole mess from a different angle . . . starting with Aguila and Ramon.

I made a list that went like this:

1. Aguila and Ramon Cruez are working at Tyra Grimes's illegal labor camp.
2. They get T-shirts and come to Paradise, and start selling a few.
3. They don't hurt anyone (although another mystery couple, the Crookses, posing as writers, say they are dangerous, especially to Tyra).
4. Tyra also came to Paradise . . . but not to put me on her show. Why? Because of the T-shirts? Or because of Aguila and Ramon?
5. Tyra has accused Elroy of attacking her and Lewis, and now Lewis is dead.
6. Paige lied about the cocoa stain on her sweater—she was definitely somewhere muddy. Why did she lie? Was she out at the site where I found Tyra, Lewis, and Elroy?
7. Lewis was totally against Tyra's coming to Paradise. Why?
8. Tyra was very interested in Lewis, somehow met with him out by the old mall site. Why? What's the connection between them? Could Lewis be why Tyra came to Paradise?
9. Vivian Denlinger also was against Tyra's coming to Paradise and was upset that Verbenia was wearing one of those T-shirts. How did Verbenia get the T-shirt, and why was Vivian so upset?
10. T-shirts stored at orphanage then disappear—but the "Smiths' " truck is broken down at orphanage. How did the T-shirts get out of there? Probably it was Billy and the Smiths who took them out—in Paige's SUV? Where did the T-shirts go? Why move them? Why would Paige want to hook up with these three?

I looked over my list a few more times, then staggered over to my couch and collapsed. I'd learned a lot today, and although I had a lot of new questions, they all seemed to come down to two things—figure out why Tyra really came to Paradise, and figure out what was going on with Aguila and Ramon and those T-shirts.

I'd done more than enough detective work for one day. I'd think about this again tomorrow. Right now, my brain was tired, my body was worn out, and my head was still itching like crazy, despite my shower.

All I wanted to do now was make a sandwich, since I hadn't had dinner yet and the cookies only counted as a snack, watch a *Mary Tyler Moore* or *I Love Lucy* rerun on the TV Land cable station . . . or maybe even skip all that, and go right to sleep, right here on my couch . . .

The doorbell rang.

I got up and answered my door. Owen staggered into my apartment. There were dark blue circles under his eyes. His hair was sticking out in all different directions, like he'd run his hands through it a thousand times. His shirt was un-tucked. He was also carrying two large shopping bags from a mall all the way up by Columbus.

Owen's arms quivered, but still, he held onto the shopping bag handles. "Shopping," he wheezed. "She made me go shopping. Said there were essentials that were missing from the apartment . . . the right soap holder to go with the right toothbrush holder . . ."

It was around six o'clock. I just figured Tyra hadn't been ready to be released yet from the hospital, and that's why I hadn't heard from Owen.

"Owen, what time was Tyra released from the hospital?" I glanced behind him, into the hall, looking for Tyra.

"Ten," he said. "Ten this morning. Just a quick trip, she

said, for a few essentials. Scented soaps, candles, lotions . . ."

"Owen, set the bags down and stop moaning," I said.

Tyra breezed into my apartment. She held out keys to Owen and said, "Owen, be a dear, put those bags in my little apartment, won't you?"

I was horrified to observe my dear Owen obediently put down a bag, take the keys, stick the key ring in between his teeth, pick up the bag again, and stagger back out of my apartment. This, from a man with two PhD's, a man who can quote Shakespeare at will, a man who hates even shopping for groceries. Something terrible must have happened to make him act this way, all cowering and catering before Tyra. Maybe she'd hypnotized him.

"What have you done to Owen? You're treating him like— like some servant." I stopped. I was so mad, I was panting, which was getting in the way of my speaking clearly.

"I've merely asked him to put away a few things I had to pick up. Essentials. It's been a trying experience, I must say. So hard to find the proper things around here."

"Well, now that you're all stocked up, you'll want to go to your apartment—or my apartment, that I'm letting you use, for free, and—"

"Where's Paige?" Tyra was looking all around, as if she expected Paige to just materialize, perhaps offering a soufflé for dinner or a neck massage or something to soothe her boss.

"She's not here. In fact," I went on, feeling a little triumphant over the news, "I have no idea where she is. No one does. It looks as though she's run off. She checked out of the Red Horse last night—with no forwarding address."

I'm not sure what, exactly, I expected Tyra's reaction to be. Maybe outrage. Maybe fear. Maybe shock. After all, Paige was a longtime employee.

Instead, Tyra just stared off into the distance for a minute. I wondered if she'd even heard me.

Then she looked back at me, gave me a smile that was—
even though I was angry with her—endearing. "You'll have
to drive me tomorrow, then. Thank you so much dear. I appreciate it." She started for my door.

"What? I'm not driving you around. I have a business to
run."

Tyra stopped and said without turning around, "I need to
be at Stillwater Farms, tomorrow, for a 10 A.M. meeting.
Paige has disappeared with my only means of transportation.
So I need a driver tomorrow, plus I'll need to go back later
this week, as well, for a press conference I'll be holding
there."

Then she walked out.

And I knew I'd drive her, because I was curious why she
wanted to go to Stillwater Farms, of all places. Why she'd
hold a press conference there. What she was up to there . . .
and I suddenly felt a little fearful for Guy, although I had no
logical reason to feel that way.

And what was worse, I knew I'd drive her just because
Tyra had told me to. She had that affect on people.

"I wish I could say I'd learned something from Elroy," Owen
said. "He just kept babbling about how he was so glad to
learn that it was the mushrooms that must have made the
workers sick, not his tuna salad."

Owen and I were sitting on my couch. Owen was drinking
Scotch and water. I'm not a Scotch drinker, myself, but I keep
it here for Owen. While Owen got Tyra settled in the apartment next door, I ran down to my laundromat and thanked
and paid Chip Beavy for watching my business for the day.
Then I locked up my laundromat and came back up to my
apartment, where I made us a dinner of turkey hot shots,
which is slices of turkey on top of white bread and mashed
potatoes, all covered in turkey gravy. I put plenty of salt on

mine. If I'm eating comfort food, I want it good and salty. Unless it's chocolate.

After we ate, while Owen cleaned up and poured himself a Scotch and me a Big Fizz diet cola, I called Winnie's house, worried that I hadn't heard from her yet. Her husband Tom sounded mighty grumpy, said Winnie's been gone all day on some important research project over at the library, and he had no idea what it was, why it was so important, or when she'd be back. I wondered if she was at the library so long because she was finding out so much about Tyra—or because she wasn't having any luck finding anything.

Then, after we sat back down at the kitchen table with our drinks, I told Owen about what all I had learned. We talked really quietly, just in case Tyra could hear us. We hadn't heard a peep out of her since she'd gone into the spare apartment, so we guessed she'd just gone to bed early after her ordeal the night before. On the other hand, she could be standing with a glass to the wall. The walls are so thin between the apartments, a paper cup would have picked up everything we said.

Now, Owen sipped his Scotch and shook his head. "I don't know what gave Elroy the idea that those businessmen from years ago got sick on mushrooms, but that's all he would talk about."

I felt a little guilty—because I knew how he'd gotten the idea. From me. "He didn't say anything about Lewis or Tyra, or seeing them out there?"

"No. But I did ask him, directly, what he knew. All he said was that the first time he saw them was when you and he found them together—Tyra knocked out, poor Lewis already shot. And he says he does have a gun, but he doesn't remember loading it or bringing it from home." Owen shook his head again. "He didn't even seem to care when the hospital released him to Chief Worthy. He just kept talking about those damned tuna sandwiches and mushrooms."

"Does he understand that Lewis is dead? What he's being locked up for?"

"I don't think reality has hit poor Elroy yet. Maybe the mushrooms, which the doctor at the hospital did confirm they found when they pumped his stomach, scrambled his brains. Apparently, he's lucky to even be alive, after eating as many as he did, and . . ." Owen sat his glass down on the coffee table. Suddenly, there was a gleam in his eyes. Or maybe it was just lamp glare on his glasses. In any case, he waggled his eyebrows at me. "Do you know your voice is really sexy when you whisper?"

He moved toward me on the couch.

"No, I didn't know that. Now Owen, what am I going to do tomorrow? Tyra expects me to take her to Stillwater, and I want to, because I want to find out why she's going there, but I can't keep leaving the laundromat alone or hiring Chip Beavy—who says he has classes at the community college tomorrow anyway, and—"

Owen shrugged, and the gesture moved him even closer to me. "I don't know what you'll do, but I'm sure you'll think of something. You know, in this light, your hair looks even prettier than usual. I really love this new look on you . . ."

With that, he pulled me closer and started kissing me.

I enjoyed his kisses. Enjoyed them so much that I forgot, for a moment, about my worries about Elroy and Lewis and Billy and Paige and Tyra and the Cruez couple and Paradise. Enjoyed them so much that I didn't care that as Owen stroked my hair, my scalp began to tingle and itch even more. Enjoyed them so much, that I ignored the pounding that started suddenly upon my door.

But I wasn't able to ignore Tyra's yelling, in a panicked tone I would never have thought possible for someone as smooth as Tyra, "Josie Toadfern, you answer this door right now, or else I'm calling the police—you, you thief!"

10

"I want my papers back—now," Tyra said. This was a side of Tyra I'd never expected to see. On television and in Paradise, Tyra had been, by turns, either truly charming or manipulatively charming—but always charming. Now, she was angry, her hands on her hips as she stood in my doorway. But beyond the glare of anger in her eyes, I saw something else. Fear. This sudden switch in Tyra's emotions was scary, somehow, and I backed up.

Tyra scooted forward, matching me step for step. We did our Tyra-mad, Josie-nervous shuffle, all the way back to my couch. When I hit the couch, I went down hard, right on a spring that had long ago sprung. I winced.

With a sideways glance, I saw Owen tiptoeing off to the kitchen. I figured he was either going to call 9-1-1 or grab a skillet to whack Tyra over the head for me. My hero.

But then, suddenly, Tyra collapsed onto the floor, clasped her hands together in a prayerful pose, and as she stared up at me, started crying. Apparently, scared had won out.

"Ple-e-e-ase," she wailed. "You have to give those papers back, Josie. Look, I'll pay you for them. I'm begging you—"

I looked over at Owen, who was holding the phone near, but not quite to, his ear, as if he had frozen in mid-movement from shock at Tyra's sudden mood change. I sighed and shook my head at him. Bringing the portable phone with him, Owen came into the living room, sat down next to me, and took my hand. I moved closer to him, partly to get my tailbone off the couch spring, and partly because I just wanted to be near him.

"I need those papers back," Tyra went on. "You don't understand how important they are! You have no idea how many lives will be affected—no, ruined!—if I don't get them back!"

I had a pretty good idea that one life in particular would be ruined—hers. I also had a pretty good idea who had the papers, and it wasn't me. It had to be the Crooks duo. Or . . . the thought gave me a sudden shiver . . . maybe Paige had taken them the night before, while she'd been in Billy's old apartment adjusting Winnie's decorating efforts to more closely match Tyra's taste. I wasn't sure which option would be worse.

In any case, Tyra's belief that I had these papers seemed to give me some power over her. I guessed that they had something to do with the T-shirts and the forced labor camp.

"I'm open to negotiation, Tyra," I said.

She snuffled, still prone on the floor.

"I can get your papers back," I added, "but you have to promise me something first."

"Anything! How does five thousand dollars sound?"

I stared at her. Five thousand dollars sounded like a lot of money.

Tyra took my silence as a challenge. "Okay, ten thousand,

then? Or, look, I have this fur, a really nice one, mink, I could give you that and—and—" Tyra started yanking at the big diamond cluster ring she wore on her right hand.

I wrinkled my nose. This was getting distasteful. "I don't want money or a fur or a ring," I said. Well, the money and ring part sounded okay, but I needed information, and material things couldn't distract me. "What I want is information," I said. "Why don't we start with you describing these papers to me—"

Tyra stopped yanking at her finger and wailing, sat up suddenly, and stared at me. "You mean, you don't actually have my papers?"

"I have a pretty good idea who does have them. But, um, to be sure, I'll need you to describe them to me."

Tyra snuffled, calmer now. Owen, always the gentleman, offered her a tissue. She blew her nose. Then she said, "Apparently I've made a mistake. If you don't know what the papers are, then you must not have them." She stood up, gave us a wavery smile, and started backing up to my door. "Forget this little outburst. I'm not sure what came over me. I must just be really shaken from all that's happened, you know . . ."

"Fine," I said, standing too. "We'll just call the police, then. Report these papers stolen . . . you can give *them* a nice, detailed description of what these papers are all about."

With that, I grabbed the phone from Owen.

Tyra stared at the phone in my hand. "Oh, no, please don't. They're just papers that have instructions on various napkin folds. You know, the parson's fold, fan fold, pope's hat fold . . ."

I shook my head. "C'mon, Tyra. I know those papers are about something more important." I made a show of starting to punch numbers on my phone's handset.

Tyra surprised me yet again, lunging forward and grabbing my phone. I hung on as she jerked it, and me, toward her.

"Please don't call the police," Tyra said. The pleading in her voice was edging back over to anger.

I yanked back, pulling Tyra toward me now. "Oh, yes, I'm calling the police. The papers were stolen from my property, so it concerns me, too."

Tyra yanked. "If you know who has them, then why don't you just tell me? I'll pay you a handsome sum, and—"

I pulled, and we tug-o-warred again over top of my coffee table. "For all I know, by leading you to those papers, I'll be aiding and abetting you in some crime."

"Well, I never!"

"What am I supposed to think? You're being so guarded about those papers. Yep, we're calling the police. It's time we reported Paige missing anyway."

"Don't be silly. Paige disappears like this all the time. Usually, she does leave me a note, always something ridiculous, like she's gone to find work that's truer to her ideals, as if saving the poor masses from decorating and entertaining mistakes isn't enough of a mission for anyone . . ."

This was interesting information about Paige, adding new insight to the ripped up letter I'd found in Paige's motel room. But it didn't fit what Paige had said about doing anything for her boss. Maybe Tyra was lying.

In any case, I wanted to know why these papers were so important. So, I hollered, "Don't try to sidetrack me! Either we're calling the police, or you're telling me what's on those papers and why you really came to Paradise!"

With that, I gave my hardest pull yet, and the phone went flying up in the air. Unfortunately, my Big Fizz diet cola, which was right between us, also went flying up in the air—and landed on Tyra. She yelped, lost her balance. Her arms flailing, she grabbed wildly for something to help her steady herself. What she ended up grabbing was my hair.

Suddenly, she went down with a thump and another yelp, landing on the floor on her butt.

I yelped, too, at the sudden sore spot on my head. My hand went to the spot, and found smooth skin.

And then we all stared at the fistful of my hair that Tyra clutched in her hand.

The chunk of hair was missing from the right side of my head. I rubbed my new little bald spot while I stared at the hair in Tyra's hand. What was really weird was that my head felt better where my hair was missing.

The awareness that she had yanked out a handful of my hair seemed to have calmed Tyra down.

So there I was, a chunk of hair missing from my head, staring at the famous designer who'd given me a bald spot, who was, herself, drenched in Big Fizz diet cola.

I had two choices. One was to run out of the room. The other was to use this to my advantage to get Tyra to talk to me.

I held out my hand, staring pointedly at my lock of hair in Tyra's fist. She handed my hair to me, like she was letting go of a snake.

I waggled my lock of hair at her. "This," I said, "constitutes proof of assault and battery by you on my person. And I really will call the police and file charges against you if you don't tell me what I want to know."

Tyra looked up at Owen, tears in her eyes. "She started it!"

Owen sighed. "I think," he said, "you'd better talk to Josie. I'll get you a towel."

"My blouse . . . I'll have to pretreat it with something . . ." Tyra started.

"No," I said wearily. "Cola's a tannin stain—like coffee, and tea. Putting soap directly on it will probably set it in. Go change, then we'll wash the blouse in warm water. That'll probably do the trick. If not, there's always all-fabric bleach."

Tyra stared at me and echoed what Paige had said the night before. "You really are a stain expert!"

Hah. I'd finally bested Tyra Grimes at something.

A bit later, we were all back at my kitchenette table—Tyra changed into another blouse, her blouse washing down in my laundromat, the cola dabbed up off my carpet . . . and my lock of hair, wrapped up in a paper towel, and stuck in my pocket— just in case I needed to get it out again as a reminder to Tyra of my threat to file assault and battery charges against her. I'd have to think later about what to do about my new bald spot.

"All right," I said. "Let's get down to business. First things first. Why did you accuse Elroy of killing Lewis?"

She looked at me evenly. "Because he did. Just like I told Chief Worthy."

"I don't believe you. I think you're covering for someone."

Tyra gasped and looked away. I leaned forward. "Was Paige out there that night?"

"No," Tyra said too quickly. "No . . . and besides . . . Paige would never do anything like that. I mean, she's tough, but . . ." She shook her head. But there was a moment of fear in her eyes, much like I'd seen earlier.

Tyra, I thought, was covering for Paige. But if she wasn't—if instead, say, the Cruez couple had come after her and instead accidentally killed poor Lewis, why wouldn't she say so? I'd have to get to the Cruez couple in a moment.

For now I had another question for her. "Tyra, why did you come to Paradise in the first place? Did it have something to do with Lewis?"

Tyra looked surprised and then laughed. "Lewis? Heavens, no. I never met him until I got here. I only came here to do a show with you on stain removal techniques."

I shook my head. "I was out at the Red Horse Motel to-day—Paige never booked rooms for a film crew. You never intended to have me on your show. So why did you really come here?"

Tyra frowned. "I thought you wanted to know about my missing papers?"

Now that, I thought, was interesting. She'd rather talk about her missing papers than why she'd really come to Paradise.

"Okay," I said. "I have a hunch your papers and why you came to Paradise are related, but we can start with the papers."

"You know about my designer T-shirts?" Tyra said.

"Sure."

"Well, the papers have to do with their manufacturing at a—a plant in California. The papers are legal documents and letters from my attorney, because, you see, there have been a few, um, labor problems at the plant. Something about whether or not the workers are actually, uh, legal to work in this country." She gave a nervous laugh. "It's so unfair! I've never even been out to the plant in California—I delegate all that. I pay people to oversee things like manufacturing."

"So you're saying that you didn't know that illegal labor practices were going on—"

"No, of course not! All I did was hire some plant managers and tell them to get the T-shirts made as cheaply as possible." She stopped, considering what she just said, then smiled. "While preserving quality, of course. I wouldn't want anything bearing my name to be shoddy." Tyra sighed, impatient all of a sudden. "Beside, no one ever thinks about how or where the clothes they are wearing are made, do they? Do you know where your jeans were made—under what conditions? Or your shoes? Or your T-shirt?"

"Uh, no," I said. "But it seems to me that as the owner of your business, you'd care about—"

Tyra waved a hand at me. "Like I said, I delegate all that.

My role was to design the T-shirts, and the other clothes that would go with them. I'm the talent behind the operation."

I wondered just how much talent it takes to design a T-shirt. A T-shirt, it seems to me, is just a couple of squares of cloth with two short sleeves sticking out of them. In fact, once upon a time, a T-shirt, I remember my Aunt Clara saying, was considered underwear. Now people pay big bucks to wear T-shirts with other people's names on them, and I had no doubt that people would pay big bucks to wear Tyra Grimes's T-shirts, too.

And I couldn't blame her for wanting to cash in on people's willingness to be walking advertisements for her. After all, I'd had T-shirts printed up with my slogan—Toadfern's Laundromat, Always a Leap Ahead of Dirt. I'm the only one who wears them, but even so, it makes a nice statement. Still, I didn't see that it takes much effort to design a T-shirt, other than to say, "Make them red and put my name on them in a fancy script." But I decided not to comment on that.

"What people would care about is that the T-shirts have my trademark name on them," Tyra was saying. "That's what people care about. And what I cared about was getting them done quickly and at a low overhead."

"So it's not your fault that maybe they aren't being made with legal labor, under lawful and fair conditions, because you delegate that part of the operation."

"Exactly!" Tyra looked genuinely pleased that I understood. She had this tendency, I was noticing, to mistake understanding for approval. "So you can see why I'd want these papers back. If they get out to the media . . ."

She suddenly looked worried again.

I considered what Tyra had just told me. I didn't for a minute believe that she had told me everything, or that she'd innocently and naïvely turned her business over to someone else to run. She struck me as someone who'd want to control every aspect of her business. My gut told me that she probably knew exactly what was going on, had approved it, probably even ordered it. And my gut told me that those papers showed exactly that.

I started to bring up Ramon and Aguila Cruez . . . but a warning bell went off in my head. If I did that, she might get scared and run. And if she ran, then we might not ever get to the bottom of who had really killed Lewis—and Chief Worthy would just let poor old Elroy languish in jail, and chalk Lewis's murder up to resentment over being taunted about tainted tuna fish.

And surely Tyra would be safe for a day or two, right? After all, the Cruez couple wouldn't be likely to come into town, where Tyra would be surrounded by people. And without her SUV and Paige, Tyra could only go where I or other volunteer drivers would take her. And after her experience last night, I couldn't imagine she'd go off walking by herself again.

"Here's the deal," I said. "I know who has those papers and I can get them back for you." In truth, I wasn't sure who had the papers—the Crookses or Paige—but I'd worry about that later. "But you have to tell me something first."

Tyra looked wary.

"Why did you come here to Paradise?"

Tyra sighed. "All right. I was going to come here anyway, but then your letter showed up. It made the perfect cover. I'm in town to make a sizable donation to Stillwater. I'm meeting with the director tomorrow to iron out the details—that's why I need you to take me there. Then I'm going to have a press conference on Friday to reveal my donation. Your wanting to be on my show made a good cover for coming here—that way no one would try to figure out why I was coming here until I was ready to announce my donation." She gave a pacifying smile. "But I did want to talk with you about possibly being on a future show."

I decided to ignore that last comment, as unlikely as it was. "You came here just to make a donation to Stillwater?"

"Why, yes," Tyra said. "What's so odd about that? I make donations all the time." She leaned forward, said in a hush-hush tone, as if sharing some insider business secret, "They make a good tax write-off."

"But wouldn't sending a check have been easier?"

Tyra glared at me. "This is a sizable donation."

I thought about Guy. I thought about how upset Vivian had been at the Tyra Grimes T-shirt Verbenia had been wearing. Something didn't seem right. I mean, I could see that Tyra would want do something that looked really good, to offset the fact that she was about to get in trouble for using illegal labor in her business, but something about it was really troubling me.

So, I blurted out, "Why Stillwater?"

Tyra looked at me evenly, as if daring me to question what she was about to say. "I read about the institution in an article recently. It sounded like a worthy cause."

"Where was the article published?"

Tyra shrugged, then yawned. "Can't remember. I read so many things, you know."

She stood up. "Sorry about all the fuss earlier," she said. "But now that I've told you what you want to know, I trust you'll track down those papers for me?"

I nodded. Tyra started to the door. Then she turned and gave me her trademark charming smile. "You might try parting your hair in the middle. It would look better, anyway."

And with that, she let herself out the door.

When she shut the door, I stepped into the living room, asking Owen, "Was I just had?"

But he couldn't answer. He was fast asleep on my couch. Poor guy. He'd had a long day.

I stared at him, daring myself to wake him up. Then I

heard it start to rain outside. Somehow, that just made me feel melancholy—not a good mood for what I'd been thinking of doing with Owen.

So I covered him up with a spare blanket, then gave him a little kiss on the temple, and went to bed myself.

I woke up early the next morning, even before my alarm went off, after a blessedly deep and dreamless sleep. No visits from old Mrs. Oglevee, haranguing me about all I was doing wrong.

I took a shower, noting with a little alarm the wad of hair that tangled itself around my drain stopper. My scalp was even itchier than before, so I put on a generous amount of conditioner, which made my head feel better. Then I toweled off and put on jeans and a plain blue T-shirt, with no one's name on the outside of it, not even mine. I parted my hair in the middle, blew it dry, and studied myself in the mirror. I had to admit that Tyra was right—a middle part looked better on me than a side part, an admission which kind of made me grumpy, since all my life I'd worn a side part. I told myself it was just a trick of the bathroom lighting that my hair was starting to look a bit more brassy than strawberry blond, a bit more kinky than curly.

I went out to the living room, all ready to make a nice big breakfast to share with Owen. But he was already gone. He'd left the blanket folded up neatly on the couch, but no note.

I told myself, as I went into the kitchenette, that I wasn't surprised. Or disappointed. Owen and I were really just friends, after all. And unlikely friends at that. Me, a laundromat owner. Him, a professor of philosophy, religion, and literature. Nope, I wasn't a bit disappointed. But for breakfast I had Choco-puffs cereal, topped with chocolate milk, anyway. And just a dash of chocolate syrup. Plus a leftover chocolate chip pancake.

Then I went down to my laundromat.

I love the ritual of opening up my laundromat in the morning.

Even this morning, when I had so much on my mind—like how poor Elroy was doing, and Lewis being dead, and wondering what Tyra was really up to with Stillwater, and the T-shirts and Billy and Paige and the Cruezes and the Crookses and the missing papers, and of course Owen, and my hair coming out, and wondering if I'd ever hear from Winnie—even with all that on my mind, I felt that little thrill of eagerness I always get when I'm unlocking the doors to my laundromat. Even with my toad painting gone, and my name misspelled to "Todeferne," and my coffeemaker replaced by a cappuccino machine (all of which I was going to correct as soon as I got the chance), I felt that bit of excitement that comes with opening up my own place of business, with taking in the whole place with one glance and seeing how neat and clean it is, because I always make sure my place is clean each night before I lock up, and there's something about the quietness at the start of a day—before all the washers and dryers are making noise and there's people inside my laundromat.

I started back to my storeroom office, to make a sign—leave a message for Josie if you have any laundry questions. I didn't like it, but I was going to have to leave my laundromat opened, but unmanned today. I didn't see as I had a choice. I told myself that my laundromat had been all right in my absence on Monday, that my sudden uneasiness was unfounded. I had to open up for my regular customers. Still, I wished Chip Beavy was available to watch it. Or Billy.

I also knew I couldn't not take Tyra to Stillwater. One way or another, even without Paige around to chauffeur her, Tyra would find a way out to Stillwater, and I wanted to be there to figure out what she was up to. I didn't believe she just wanted to be nice and give a donation to a place she had just read about in an article. I doubted there'd even been an article. Don Richmond, the director at Stillwater, was always good about letting the families know when news about Stillwater was going to come out. I would ask Winnie to check all the news resources she knew about—if I ever got in touch with her again, that is.

I was almost back to my storeroom, when I noticed, right under a folding table, a lump of dark clothing.

Then I saw the clothing stir. I blinked. The clothing stirred again. And groaned. And started snoring.

So I did the only thing I could think of to do. I went right over and kicked it.

The lump of clothing yelped and quickly unfolded itself to reveal Billy Toadfern, unshaven and unkempt in a wrinkled black raincoat, black shirt, black jeans, and black baseball cap.

Billy blinked up at me, licked his lips, yawned, and licked his lips again. Then he said, "You're early."

"Billy, get out from under that table. And tell me what you're doing here. Plus where you've been."

He crawled out, stood up slowly, his knees popping loudly. Then he staggered forward and hugged me. Suddenly, he pulled away, glancing back at the big glass window.

"Come on, back to the storeroom," he said, shoving me along. "Before they see me!"

"Who is 'they'?" I tried to keep my feet firmly to the ground, but Billy pushed me on.

"Come on! I can't let them see me!"

So we staggered on back to my storeroom.

He slammed the door shut, began looking around, as if "they" might be back here, too. I knew "they" weren't. Between my desk and the three shelves, there was barely room for two adult people, and definitely no hiding spots. The only "they" my storage room/office would be able to hide was a few mice, and if any "they" of the mouse kind were back there, I didn't want to know about it.

I grabbed Billy's shoulders, shook him, and said, "Billy! Settle down. Now, tell me, what's going on? Who's this "they" you're worried about? Is it the couple from the Red Horse—Aguila and Ramon?"

Billy stopped looking around and focused on me with wide eyes that were fearful.

"How do you know their names? Who told you?"

"I'm not answering that until—"

"Was it a couple? The man—tall, cute, and dark? The woman—short, cute, and blond?"

"Well, um, yes, as a matter of fact, they were just here yesterday . . ."

"What did they say about Aguila and Ramon?"

"That they're armed and dangerous and—"

Billy cut me off with a loud groan. "Oh, geez, Josie, please tell me you didn't believe that, that you didn't tell them anything . . ."

I frowned. "I didn't really have anything to tell them. Except that apparently you and Paige ran off with Aguila and Ramon, from what I heard. But I didn't even tell them that." I didn't mention that Paige had been writing an incriminating letter to Tyra, since doing so would mean I'd also have to mention I'd been snooping through trash cans in their motel rooms. "Now what is going on here, Billy—"

Billy grabbed me, hugging me really hard. "Oh, Josie, you're the best! Okay, look, you must not trust these two, must not tell them I'm here—"

I pushed away from Billy, gasped for air, then said, "Why are you afraid of the Crooks pair, for pity's sake? They're just writers—at least, that's what they say they are—although—"

Something in the serious way Billy was looking at me

made me stop. Billy usually always has a twinkle in his eye, like he's not really taking very seriously what's going on around him, like whatever he's doing is just for his own amusement. He was that way with the Cut-N-Suck demos. He was that way with preaching. But now, he looked really serious.

"They're not writers. They're FBI agents."

I stared at Billy. No, he really didn't look amused.

"How do you know that?"

"Just trust me—I do. And it is very, very, very important that you not let them know Aguila and Ramon are around here."

"From what they said, they're interested in Tyra Grimes. Billy—what have you gotten yourself into?"

"I'll tell you sometime—but not right now. Has Tyra said anything about why she's in town?"

I lifted my eyebrows at that. "Why, because she wants to interview me for her show, of course."

We looked at each other for a long moment. I sighed. "Right. Okay, it seems she wants to make a donation to Stillwater. She says she read about it in an article, came here with my story as a cover, so that her donation could be a big surprise."

Billy looked stunned. "Stillwater? She's here because of Stillwater?"

"That's what she says. Why did you think she was here?"

"We were worried that it was because of the T-shirts, but if she's here for some other reason, and if she doesn't know about the T-shirts, then we can go ahead with our plan . . ."

Billy gazed off, as if he were previewing the steps of the plan taking place in some not too distant future.

All the chocolate I'd had for breakfast suddenly curdled in my stomach. "Uh, Billy," I said, "just what sort of plan have you cooked up?"

He snapped his focus back to me. "I can't tell you right

now. But you've been a lot of help. Just don't let anyone—especially Tyra or the Crookses—know I've been here. Or that Aguila and Ramon are around."

He turned and stepped to the back door.

"Uh uh, Billy. Not so fast. I'm going to tell everyone—especially the Crookses—that they're around and that they're up to something with stolen goods, unless you give me more information."

Billy turned back around, looked at me with disappointment. "Josie, now, that's not like you. What's gotten into you?"

I could have told him that I was still hurting over Tyra using me as a cover for her real reason to come here, a reason that had me uneasy. That I was not looking forward to being the laughingstock of the town once the truth came out that Tyra had never really planned on having me on her show. That I was still sore over Owen leaving this morning before I woke up, without even writing me a note. That I knew just what he, Billy, meant by his question—good old Josie, always the soft pushover, always eager to please, how could that change?

But I have a stubborn streak, too, and getting irked makes it widen, and I was mighty irked at Billy taking for granted that I'd be a pushover for him.

So I crossed my arms and said again, "Billy, I need information. So give it to me. Or else."

Billy sighed. "All right. What do you want to know?"

"What's Paige doing with you?"

He looked surprised at that, which made me grin. I was always able to surprise him into telling me stuff, even as a kid, like who his latest crush was on. It worked now, too.

"We told Paige the situation, what Aguila and Ramon are up against," Billy said. "She's helping us."

"Voluntarily?"

Billy nodded . . . and something in his gaze softened. "Paige is really . . . a woman of great depth."

Uh oh, I thought. Looked like Billy had found his latest crush. But I didn't want to get sidetracked by pointing out to Billy that Paige was also a woman of great sophistication, and wouldn't want anything to do with the likes of him. So I said, "Okay, then, did Aguila and Ramon somehow know Tyra was going to be here in Paradise?"

Billy shook his head. "In fact, they're really upset that she is here."

"Then why are they staying around these parts? Why don't they just skedaddle elsewhere? It's a big country."

"They're here to sell the T-shirts. That's part of the plan."

Oh fine, now my cousin Billy was helping a pair of illegal immigrants—escapees from a labor camp, true, but still, illegal immigrants who were described as armed and dangerous by undercover FBI agents—traffic in stolen goods. Stolen from an illegal labor camp, true, but that somehow probably made it doubly illegal to be selling them. I couldn't stand trying to stay all calm and logical, with all of this information—which I had asked for, true—swirling in my head.

"What plan?" I burst out. "Why do they have to sell the T-shirts here? Why do they have to sell them at all? Why, why, why are you hooked up with them at all?"

Billy gave me one of those long, fiery looks he used to give from the pulpit, a look that was always accompanied by silence, like it was now. Just Billy staring right into me. But this time, his stare did not seem to be just for effect. He seemed to really be trying to see something, to be struggling to make a decision from whatever he saw in me. It made me uncomfortable, but I stared right back at him.

At last, he said, "All right, Josie. Here's what I can tell you. I'm hooked up with them because they need help. Because a young child's life depends on getting the right help. And right now in my life, helping someone else is what I need to help me, too. Anything else you want to know, I'll have to show you."

I wanted to scream again—this time, what child? Show me now! But I still had to get Tyra to Stillwater. So I said, "Fine. How about this afternoon."

"All right," he said. "Come to the Red Horse this afternoon, about three o'clock."

"Why there? You just checked out of there—"

"Josie, don't ask so many questions right now. Just trust me."

Billy moved to the storage room door, opened it, and stuck his head out, looking around. Then he stepped back in and looked at me. "Listen, thank you. You've helped more than you know."

"I don't suppose you could repay me by watching my laundromat today?"

He grinned, shook his head. "I have my own business to attend to." Then he pointed his finger at me. "Three o'clock. Sharp."

He darted out the door again.

This whole situation, I thought, was as wrinkled and knotted up as a bunch of socks stuck in a spin cycle.

I went to work, making sure the lint traps were cleared out, the change machine full, everything in order. I'd be gone for a few hours, I told myself, then I'd go back to paying attention to running my business.

Then, I went to meet Tyra to take her to Stillwater, wondering again what she was really up to. I just couldn't fully believe her mission here in Paradise was to be a generous benefactress.

11

In fact, Tyra was not in a generous mood at all as we headed up the state route toward Stillwater, even though it was a beautiful spring day—one of those days with an impossibly bright blue sky—and even though I kept diligently pointing out, in the cheeriest voice I could muster, numerous items of local scenic interest: fields being plowed for corn and soybeans, farmhouses and stands of trees, horses out grazing in a field, the Raybells' free-range chicken farm, Margo Putney's dairy farm and ice cream stand, and the Bloomin' Beauties Garden Shop.

I'd say, "Look, Tyra! Horses!"

Or, "Look, Tyra! A tractor trailer!"

Or, even, "Look, Tyra! Mrs. Susy Whitfield's got out on her clothesline the choir robes from the Second Reformed Church of the Reformation—that's where my cousin Billy used to preach, but Harvey Welter's taken over now. 'Course, the choir robes will be wrinkled, because I'm not doing them anymore since Billy was let go from preaching. I always did them at half price . . ."

But Tyra just wasn't interested in items of local scenic interest . . . or in local gossip. She was just plain nervous. The only thing she wanted to know was if I had her papers back yet, and when I told her no, she kept fussing with trying to adjust her seat just so. Finally, she pulled the seat adjustment lever so that she and the seat were leaned all the way back. She gave a little moan of dismay.

"You know, if you keep doing that," I said, "you're going to break the springy things that adjust the seat, and—"

"Ow! Gosh darn it!" Tyra howled. Well, she didn't really howl exactly that. But what she did say, I don't feel quite bears repeating word for word. No need to offend the good Lord twice through the retelling.

I glanced over at her. She'd pulled on the seat adjustment lever yet again, and now she and the seat were folded in half, pitched all the way forward.

Then I focused my attention back on the road.

"I'm going to throw up if I stay like this," Tyra gasped.

"Straighten the seat up, then," I said, pushing back a wave of panic at the thought of Tyra puking into the passenger side foot well of my car. The sickly cloying smell of puke stays around long after the stains are gone.

"I can't straighten back up!" Tyra gagged.

"Okay, look," I said desperately, trying to find some place I could pull over without my car getting stuck in the mucky mud left from the previous night's rain. "Take some deep breaths—slowly, in and out, in and . . ."

"I can't breathe at all like this." Tyra gasped, as if each word were being squeezed out of her.

Just then we went over a bump in the road—a small bump, one I barely felt, considering how slowly we were going, but I guess being all bent over with her face nearly in the floorboard, Tyra felt it mightily, because just as we went over it, she hollered, "Damn it! I bit my tongue!"

"Are you bleeding? Do you need a tissue? I keep a box in the glove compartment—here, let me open it for you . . ."

I reached over and unlatched the glove compartment. It fell open onto Tyra's head—barely tapping her, really—but she started bobbing her head up and down and around, like a panicked mule in a too-tight harness, and jolted the compartment door so that the entire contents showered down on her head: papers from Elroy's shop, from the times I'd had my oil changed or repairs done. A tire gauge. A flashlight. And the box of tissues.

"What is going on here? Are you trying to kill me?" Tyra thrashed about as she hollered. Apparently the barrage of stuff on her head made it possible to breathe, and also holler again, "Be careful!"

There was the gravel driveway to Ed Crowley's farm just ahead. I could pull in there.

Tyra's fist hit the center gearshift hard enough that she knocked the shift to neutral. My car slammed to a stop. The force was enough that it threw Tyra, and her seat, all the way back. She started screaming. I started screaming too, mostly because I was horrified at the thought of my car's gears being stripped and having to deal with one very large repair bill.

Then I heard a siren. I looked into the rearview mirror and saw a police car coming up the road behind us. If I didn't move, and fast, the cruiser was either going to ram right up my tailpipe or have to swerve around us—and on this narrow country road, that would be dangerous. I needed to move. I grabbed for my gearshift, got us into drive, and suddenly— just as the police car was about to plow into the back of mine—we were moving forward again.

I glanced into my rearview mirror. Yes, that really was Chief John Worthy in the car behind me, right on my tail, his mouth hanging open like the shock of seeing me careening all over the road had unhinged his jaw.

I gave a little oops-sorry wave—to no effect, as Chief Worthy kept on his siren and his flashing lights.

Now, you know how in a traumatic situation your brain kind of splits off, and while the main part is still dealing with the situation, the split off part is kind of analyzing it and thinking about it, and in a half second can go through thoughts that would normally take minutes . . . or longer?

I am ashamed to admit it, but that little split off part of my brain had this idea—just for a little bit, as I am a law-abiding citizen—that I should just put my gas pedal to the floor and try to outrun Chief Worthy. I had this momentary fantasy that if I did so, maybe the passenger side door would fly open, and Tyra would go flying out, and Chief Worthy would be obliged to stop and help her. I only envisioned her scratched up a little. With a few bruises. Maybe bleeding here and there. But definitely not too hurt, or dead, or anything like that. Then, with Chief Worthy delayed by Tyra's needs, I could drive on and on, beyond Paradise, beyond Mason County, even beyond Ohio . . .

My mama had done that. Just up and left after our trailer burned, left behind whatever problems plagued her. I never found out what those problems were. I've never tried. I've never really wanted to know. Knowing can be worse than imagining.

But just before our trailer burned and she ran off and left me alone, she'd told me, "Mark my words, little girl, you can't run away from trouble, it'll just stink worse as it follows you."

I guess I only remember her saying it because she left after that. But even though it was advice she hadn't taken, it was advice that was still good. And even as my foot pressed down just a little on my gas pedal, I thought of Guy, over at Still-water. He needed me.

And I thought of all the folks in Paradise who depend on Toadfern's Laundromat to get their clothes clean—working clothes for construction jobs or nursing jobs or teaching jobs all around Mason County, or going out on Saturday night clothes, or going to church on Sunday morning clothes . . . who would run my laundromat if I left? So lots of folks in Paradise needed me, too.

I thought of Winnie. Who else would debate the merits of the latest books with her, or discuss Dickens or the Brontës with her? She needed me.

I thought of Owen. I wasn't sure he needed me. But I'd like to find out.

So in that split-second—Tyra still screaming, Chief Worthy's sirens still blaring—I thought all that through, and then we were coming up on the Crowley farm. So I moved my foot from the gas pedal to the brake, slowed down, and pulled into the gravel drive.

Chief Worthy pulled in right behind me.

I swatted Tyra on the arm and hollered, "Hush up!"

She stopped screaming, looked up at me—she was still prone with the passenger seat most of the way back—then moaned, "Where are we? Are we dead? Oh, God, I don't want to be dead . . ."

"Stop blubbering," I said. I picked the box of tissues up off my floor, tossed the box in her lap. "Blow your nose and smile. Chief John Worthy has just pulled us over—and I sure don't want any trouble with him."

Chief Worthy tapped on my window just then. I rolled it down, smiled out at him. "Hello, Chief," I said, making my voice as cheery as I could. "Were you wondering what was going on just a minute ago there? See, Tyra here was fiddling with her seat—frankly, I think she broke the seat adjustment thingy—and . . ."

"Josie, have you been drinking?"

I was genuinely shocked at Chief Worthy's suggestion. "Of course not."

"I cannot vouch for her," Tyra said. "I had to fend for my-self for breakfast. There wasn't much to choose from—"

I turned away from Chief Worthy and glared at Tyra. "Now, you know as well as I do that Winnie stocked up the cabinets and fridge with plenty of—"

"Josie, I'm going to have to ask you to get out of the car."

I got out, shut my car door, and turned and faced Chief Worthy, who was already shaking his head at me. He was holding a pen and pad, all ready to write me up for something or other, I could see. Tyra, meanwhile, was still in my car.

"Josie, I want you to walk up this lane, about twenty steps, then turn and come back."

He was doing the old walking a straight line test to see if I was drunk or not. Just the fact that he would think such a thing of me was making me shake—and being tested to see if I could walk straight on wet gravel hardly seemed fair. But I figured protesting would get me nowhere except into one of the two jail cells over at the Paradise Police Department. And I didn't relish the idea of being neighbors in the local jail with Elroy, as much as I was worried about him.

So I walked, counting out twenty steps, trying to keep it even, trying to keep it natural, then turned and came back to-ward Chief Worthy, who didn't say a word. Just stared at me.

I walked right up to him, so his black boots and my white sneakers were just about toe-to-toe, so my nose was practi-cally on his chin. I opened my mouth and exhaled. Let him detect for himself that I'd been guilty of too much chocolate for breakfast, but nothing worse.

Chief Worthy frowned, looking displeased. He couldn't pull me in for having too high a chocolate level in my blood count.

"All right, Josie Toadfern, what's going on here?"

"I'm driving Tyra somewhere. Her seat got stuck in a posi-tion she didn't like. She started flailing around, hit my gearshift, and sent us into neutral. I'm lucky she didn't strip the gears."

"You're lucky you didn't cause a crash." Chief Worthy stepped around to the passenger side of my car and tapped on the window. Tyra struggled to roll it down, but quickly gave a little hands-up gesture, along with a little damsel-in-distress smile. It was all I could do to keep from rolling my eyes—not that either of them would have noticed. No, Chief John Worthy was busy being all knight-in-shiny-armor-ish, opening the door for Tyra, helping her out, asking her if she was okay, looking all concerned, even calling her ma'am.

"Well," Tyra said, "while I do appreciate that Josie here is willing to be my chauffeur, I must say that she has the most difficult automobile. I was simply trying to adjust the seat—"

"You weren't adjusting it! You were mauling it!"

"Don't interrupt Ms. Grimes, Josie," Chief Worthy said. "Now, you're sure you're voluntarily with Josie?"

He gave me a hard look as he asked Tyra that. Oh, fine. He couldn't get me on drunk driving. Now he was going to try to get me on trying to kidnap Tyra Grimes for some awful purpose.

"Well," Tyra started, drawing the word out, giving me a sly look, "now that you mention it . . ."

The woman was about to play along with the idea that I'd kidnapped her—and why not? She could get me out of the way, find someone else—probably Chief Worthy—to escort her around town. I probably wasn't being as accommodating as she would like. And I sure had had a lot of questions about her business the night before that she didn't like. But I wasn't about to let her get away with giving Chief John Worthy an excuse to haul me down to the police department. I wanted to figure out what she was up to at Stillwater, for one thing. And I didn't want any trouble with the police, for another.

So I said, "Why, Tyra, don't you recall our conversation last night? We were talking about your need for me to drive you around today . . . and then you mentioned some papers of yours that you say were stolen . . . and I suggested we call the police, so I guess it's a good thing Chief Worthy stopped us today—"

"You had some papers stolen?" Chief Worthy said eagerly. "Ms. Grimes, you should come file a report—"

"No, no," Tyra said, shooting me an unhappy look. "Josie's mistaken. I'm sure I just misplaced the papers."

"And—" I urged.

Tyra sighed. "And Josie is being so kind to drive me on my—my errands today. I asked her to."

"And—" I pressed.

"And it was my fault about the car going in neutral," Tyra said. "So, please, Chief Worthy—"

"You can call me John—"

"Okay, John. If there's any ticket you need to write, or anything like that, please write it out to me—"

"No, ma'am, that's not necessary. I'm glad everything's all right. Perhaps I should follow you, to make sure everything stays all right?"

"Oh, not necessary," said Tyra.

"Fine. Good day, then."

Chief Worthy started back to his cruiser. But suddenly he stopped and turned with the smug grin that had served as a warning sign way back in high school. Uh oh, I thought. This was going to be bad. Even Tyra looked nervous again.

He looked at Tyra. "Don't hesitate to call me if you need anything, Ms. Grimes," he said. "Josie has good intentions—but she can be too nosy for her own good. Puts people off, but that's never stopped her. It's just one reason we called her Nosy Josie back in high school."

With that, he gave a little laugh, got back in his cruiser, and backed out.

I just stood there a long minute, watching him go, blinking back tears, not wanting to feel a thing, but instead, feeling everything I wanted to push down. Hurt. Humiliated. Angry.

Tyra and I got back in my car.

First, she picked up everything that had fallen out of the glove compartment, put it back in neatly, then shut the door. Then she sat back. She didn't even complain that she was more or less lying down, the seat was so far back. She didn't fiddle with the seat lever. I started the car and we pulled out.

"That true, what John just said? About your nickname?"

She asked the questions softly, gently.

"Yes," I said, finally, my voice thicker than I liked.

"Why?"

I waited, swallowed a few times before I answered. "I was always interested in what other people were up to. I worked on the school paper. The combination gave me the nickname Nosy Josie. Funny, huh?"

"No. Sounds mean. And Chief Worthy was a prick for saying what he did," Tyra said firmly. I was surprised to hear Tyra say that. It didn't fit her prim and proper image. But she said again, "A real prick. And you shouldn't listen to him. You seem to have lots of friends."

I didn't say anything.

"Really, I mean it," Tyra said. "Several people commented to me at the party about how much they like you, and look up to you, how proud they are of your expertise and your contacting me to get on my show."

Although, of course, I wasn't going to be on her show, but I didn't say anything about that, either. I was too intrigued by the fact that Tyra sounded . . . wistful. Envious, even.

Silence, as my car chugged toward Stillwater.

Then, "And Owen, now he really seems to like you," Tyra added softly. "Relationships are important, Josie. Having people who really care for you, not for what you represent. Or earn. I learned that too late. And I wish I could go back and fix a lot of things so that I could have relationships like you do now. You're lucky."

The pictures I'd found in Tyra's purse came to mind. Maybe they were of people who had once been important to Tyra, or should have been. Then Lewis came to mind, and I gasped at the idea that maybe Tyra and Lewis had once had a relationship—a real relationship, not just a passing connection of some kind. Certainly, his feelings about her were too strong, too out of character for him, for them to have developed simply because she wasn't his favorite media star.

My imagination took off. Had Tyra and Lewis known each other in the past, as lovers? Did his anger rise from her having jilted him to pursue her career? Was the Stillwater donation Tyra's excuse to come back and see Lewis?

I glanced over at Tyra, trying to find the right words to ask my questions of her without putting her off, but Tyra was dozing. I'm not sure if I'd have had the nerve to ask, anyway.

I turned my focus back to the road. I'd just seen a soft, lonely side of Tyra Grimes that didn't fit the chirpy, busy-busy-busy TV-Tyra person that I and thousands of other people had come to admire. A side that talked about relationships and feelings and people, instead of just about how to make and improve things.

It amazed me.

And it made me uneasy. It reminded me too much of seeing a surprisingly personal side to Lewis, too, just before he died.

* * *

By the time we got to Stillwater, I had my emotions back under-
der control, and Tyra had awakened. I parked in the visitor's
lot and started toward the main building, with Tyra walking
alongside me. We didn't say anything to each other. Tyra
seemed withdrawn and nervous again, maybe a reaction to
having opened up to me for a few moments, maybe because
of her upcoming meeting.

Stillwater's director, Don Richmond, was waiting for us at
the main building, an old farmhouse in which a parlor had
been left in place and the rest of the space was a kitchen and
dining hall on the main floor. Office space for the director
and a few other folks was on the second floor. Sleeping quarters for the residents had been added on.

Don was a tall, bulky man, with a dark brown beard that had
gone half gray, but unevenly, so it looked painted on. He normally wore flannel shirts and jeans, or T-shirts and jeans, depending on the season, and had a big smile on his face—a smile
that showed he was friendly, but hid how firm he could be when
he had to. He was a genuinely nice guy who'd quit his job at
some big legal database company to work here because, as he
said, work should be more than a paycheck. And he always
looked genuinely happy, even when dealing with problems.

But today he looked worried. And he was wearing a suit.
The combination startled me.

I started to introduce Don and Tyra, but Tyra rushed right
ahead. "You must be Don Richmond," she said, holding out
her hand. "So nice to meet you in person, after all those
lovely phone conversations."

I guess she figured she needed no introduction. Who
wouldn't recognize Tyra Grimes, right? Sure enough, Don
took her hand, shook it, and said, "It's nice to meet you, Ms.
Grimes."

But he didn't sound like he thought it was all that nice.
Truth be told, he looked and sounded scared. He was shaking.

He looked past Tyra to me, started to say something, but Tyra jumped in. "Oh, this is Josie Toadfern. She's my chauffeur, since my assistant is otherwise occupied." Tyra smiled kindly, warming to her benefactress role. "Perhaps Josie can just wait out here in this charming little parlor—"

"I know Josie quite well," Don interrupted.

"Guy over at the greenhouse?" I asked, acting like I didn't see Tyra now staring from one to the other of us.

Don nodded.

"I'll just sign in, then, and go see him."

I turned, walked over to the reception desk, and signed in. By the time I was done, Tyra and Don had gone up the stairs.

I went on out, walked around to the greenhouse. Verbenia was the first person I saw. She was misting little cups that had seedlings in them. She looked up at me, then quickly tucked her chin down to her neck so that her long blond hair fell in front of her pretty face.

Then she stared up again, her blue eyes piecing me together, and finally coming up with a whole she recognized. I was rewarded with a smile. "Hi, Verbenia, I'm here to see Guy."

"Verbenia hi, hi Verbenia. Josie hi, hi Josie," she said. "Guy by the pumpkins. By the pumpkins Guy."

Verbenia is pretty verbal for a resident of Stillwater, but she doesn't like long conversations, and she doesn't like to be touched, except by her sister Vivian, who could calm Verbenia down with tight hugs. I sidled down the narrow aisle past her, seeing Charles, who stopped me, as always, to ask me how many miles I'd driven to get here, how long it took me, and the route I'd taken. I told him, and he thought a minute, then told me it had taken me seven minutes and 28 seconds longer to get here than the last time. That's what Charles did—somehow, he kept track in his head of how long it took people to get to Stillwater, and figured out the difference. He had those numbers for all of the regular Stillwater visitors.

As I moved on, I wondered over the fact that the whole scene with Chief Worthy had only taken seven minutes and 28 seconds. I knew Charles was right. But it had seemed like a lot longer than that.

Fred waved at me, then, in his funny way—he keeps the top part of his arm pressed into his body, then flaps around his forearm like a flipper. Fred never says much of anything. I waved back at him, then saw Guy. He was over with Celeste, one of the activity supervisors. She smiled as I came over.

"Hi, Josie! Guy, show Josie the pumpkin starts," Celeste said, with a bright but firm tone to her voice. "Show her how the pumpkins are doing." Celeste is just out of college, but she knows how to handle the Stillwater residents.

At Celeste's suggestion, Guy picked up a pumpkin plant in its peat pot, carefully explaining how he'd put in the seed, covered it with dirt, watered it, and made sure it got plenty of light, and then a baby pumpkin plant came up. Then he picked up another pumpkin seedling and repeated his explanation. He did that for every plant he was responsible for—thirty-six pumpkin plants in all. He told me the same way, each time, and with pride, each time. And I didn't rush him at all.

I was glad to listen. It made him feel good. It made me feel good, listening, and glancing around at the others working, some of them watering, some carefully transplanting other plants to bigger pots. It was warm and moist and cozy in the greenhouse, and I liked the sight of all those tables, covered with all those flats of plants, and the smell of green and life and warm and dirt. A greenhouse is the only place I know where you can smell all that at once.

And Tyra Grimes was here. Up to something. And it scared me. Because ever since she came to Paradise, weird things had been happening. I wondered how whatever she was doing here might hurt Stillwater's precious balance of quiet

work and routine. A balance that worked for the residents of
Stillwater. A balance that Tyra might turn topsy-turvy.

On the other hand, maybe she really did just want to make
a donation to Stillwater. After all, what could someone famous like Tyra gain from a place like Stillwater other than a
tax write-off? It was impossible to imagine. Yet Stillwater
was the reason she had really come to Paradise. And I found
it hard to believe she just wanted to make a nice donation.

Guy was staring at me. He'd gone through all thirty-six
of his pumpkin plants, and he was waiting for me to say
something.

"They are wonderful," I said. "The healthiest, most wonderful you've grown yet."

Guy beamed. "Big pumpkins? Big, big pumpkins?"

"Yes," I said. "They will be very big."

The others were lining up behind Celeste now. The time to
work in the greenhouse was over. I walked with Guy to the
end of the line.

"Lunch duty today," Guy said, letting me know what was
next on his schedule. "Wash up first. I'm chopping onions.
Sloppy joes. You like sloppy joes."

"Yes, I do," I said. His statement was his way of asking
me to stay for lunch. But I didn't know how long Tyra
would be staying to talk with Don. And somehow, I didn't
want her to linger here. I wanted to get her away from here
as quickly as possible. I was panicking—not going on
logic—but sometimes a gut feeling is more telling than
logic. So I said, "I'm sorry, Guy. I don't know if I can stay
for lunch today."

He put his hands over his face, which meant he was upset. I
touched his arm, but he pulled away. He kept his hands like that
as he walked out behind the others, looking through his fingers
spread apart over his face. I followed along, stopping outside

the greenhouse. Charles led the group on around to the main house. I stayed outside, went around the back to see how the flower garden was doing. And there I saw Vivian Denlinger.

That was a surprise—Vivian's a nurse up in Columbus, and it seemed unlikely she'd be able to visit today. But then, it wasn't like me to be here in the middle of the week, either.

Vivian was wearing a black dress—something else that surprised me. She never wore dresses—always khaki pants or jeans and some simple top. She sat on the bench and stared at the bed of tulips—mostly yellows and pinks and purples. Only a few reds, which was good for Guy. She looked like a lady out of a painting in a book of artwork Winnie'd loaned me once. A lady in a garden, staring at the beautiful flowers, but really seeing something far away. A lady in mourning.

Now, I was still smarting from what Chief John Worthy had said. But nosy or not, one thing was certain—I know something that needs checking into when I see it. And Vivian here on a Wednesday, when she was supposed to be up in Columbus being a nurse, dressed in a black dress like some widow in mourning, definitely bore investigating.

I walked over and sat down on the bench next to her. She had on some thick, cloying perfume—a mixture of vanilla and gardenia—the kind of thing much older ladies wear, along with a hat and a churchy dress, when they want to look fine for some special occasion.

"Hi." My greeting was gentle, but it still startled her. "Sorry. You okay? You're usually not here mid-week, and—"

"Neither are you," she snapped. Then she shook her head and rubbed her eyes. "Sorry, Josie. I took off today after hearing about Lewis's death. I've really been struggling with how to tell Verbenia and whether or not to take her with me to his viewing in a few days. I think, though, that would be too upsetting to her. I'll just have to tell her about his death this afternoon."

I stared at her. Surely there couldn't be two Lewises in the Paradise area who were dead . . . still, I was taken aback. "You mean . . . Lewis Rothchild? You knew him? You're going to his viewing?"

Vivian's expression became guarded. "Yes, Lewis Rothchild. He is—was—a—a friend of our family's."

Vivian and Verbenia's family . . . now, *that* was a new idea . . . I'd always just thought of Vivian and Verbenia as having only each other. I'd never given any consideration to a dad or mom, or other sisters, or brothers, uncles, aunts, cousins . . . but surely those folks were out there. Still, I'd never seen any of them around. Or Lewis, for that matter. Vivian and Verbenia were so close I just thought of them as having only each other.

I gave Vivian a little pat on her arm. "Then I'm sorry for your loss. I didn't know you knew Lewis. How did you and Verbenia know him?"

Vivian looked away, tensing up even more than usual. She smoothed her already perfectly smooth hair, which was captured in a tight bun. "It's a long story. But I—we—will miss him."

Her voice trembled.

"Is that what you were talking to Celeste about? Having to tell Verbenia?"

"That—and that damned Tyra Grimes T-shirt."

Vivian's voice shifted from sadness to anger so suddenly—and so completely—that I was again startled. "Yeah, uh, that T-shirt really upset Guy, too. You know how he is about the color red. So, um, did you ever find out how Verbenia got one?"

Vivian's frown tightened. "Charles's mother saw this couple selling those T-shirts out of the back of their truck. I guess she's a real Tyra Grimes fan." Vivian said that as if instead of being a popular media star, Tyra was a fiend anyone with sense would hate. "I guess the couple gave Charles's mother some sob story about needing money. So she bought three or four T-shirts. She gave one to Charles—and when Verbenia saw it, she really reacted to it, tugging on his sleeve like she wanted one too. So Verbenia got one."

Vivian pressed her lips together. She got that faraway look she'd had when she'd been staring into the garden, only this time she didn't look wistful, just bitter. When she spoke, her voice was nearly a whisper, it was so thin. "I got the T-shirt back. And made it very clear that Verbenia was never to have anything else given to her without my prior approval."

Suddenly she shook her head, her expression clearing. "So, Josie, I haven't asked yet—what brings you here today? Don't you normally visit on a Sunday, too? Everything okay?"

A few seconds passed after I opened my mouth before words came out. Even then, I stuttered. "I—uh—yeah, sure, I normally come on Sundays, but there's a, uh, visitor who wanted to, uh—"

And then I stopped. Vivian wasn't listening to me anymore. She was staring beyond me. And her face had gone ghostly white, and hard.

"Vivian?" I said.

She stared.

I turned to see what had made her react so strongly.

It was Tyra Grimes, walking toward us, now yoo-hooing across the lawn at me.

I turned back to Vivian. But she was gone, nothing left of her but a waft of her perfume. She'd left so silently, so fast, I was glad of her perfume. It was the only proof I hadn't imagined her.

* * *

On the ride home, my and Tyra's conversation was quick.

I said, "So how is it you know Vivian Denlinger?"

"I have no idea who you're talking about."

"The lady I was sitting with when you came out from your meeting with Don."

"I only caught a glimpse of her, but I'm sure I've never seen her before in my life."

"Well, she seemed to know you."

"Everyone knows who I am."

"No, she seemed to *know* you. I don't think she likes you."

"Hmm. Must have seen the show I did on why soup should always be served as a course unto itself—never as a meal." Tyra yawned. "Got a lot of complaints about that one. Riding in a car makes me sleepy. I think another nap is in order."

Tyra's nap gave me time to think.

What I thought about mostly was Vivian. There was definitely a connection between her and Verbenia and Lewis. There appeared to be a strong connection between her and Tyra—why else would she have such a strong reaction to a simple T-shirt? Or react that way to seeing Tyra? And of course I already suspected a personal connection between Lewis and Tyra. So somehow Lewis, Tyra, Vivian, and Verbenia were all connected . . . and Lewis was dead, while Tyra was planning on making a sizable donation to Stillwater, a fact that should have made Don happy . . . but he'd looked miserable when I'd dropped off Tyra.

This was all new information—but I wasn't sure how it connected with Billy and the two runaways from Tyra's labor camp, or with the Crookses being in town, or with Paige apparently running off with Billy, or . . .

My car swerved. I refocused on the road. My head was spinning. Thinking would have to wait.

So for the rest of the drive home to Paradise, I concentrated on driving, on staying calm. Which was a good thing, because as soon as we got back to my laundromat, I discovered that all hell had broken loose—again. And then things got even worse.

When we'd left Paradise that morning—Tyra and I—it had been the same sleepy little Ohio town I've always known. Three pickup trucks—one blue, one yellow, one red, all rusty—were parked in front of Sandy's Restaurant. Mayor Cornelia's lilac Cadillac (she's a Joy Jean Cosmetics sales representative when she isn't mayoring) was in front of Town Hall. Otherwise, the streets were pretty empty.

But when we got back to Paradise, I could barely get my car through town. The streets were packed with vans with satellite dishes on top and cars—big, new, shiny ones that I didn't recognize—parked everywhere there was a niche of space, in front of my laundromat, and in front of Sandy's Restaurant, and in front of the drugstore and the police department and Town Hall and the theatre. I saw a van that had a little satellite dish on top and CHANNEL 4, MASON COUNTY'S TOP TV NEWS SOURCE on the side (it's actually Mason County's only news source), plus two vans from Cincinnati, three from Columbus, even one from Dayton.

Word had finally gotten out—Tyra Grimes was in Paradise.

And so the world had at last discovered Paradise.

We were about to get the fame I'd wanted for my hometown. My wish had come true.

I should have been happy. But there was this sick fluttery feeling in my stomach, and I heard the words Mrs. Oglevee used to say: "be careful what you wish for . . . you just might get it."

I had to park all the way down by Lewis's Funeral Home, four blocks from my laundromat. Then, I had to wake Tyra up, which made her grumpy, like a kid who's napped too long. But when she saw the media vans, a switch went off. She was suddenly Happily Beaming Tyra, Meet-the-Media Tyra, Gracious Tyra.

To get ready for the role, Tyra whipped a lipstick out of her purse and peered into a little mirror while she freshened up her lips, then finger-combed her hair.

"Did you see where they all are?" Tyra asked. She meant the media, of course.

"Everywhere," I moaned.

"They have to be somewhere big. Where would that be?"

I thought. There's no really big gathering spot in Paradise—not big enough for all the people who were currently clogging the streets.

"Even during the Beet Festival Parade, the streets aren't this crowded," I said. "The only place in town with lots of space is the Paradise Theatre—but it's closed—or . . ." I stopped, the terrible truth hitting me, then wheezing right back out again in a thin stream of words. "Or . . . my . . . laundromat . . ."

Tyra got out of my car, hurried off without waiting for me. Of course, it wasn't like I needed to introduce her.

I got out too and started hurrying down the sidewalk—I was mighty worried about what was going on in my laundromat—but I stopped when I saw, on the corner down by the

Rothchild Funeral Home, Vivian, staring at me. She looked quickly away and ducked into Cherry's Chat and Curl.

She'd followed us. That had to be the truth. Vivian wasn't likely to go in and get her hair trimmed into some chic new style, not when she'd been wearing the same bun for years.

But I didn't have time to run into Cherry's to question her—I needed to get down to my laundromat. Now, I kind of wish I had. I could have talked with Cherry about why my scalp was itching all the time. I could have talked with Vivian, maybe even found out what was bothering her, then and there . . . instead of later, when it was too late.

But truth be told, I was more worried about my laundromat at the moment than about anything else—than about Tyra and whatever she was plotting at Stillwater, than about Billy and why he wanted me out at the Red Horse Motel at three o'clock. Toadfern's Laundromat is my livelihood.

I ran. By the time I got there, I was huffing for breath.

But when I stepped in, what I saw took my breath away.

Reporters.

Everywhere.

Like an infestation of ants.

Not just Henry Romar, the publisher/editor/reporter for the *Paradise Advertiser-Gazette*, although he was there too, eyes wide, taking pictures of all of the reporters. This would be Henry's biggest scoop—this many reporters had never been in Paradise before.

And it wasn't just reporters and photographers crowded into my laundromat. As I picked my way through the crowd, trying to get to Tyra, I ran into Mayor Cornelia. And stumbled into Pastor Whitlock, from over at the Baptist Church.

It was so noisy that when I shouted, "This is a place of business! Unless you've got something to wash . . ." my voice was picked up and drowned in the thundering voices all around me.

It was so crowded that to see what was going on I finally climbed up on one of my folding tables and stood up on it and peered out over the crowd.

I took in what was going on in the center of my laundromat. There stood Tyra, a little circle of space around her, silent but smiling for camera after camera as reporters jostled to take her picture. She turned slowly, an eye of calmness in the middle of all these people storming around her, like she knew that her worth, in that moment, was in being seen, being photographed, being filmed. She knew it, and she liked it, and she relished it, so she played to it. It made me wonder how it felt to be someone like Tyra Grimes, when she was all alone. From what she'd said in my car on the way to Stillwater, it felt lonely. My thought from my last visit at the old orphanage echoed through my mind . . . two different things, alone and lonely. And not an easy combination to live with.

I could only pick up bits of the questions being hollered—"Ms. Grimes, what brings you to this little town?" "Ms. Grimes, can you address the allegations about illegal workers at your manufacturing site in the California desert . . ."

Tyra held her hand up. The people in the room got quiet, more or less, although there were still people taking pictures.

About this same time, a hefty reporter with a camera noticed me standing up on my folding table, and climbed up too.

"Get down," I hissed at him. "I own this place . . . this is my table . . . I'm the only one who can—"

But he ignored me. Trouble was, other reporters and photographers noticed the vantage point this big fellow had gained by joining me up on the folding table, and so they started climbing up too. I swatted at them like horseflies, but they were just as stubborn, and swarmed on up.

Meanwhile, Tyra was speaking. "I'm so glad you are all here. I do have important news to share with all of you." The room got really quiet after that—except for the creaking sound of the table that I and about five other people were standing on, plus the sound of me swatting and hissing, "Shoo, shoo!"

"I will be holding an official press conference day after to-morrow, on Friday afternoon." A groan went up and someone hollered, "Why do we have to wait so long?"

Tyra held her hand up for silence and the crowd quieted. "Please, the conference will be two days from now at Still-water Farms. I'm sorry to wait that long, but I have to wait for a few, um, details to be finalized." She paused, as if unsure of what to say next. She missed Paige and her counsel, I thought. Then Tyra smiled and went on. "I also need to wait until after the funeral of Mr. Lewis Rothchild, out of respect for his family." The crowd buzzed at that. Tyra finished, rais-ing her voice, "At that time I will answer your questions— and make a significant announcement of both a personal and business nature."

There was a lot more buzzing after that—people trying to get Tyra to answer more questions about the questions she wouldn't answer yet—and picture taking. And me, saying "please get down off my table . . . please get out of my laundromat . . ."

And then, just what I was afraid would happen happened. The table legs buckled and the table swayed and then crashed. Some of us went down in a heap, some of us tum-bled into other parts of the crowd, so people in those parts fell down, too, knocking down other people who hadn't even been near the table to begin with—in a kind of willy-nilly people-domino way. Me, I landed right on the reporter who had gotten up on the table with me to begin with. He cush-ioned my fall, for which I was grateful, although he was moaning pitiably.

Still, I had a whole split second of prayerful hopefulness that everything would be all right, but then someone landed on me, and someone else hollered that they were pinned under the table, and then I heard first one crashing sound from back in the storeroom, and then another crashing sound, from over where the cappuccino machine was, then a sort of tumbly thump-thump sound.

And over and around all those sounds, people hollering and moaning and cursing, and I thought, oh Lord, we're gonna have one of those panic-induced stampedes, like what you read about happening at rock concerts, where everyone gets crushed to death, only it was going to happen right here in my laundromat.

Then, rising above all the other noises came a new sound—a long, high thin voice mewling one plaintive word—*"M-a-a-ma!"*

A little kid—somewhere in this crowd, in my laundromat . . . I scrambled up, not sure what to do. Suddenly, there was a roar, "Get out of my way!" and parting the crowd in a manner that would have made Moses proud was Becky Gettlehorn, holding Tommy on her hip. The crowd hushed and pulled back as she got to the little girl—Haley—who was sitting in the middle of the floor, crying, her lip bleeding and cut. I remembered how Lewis had rescued Haley from the crowd out front just the day before yesterday.

Becky swooped down, scooped up Haley, murmured at the child until she calmed down, then glared at me.

"I just got my last load out of the washer," Becky said, spacing her words out evenly, so each one sounded like a judgment coming down on my head, "but I guess I'll take the clothes home wet, and hang them up to line dry."

With that, she put down her kids, grabbed up a stack of three laundry baskets, and staggered out with Tommy and Haley following her.

Before the crowd could close over the path she'd cleared, or start talking again over the hush her righteous mama's wrath had made, I said, "Anyone who isn't doing laundry in here—get out!"

Everyone ignored me.

Their attention was back on Tyra, who'd somehow remained calm, standing and unruffled through everything. The eye of the storm.

"Thank you for your time and attention," she said sweetly, as if she'd just completed a public service announcement. "I'll look forward to seeing you all over at Stillwater in a few days."

With that, she grabbed Mayor Cornelia's elbow and started moving toward the front door, all the while chatting at Cornelia as if they were old school chums miraculously reunited. Cornelia had a shoeprint on the shoulder of her white blouse, and loose ends of hair were sticking out of her usually smooth coif, and she was limping—I had heard her high voice among those hollering after getting knocked down—but she still looked thrilled to be receiving Tyra's attention.

I watched the rest of the crowd follow them out. At the tail end of the crowd was Vivian. I hadn't realized she'd followed us in here. She didn't even notice me as she moved by me—her gaze was glassy, far off again.

I didn't stop her or anyone else. I was glad to see them all go.

Finally, I was alone in my laundromat—and able to take in the mess it was in. The folding table was bent in the middle, its legs broken. The bookshelf had fallen over, and books were scattered everywhere. Two of my laundry carts were knocked over. There were soda cans and plastic coffee cups and even cigarette butts on my once clean floor and tables. And the cappuccino machine had gotten knocked to the floor, where it was in pieces.

Some sample packets of powdered soap had gotten trampled, so a fine powdery residue was everywhere. A trash can was knocked over, so wads of lint and fabric softener towels and soda cans and other trash were all over the floor. My laundromat looked just plain shameful.

I went to the front door, locked it, and turned my sign from OPEN to CLOSED. I pulled down the miniblinds over the big plate glass windows that front my laundromat. Then I checked my washers and dryers. At least they seemed fine.

But still, I felt just plain sorrowful. I had to go see what Billy wanted to show me out at the Red Horse Motel, but after what had happened, I couldn't leave my place standing open. Even if it was fit for customers—and it would take hours of work before it would be again—I just didn't want to risk it after what had happened.

Poor little Haley had been scared in my laundromat—and it could have been a lot worse. She could have been really hurt. Maybe even trampled to death. My head spun as I thought about that.

No, I'd have to lock up my place while I was gone.

Because for the first time ever, I didn't feel safe enough in my own hometown of Paradise, Ohio, to leave Toadfern's Laundromat open and unattended for a few hours.

So for the first time ever, it would be closed in the middle of a working day.

In fact, for the first time ever, Toadfern's Laundromat would be closed for several days running—until Tyra and all the reporters were out of town—because I sure didn't want to risk a repeat of what had just happened.

I didn't see that I had a choice.

And not having a choice made me feel even more sorrowful.

My plan was to leave by the back door, being sure to lock it too, then see what Billy wanted out at the Red Horse, then come back to start cleaning up.

I crossed to the stock room and saw, on the floor, a tiny kid's T-shirt. I picked it up. It was still damp. One of Becky's kid's T-shirts. An old worn-out one, with a patchy bit of teddy bear picture still on the front. Folks like Becky, I thought, sure wouldn't be buying Tyra Grimes's T-shirts.

I hung the tiny T-shirt over a hanger on one of the laundry carts before leaving.

Billy was waiting for me in the bar of the Red Horse Motel. He was sitting with Luke Rhinegold, Billy drinking a beer, Luke nursing a cup of coffee. They were both staring up at the big-screen TV, watching a wrestling match. Somehow without flicking his eyes away from the television, Luke saw me coming in, stood up, and moved back to the bar.

I sat down in the chair he'd left. Billy kept staring at the television. "You're early," he said.

I stared at the TV too, uncomfortable with looking at Billy in case he decided to make eye contact. Billy had changed. I hadn't really had time to think about it this morning, when he'd been waiting for me in my laundromat—but he was different. Serious. Even as a preacher, even when he was worked up to a good preaching froth on his favorite topic—the glories of heaven and the agonies of hell—he hadn't been so . . . serious.

I made myself look at him, take him in. Yes, there was a new set to his jaw—determined. A new set to his shoulders—confidence, instead of the old cockiness. Billy was on a mission—and it was finally something he really believed in.

I put my hand on his arm. "I'm in trouble," I said. "*We're* in trouble. I mean—Paradise is in trouble."

Billy looked at me then. And I told him everything, about the visit to Stillwater, about what had happened when we got back.

After I finished, he said, "I don't know what Tyra is up to at Stillwater, but I want you to come with me to meet someone. At least it'll help you understand a few things."

Rosa walked in the bar then. I gave her a little wave, figuring she was going back to the kitchen to find Luke for her paycheck—the only reason I could figure Rosa, a truly God-fearing woman, would come in here. After all, every time I'd seen her even walk past the entrance to the bar, she'd crossed herself and muttered a prayer, eyes cast heavenward.

But Rosa came over to our table. She didn't sit down, but just stood and stared with an uneasy air at me, then looked at Billy.

"You ready?" he asked.

She nodded and cast another glance at me. "We can trust her?" she asked in her thick accent.

Billy didn't answer right off. Then he said, "Pretty sure."

Now, this was real nice, I thought—Billy being the trusted one. Rosa—even Billy—doubting me. But I didn't say anything as I followed Billy and Rosa out. I had no idea what they were taking me to see or do, which made me nervous . . . and curious.

As it turned out, Billy rode with me and I followed Rosa's little blue Tercel.

"Where are we going?" I asked Billy after we'd driven about a mile or two north through the countryside.

"Rosa's house," he said, without looking at me.

I didn't ask him why. I figured I'd find out soon enough. I flipped on my barely functioning radio to the one station I could get—Masonville's golden-oldies station, which played mostly songs from the mid-seventies through the late-eighties, covering the years from my birth through junior high—when I'd met Mrs. Oglevee. Thinking of her made me squirm. She'd surely view with disdain the activities of my day so far. I tried to focus on the song that was playing—something about a disco duck—and longed for a fully functioning radio that would pick up more than one station. I'd been promising myself a new car radio—one with a tape player so I could listen to books-on-tape, too—for a long time.

Another mile or two and I realized where we must be headed: Stringtown. That's about all that's directly north of Paradise, until you hit Columbus.

One of my theories of life is that every community likes to rank itself in relation to other communities, kind of the collective version of how some people can't resist comparing themselves to others. Masonville, a county seat with several fast food franchises and a four-lane strip of state highway, sees itself as one up on Paradise but of course not nearly as swank as Columbus, which is, after all, the state capital and intersected by three major interstate highways. Paradise casts a jealous eye north-eastward toward Masonville, but can always say it is doing quite a bit better than Stringtown.

Stringtown consists of ten houses along a narrow strip of county road, pinned down at one end by a bar, and at the other by a church of unaffiliated denomination. I suppose whenever its few residents need a one-ups-man-ship fix, they focus on the fact that Stringtown is the most convenient location for either sin or redemption for the farmers who live several miles around it (although, of course, for a good laundromat they have to come to my establishment in Paradise). As for the farming families around Stringtown, I don't think they really care what anyone else thinks of them.

Rosa's house was the tiniest in the strip, a one-story porch-less clapboard painted a pale tan. It was also the best kept, with maroon shutters and door and windowboxes, and a large maple tree in the narrow front yard. Pink tulips and yellow daffodils bloomed in a neat circle under the tree.

Rosa pulled her Tercel into her gravel driveway, parking right behind a beat-up white truck. I recognized that truck.

The couple must have fixed it—maybe with Billy's help. I pulled in behind Rosa, switched off my radio, and put my hand on Billy's forearm as he started to get out of my car.

"Billy, what's going on here?"

He looked at me. "Trust me, Josie," he said. The last time he'd said that and looked at me that way, we'd been twelve years old and at the county pool over in Masonville. And he'd dunked me. Repeatedly. Until I'd kneed him in the groin and he'd gone down while I went up for air.

Still, I got out of the car and followed Billy. As Chief John Worthy had been all too happy to point out to Tyra, I am by nature nosy—although I prefer to think of it as curiosity-gifted. Besides, Billy and I had both survived the pool incident and made up. Surely we'd survive whatever awaited us in Rosa's neat little house.

But once I got inside Rosa's living room, my confidence dwindled. Huddled together on the couch, beneath a big plastic crucifix loosely tacked to the wall, so that Jesus stared down from his cross at the tops of their heads, were Aguila and Ramon. When I walked in the room, Ramon shrank further back into the couch, looking scared. But Aguila jumped up, arms crossed, a frown on her face, looking ready for a fight.

I didn't want a fight. In fact, given that they were on my list of suspects for murdering Lewis, I wanted to run.

"Billy," I said, in a tone that added, "Get me out of here."

"It's okay," Billy said, putting his hand on my shoulder. Rosa eased past us into the room and said something in Spanish to Aguila. Aguila shook her head, but Rosa kept talking, and finally the younger woman deferred and sat back down next to Ramon, who was still staring worriedly at me.

Rosa sat down next to them. "Sit down, Josie," she said, indicating a rocker over the back of which Rosa had draped a crocheted white afghan.

I kept standing. Rosa glared at me. I sat, rocking back a bit, then steadying myself. I did not think that this was going to be a cozy rocking-chair type conversation. Billy had pulled a kitchen chair into the room, and sat on the chair.

"Billy—" I started again.

He patted me on the shoulder, sending me rocking again. "It'll be OK," he said.

I looked at the three people lined up on the couch across from me—Rosa, Ramon, Aguila. Older, young, younger. Calm, scared, tough. And then I gasped, seeing something else in those faces. In Aguila, I saw the young face that had once been Rosa's. The resemblance between the two women was unmistakable.

Rosa read my face. "My grandniece. But we look like grandmother and granddaughter, don't we?" An expression of pride flared for a moment, then quickly turned to sadness. "But I never had children. So no grandchildren. So I was happy when I heard from Aguila, my grandniece, child of my sister—may she rest in peace." Rosa made the sign of the cross, while glancing in the direction of the crucifix.

"They have a child—Selena. She's only eight," Rosa said.

Aguila said something in Spanish.

"They left her in Mexico in good care a few months ago, with Ramon's people, to come to California to work."

"The work was in Tyra Grimes's T-shirt factory?" I asked.

Aguila said something else, more animatedly.

"Yes," Rosa said. "She says a man came to their town—a recruiter—who told them and others that he had visas for them. They could come work, make good money, send the money home. They wrote to me about it before they left. I still have the letters. All seemed well."

Ramon spoke next. Rosa interpreted for him, "But then they got word that their daughter, Selena, is sick back home. She has epilepsy and needs medicine to keep it under control—medicine Ramon's family back home can't afford. Ramon and Aguila wanted to leave work and go back home, but they were told no, their visas are not in order, after all, they'll be arrested if they leave the compound where they are living. But they were desperate."

Aguila spoke again, this time trembling with anger.

"She says they stole the T-shirts and got away from that terrible work camp of Ms. Grimes's," Rosa said. "They knew they could get a lot of money for those T-shirts, then go home and use it to get better care for Selena. They came here, because I am their only family here in this country."

Ramon muttered something, put his head in his hands.

"Then they had bad luck, he says."

No kidding, I thought. They come to Paradise . . . and Tyra Grimes, the very person they are trying to get away from, shows up.

"But now what? And how can I possibly help?"

Billy spoke up. "Their first plan was to get as far away as possible from here as soon as they knew Tyra Grimes had arrived in town. But we came up with a better plan."

I was afraid to ask who "we" was.

Ramon stood up, pulled an envelope out of the hip pocket of his jeans, said something in Spanish, and leaned forward, holding the envelope toward me. His hand was trembling. He said something else—and this time I made out one word: *Paige.*

I looked at Billy. "Paige . . . where is she, what's she . . ."

"You can help by taking that envelope, Josie," Billy said. "It contains a letter from Paige to Tyra. Obviously, she doesn't want to mail the letter. She could be tracked that way."

"Where is Paige?" I asked.

Billy shook his head. "I can't tell you that right now."

"You don't trust me," I said, while thinking, oh, Billy, are you trusting the right people? The Cruezes' story was moving . . . if it was true. And I knew Paige had broken into my bedroom, lied about the mud stain . . .

"I trust you—we trust you—enough to ask you to take this letter to her."

"I don't understand how a letter from Paige to Tyra will help these two or their daughter . . ."

"Let's just say . . . I got to know Paige out at the Red Horse. By then, I'd already met Aguila and Ramon and learned about their and Selena's situation. After going a little . . . nuts . . . with that T-shirt effigy in Paradise, I decided I should try to help these people. But I couldn't come up with anything, until I met Paige. When I found out who she was, I let her have it with what I think of her boss's labor practices." Billy glanced at Ramon and Aguila. "She knew the allegations, of course. She was defensive at first. But when she learned more about the truth from Ramon and Aguila, and about Selena, she came up with a plan on her own that can help out Selena. Cover her medical care . . . and take care of any, ah, legal issues there might be with Ramon and Aguila going back home to their daughter."

Aguila muttered something, crossed herself.

"She says," Rosa said, "that America is a land of great opportunity. She still thinks so, even though their experience with Tyra Grimes was not good. She hopes that someday, she and Ramon and Selena can come back. But for now, she wants to go home to her daughter, and help her get the right medical care."

I looked at the envelope, still in Ramon's shaking hand, still thrust at me. I could guess what Paige was telling Tyra. Paige probably had evidence—or could testify against Tyra—for her labor practices. But wouldn't, if Tyra would contribute money and pull strings to get help for Selena, Aguila, and Ramon.

I didn't take the envelope yet. "Blackmail?"

Billy crossed his arms, looked at me steadily with that new, serious, deep gaze of his. "If you want to call it that. I call it Selena's best hope. If you want to help her—help these people—all you have to do is take the envelope to Tyra. Paige's letter points out to Tyra why it's in her best interest to help this family."

I'd come out here, wanting to find answers. Right and wrong should be easy to tell apart, shouldn't they? That's what the law is for, isn't it—making it easy to know how to act right? That's why I'd always admired Chief Hilbrink.

But at that moment, in Rosa's little house, it all seemed pretty muddled up. Blackmailing's wrong. But so is forcing people to work against their will. Stealing is wrong, and breaking immigration laws is wrong. Certainly murdering is wrong—and I couldn't be sure that Billy wasn't trusting the wrong people, something that had gotten him into trouble in the past—and that in the heat of a confrontation Tyra was hiding, the Cruezes and/or Paige hadn't been involved in Lewis's murder.

Still, it was also wrong that this couple had been taken in by false promises of good, legal work, and ended up separated from their daughter, who was now ill.

So I did the only right thing I could think of to do.

I took the envelope.

13

So that's how I ended up once again driving down a country road with a letter to Tyra Grimes in my passenger seat.

Of course, the first letter had been from me. This letter was from Paige, and she was relying on me to get it to Tyra.

Well, truth be told, lots of people were relying on me to get it to Tyra. So this time, I drove extra carefully and slowly. I surely didn't need Chief Worthy stopping me this time around, seeing the envelope on my seat—clearly labeled "To: Tyra, From: Paige"—and asking me a lot of questions.

Billy had decided to stay with Rosa, Aguila, and Ramon. So I was alone with my thoughts about this latest development and my worries about Tyra's big announcement coming up at Stillwater in just a few days, a date that hung out in the near future like a big old stain of doom.

When I got back to Paradise, all the television vans and strange cars were still clogging the streets. Tyra wasn't anywhere to be found. I went up to my apartment and carefully put the letter in my sock drawer.

Then I went back down to my laundromat and started cleaning up the mess.

Sometime that night, I heard Tyra, coming down the little hallway, singing, "*Don't cry for me, Argentina,*" in the same warbling voice she'd used to sing show tunes when she'd arrived only a few days before. Only a whole lifetime before.

I found her in the hallway as she was letting herself into Billy's old apartment and pushed the envelope at her.

She took it and stared at it. She seemed to be having trouble focusing. I wanted to say, "Just where have you been, young lady?" I'd been worried about her.

Instead I said, "Tyra, all I know is I'm supposed to give you this. This envelope holds information that is a matter of life and death."

Tyra sucked in her breath at that and seemed finally to focus. Then she went on in to Billy's old apartment, giving me a little wave as she shut the door.

The next day, I kept busy, getting my laundromat straightened up—and then some, scrubbing the floors and all of the folding tables and the inside of the washers and dryers, even the lint traps. I worked on laundry for my customers who I knew would have normally have come in, picking up their loads, taking the clothes in, washing them for free, even doing a little ironing on a few pieces, like Mrs. Beavy's blouses, which always seemed to me just a little bit wrinkled. I figured it was the least I could do, considering that my laundromat was closed.

I also tried getting ahold of Winnie, without success. I talked once to Owen on the phone, but he seemed really distracted and distant. And my scalp itched. I tried every ointment I could think of—hair conditioner. Baby oil. Vaseline. It still itched. I even called Cherry and told her about my hair, but she just sniffed and said it wasn't her fault if I couldn't take care of my own hair, and that she did complimentary hairdos only for stars, which now that I wasn't going to be on the Tyra Grimes show after all, I didn't qualify for, so she'd be sending me a bill. Word had gotten around town that Tyra didn't plan to have me on her show, that she was really in town because of her mysterious press conference at Stillwater.

And I watched, from a distance, Tyra's comings and goings. She went to lunch at Mayor Cornelia's house, and went out, riding up to Masonville, with various members of the media.

I called Stillwater and talked to Don just to make sure none of the reporters were being a nuisance. He said some of them had come over and tried to talk with him and a few of the residents, but now they had the front gate—usually left open—locked at all times, so the residents weren't being bothered too much. Every time I talked with him, he was eager to end the conversation.

I went over to Sandy's Restaurant for lunch, for the meat loaf stack special (gravy on top of onions on top of cheese on top of meat loaf on top of mashed potatoes on top of gravy) and a slice of cherry pie à la mode, thinking a little comfort food would be, well, comforting, but I can't say I really enjoyed it. Sandy served me the food, but shortchanged me on both gravy and ice cream. The regulars there looked away when I came in and pretended they didn't hear me say "hello."

Henry Romar from the *Paradise Advertiser-Gazette* came in and asked everyone—except me—what they thought of all the reporters being in town. Bill Tiley said he didn't like all those outsiders coming in, taking up parking space. Sarah Goodsdale had seen a few of them littering and one even spitting on the sidewalk. And Micky Longensprat had overheard a few reporters talking about what a dinky little town Paradise is, and why on earth would someone like Tyra want to come here for whatever announcement she had to make?

That pretty much summed up my position in Paradise now. I'd gotten the town the attention it supposedly wanted. But now that it had it, the town didn't really like the price of fame.

So I slunk on back to my laundromat, kept on cleaning and washing, even cleaning up the stockroom.

Sounds like I was really busy, doesn't it?

But truth be told, I was really waiting.

You see, Tyra's upcoming announcement felt like a big fat dark storm waiting to break wide open and suck up all of us—Owen, Winnie, and Elroy; Tyra, Paige, and Billy; Vivian, Verbenia, and Guy; Rosa, Aguila, and Ramon; even my customers and me and everyone in town—and spin us around until we were dizzy and confused, then spit us out back to earth.

I was waiting for the storm to hit. But there were no provisions to take in, no way to prepare to protect the people I knew and loved. So I just waited, hoping I was wrong, hoping it wouldn't come at all.

But of course it would. It had to.

And when the storm finally did break, I didn't even recognize it as such.

After all, it was just Winnie calling me that Thursday evening, an hour or so before Lewis's viewing.

I was in my bedroom, digging through my dresser, trying to find something proper for going to a viewing. The last one I'd gone to had been my Aunt Clara's, but the black dress with the frilly collar and sash tie and drawstring cuffs that I'd worn at 19 didn't seem like a good idea now, at 29. Even if I still owned it, which I didn't. Or even if I could still wear a size 8, which I couldn't. So far, I'd identified fresh panties (pink), bra (white), and two options in socks—white, or black, depending on what else I could find that might work to wear to Lewis's viewing.

Then the phone rang, and I answered it, suddenly hoping against hope it was Owen. Then I could ask him just where the heck he'd been these past few days.

Before I could even finish saying hello, though, I heard these words: "Josie, you're just not going to believe what I've found out."

It wasn't Owen, and I suddenly knew I wouldn't have yelled at him if it had been. I'd have asked him to come over. I stuck the phone receiver up to my ear, holding it in place with my shoulder, then kept digging through my clothes.

"Winnie, what's going on? I've been calling and calling your place, but every time I get a hold of Tom and he says you're out. I think he misses you. He sounds grumpy."

"I've gone to earth." Winnie whispered the words. "I have a lot to tell you—but can't tell you right now. I'm at a public phone now, at the McDonald's in Masonville, but you never know who might be a reporter and overhear."

I stopped pawing through clothes, going rigid for a moment like a statue: stunned-girl-with-T-shirts-improper-for-viewings-of-dead-people.

Then I unfroze, dropped the T-shirts, sat down on the edge of my bed. "Uh, Winnie, are you okay?"

"Oh, yes," she whispered. "Quite fine. But what I've found out about you-know-who is going to shock you."

"You mean, about Tyra?"

"Shhh!" Somehow, Winnie practically shouted that. Then she whispered, "I just said, I can't tell you right now. I just want to make sure you'll be at Lewis's viewing."

"You'll tell me there?"

"Well, no. We'll either try to sneak away—or maybe I'll slip you instructions on where to meet me later. We probably shouldn't be seen together. So if I act like I'm snubbing you, don't take it personally."

I didn't think I could take much more of anything at all.

Everyone and everything I knew had gone wacky. My hometown. My cousin Billy (although it seemed almost an improvement on him). Now Winnie, the most stable person I've ever known.

I'd just asked her to do a little simple background research on Tyra Grimes, and suddenly she was acting like a spy out of some action movie. Winnie—Winnie Porter. Who takes her slushees frozen, not stirred. Uh huh.

"Look, Winnie, I'm not even sure I'm going to go to Lewis's viewing tonight," I said. "So maybe you could tell me—"

"What? Why wouldn't you go?"

"Let's see. I wasn't all that close to the man." The image of him lifting little Haley free of the sidewalk crowd arose again, and I felt sad that I hadn't ever gone beyond his gruff front to get to know him better. "Plus, the way this town's gone nuts since Tyra's gotten here, I'm almost afraid to go. Hiding seems a better idea. Plus, I'm not sure what to wear. And frankly, my head is a mess. My scalp keeps itching and the only thing that makes it feel even a bit better is Vaseline, so now my hair looks gross and greasy."

"Oh, Josie," Winnie said, sounding like her old self again, which cheered me. "Just wear something you'd wear to church, only make sure it's dark. And wear a hat, a black one."

I was about to thank her for the advice—maybe get her to chat some more while she was back to her normal self, but suddenly she was whispering again. "Gotta go. That man was looking at me funny. Can't be too sure."

With that, Winnie hung up.

I ended up wearing black pants, a gray knit shirt that was finer than my usual T-shirts, black socks, and black shoes.

My major problem, though, was the hat. The only hats I have are baseball caps—not really a proper topper for funeral home viewings. But the other choices were to go with my hair all greasy from the Vaseline I had put in, or to wash my hair out and end up scratching my scalp the whole time. Neither of those choices seemed so great, either. So I was pretty pleased when I dug out a black baseball cap. After all, black formalizes everything, from jeans to baseball caps, right?

The problem with this one, though, was it had—in white lettering—an advertisement for Elroy's Gas Station and Towing. I didn't think that would be too proper to wear to Lewis's viewing, seeing as how Elroy was in jail as Lewis's murderer. So, I grabbed a black marker from the junk drawer and colored in both the lettering and the little picture of a tow truck.

I studied my handiwork and was pleased. Unless you squinted at it hard, you couldn't see that much difference in the black I'd colored in, and the black of the cap's cloth. So, I combed up my grease-laden hair into a top knot, and put on the cap, at a kind of jaunty side angle. (My days of hanging around Tyra Grimes hadn't been completely in vain.)

Then I stepped out of my apartment and locked up. I went over to Billy's old apartment, gave a light tap, waited, then put my ear to the door. No sounds. Tyra wasn't around.

I stepped outside on the metal landing, started to lock up, but then had to clap my cap down on my head because of a sudden, strong wind that pushed me into the railing of the little landing at the top of the exterior stair and nearly knocked me over. With one hand I held my cap in place, and with the other I hung onto the railing. Then the wind died down a little. I peered up at the sky—it was strange looking. Purplish gray, angry-looking clouds . . . but gold rimmed, as if right behind them, the sun shone, bright and pure. The stinging, hard wind—but no rain.

Now, I'm pretty sure—as I told Chief Worthy later—that I finished locking up the exterior door to the second floor over my laundromat. That I didn't get so distracted by the weird weather—and almost losing my cap—that I forgot to do that. Considering what happened at my laundromat when I'd left it unlocked a few days before, I'm real sure—pretty sure, anyway—I wouldn't let a little thing like a gust of wind distract me from finishing locking up the entrance to the apartments.

But I'll never really know for sure. I'll always worry that maybe the wind did distract me enough that I left the door unlocked. That maybe—if I did leave the door unlocked—I made it just a little too easy for the second murder to happen.

There were lots of people at the funeral home. We viewed Lewis. We mingled. We tried to say nice things about Lewis, and our efforts left us staring at the floor. Truth be told, he'd been good at burying dead people, but he hadn't been much good at relating to live ones. And now that he was dead, we weren't real sure what to say about him that wouldn't sound, well, snippy.

I wanted to tell the story of how he'd rescued Becky's little girl from the crowd that had protested my cousin Billy's protest of Tyra, but it didn't seem too appropriate. And no one was doing much more than giving me a polite nod and a brush-off anyway. I was pretty sure it wasn't because of my hat.

I didn't see anyone there that I thought might still talk to me. Not Owen or Winnie. Not Paige or Billy, or even Tyra.

I did see Vivian there, kind of standing off by herself. She gave me a brief nod. I nodded back, but didn't go over. She seemed to want to be alone.

I went on up to the casket by myself. A card on an easel identified the casket as being model number 891, from the top of the Ultra line, the best Rothchild's has to offer, a little marketing touch from Lewis's wife, I guessed, as she now owned the business—a touch I was sure Lewis would have appreciated.

I looked in at Lewis. His makeup job was fine, his suit new and expensive looking. He'd have been proud of that, too. I thought about taking off my baseball cap—ever so briefly—to show my respect, but I feared I'd drip Vaseline on him.

So I kept my cap on, and in my head I thought of a few words that seemed appropriate and close enough to a prayer for me: *Good-bye, Lewis. And good luck.*

I thought that last part because I figure there's no telling what happens after a spirit's gone on from its earthly carrier (as I'd heard Lewis refer to the human body), and I figured Lewis could use the luck, wherever or however his spirit ended up.

Finally, the pastor of the United Methodist Church started a brief service. (There'd be another one, graveside, at the burial the next day.) Members from the Exalted Order of the Moose Lodge #16618, of which Lewis had been a member, conducted a brief ceremony, which consisted of each guy reciting a few lines from a poem—which was mostly about the beauty of all of God's creatures, particularly moose— then passing along moose antlers to the next guy. The final guy solemnly placed the moose rack at the foot of Lewis's casket, then stated that it was up to Hazel whether she wanted to have the antlers buried with Lewis, or to keep them for display in her home. I was sitting near the back, so I didn't hear if she said one way or the other. All in all, though, I think Lewis would have been touched by the program.

After it was over, I started to the door, wanting to go home. By now, I could hear the heavy rain and thunder, and I figured on just making a dash for it as soon as I got out the door. I'd be soaked and winded when I got home—but I could maybe comfort myself with a nice hot bath. And maybe some peanut butter on crackers.

But then someone grabbed my elbow. I turned around. Winnie, in a raincoat and scarf.

"Come on," she whispered to me. "Hazel has spread the word that there's a reception at their house for friends and family."

Well, of course there was. No one dies in Paradise without the ladies' salad, casserole, and dessert brigade mobilizing.

But there was one small problem.

"I'm not a relative, Winnie," I said. "Or a friend."

"She distinctly told me I was welcome to come," Winnie said.

"That's you, not me. Unless you want to tell me now what you called me about, I just want to get home before this storm gets any worse," I said.

"You were on the Chamber of Commerce with Lewis," Winnie said. "Plus, you found his body."

I was about to argue that that would hardly improve my relationship with him—or his wife—but Winnie squeezed my elbow hard enough to make me wince. Then she poked a note at me. I took it with my free hand.

"Directions about when and where to meet me tomorrow morning," Winnie whispered. She released my elbow, and I put the note in my wallet, in my purse. Then I started rubbing my elbow.

"Good girl," she said. "Now, we're going to the reception."

"Why do I have to go there if you're not going to tell me about what you learned until tomorrow?"

"Clues. We need to watch for clues."

"At Lewis's post-viewing reception?"

Winnie put a finger to her lips in a hushing gesture. "Yes. Just watch for anything out of the ordinary."

"Winnie, Lewis's death already is out of the ordinary." I whispered this part, trying to be discreet.

"I mean anything odd, that you wouldn't expect. Believe me, it'll make sense when you know what I know. But I can't tell you yet. It'll ruin your objectivity. Mine's already gone because of what I know, which is why you need to be there."

With that, Winnie took firm hold of my elbow again, and out we went, into the storm. We ran together through the rain the two blocks down to the Rothchild home.

I truly admire lime Jell-O.

Of all the colors and flavors of Jell-O, lime is the best. It has such a springy, grassy, leafy color that is far greener and cheerier than any actual green you find in nature.

It also is the best at letting other items shine through—unlike grape, for example, which just makes everything dark. In this particular lime Jell-O salad's case, little shreds of orange carrot, and mini-marshmallows, and tiny dots of pineapple were all perfectly preserved in a quivering lime Jell-O mold, which sat beautifully centered on a silver serving tray, in the midst of all the other casseroles and Jell-O salads and desserts, on a table set up for the occasion in the tiny front parlor of Hazel and Lewis's home. But clearly, the lime Jell-O salad was the centerpiece—the crown jewel—of all the food offerings brought to Hazel in this time of grief.

Winnie had told me to watch for anything unusual, any clues. So far, this seemed like a pretty normal postviewing repast, except that Winnie herself—although leaving her raincoat and scarf in the hall closet—was going from person to person, talking in a very low voice. Other than that, I only noted that every time it thundered outside, the lime Jell-O quivered. And it was hard for folks to keep their voices low, as seemed only proper, because the rain was coming down so hard outside, we could hear its drumming on the roof even inside.

Out of curiosity, I slipped the note Winnie'd given me out of my wallet, and looked at it. She'd written down, "10 A.M., tomorrow, old Schmidt farm."

The Schmidt farmhouse had burned down years back, and the Schmidts had rebuilt about a quarter mile down the road, but I knew where she meant.

"How are you?"

At the mouse-tiny sound of the voice, I shoved the note back into my purse, looked up guiltily. Vivian was right by me, hunched down in the same black dress she'd been wearing at Stillwater Farms. I wondered if she'd been wearing it ever since Lewis's death. She was calm, but her eyes were red-rimmed. I wondered again, about her—and her sister's—connection to Lewis. Whatever it was, she looked miserable. I felt sorry for her.

"I'm okay," I said. "How about you?"

She just shook her head. "I'll have to be okay," she said miserably. "For Verbenia's sake. She's all I live for now—"

Vivian stopped, looking to the parlor's entryway, as we all did, as Hazel came in. She gave a general greeting—with a weak smile and a wave—and encouraged us to help ourselves to the food. I was the third person in line.

I'd just gotten near the lime Jell-O, when I heard the front door open. Someone came in. I heard exclamations from the people nearest the front entry.

Then I heard Tyra Grimes's voice. "Oh hello, excuse me—what? Oh certainly, I'll give you an autograph. But quickly, darling. I'm here to offer my condolences to the poor widow."

My knees suddenly went as quivery as the lime Jell-O.

Then Tyra swept into the parlor, stood face to face with Hazel, who stared at Tyra as if she were looking at the devil himself. Tyra—doffed in a navy slicker with matching hat—smiled amiably, though. She didn't seem to notice how much she was dripping onto the hardwood floors.

"My dear Hazel," Tyra started. "I just had to offer my condolences." She glanced around the room. "What a lovely buffet—although some black bunting on the table would have added a somber yet decorative effect, don't you think? Anyway, I just had to tell you how sweet Lewis was, how gentlemanly, to stop and check on me when he saw me along the road that dreadful evening. Why, if we'd have known what would happen—"

"Get out of my house," Hazel said, her teeth so tight that the words barely gritted out. Suddenly, the whole parlor was quiet—except for the sound of the steadily pelting rain outside. "You are not welcome here. You haven't been welcome here since—since—years ago—when—"

She stopped herself, glancing around, suddenly seeming to realize she couldn't finish saying what she had to say with all these people in her home. I wanted to look away—whatever she and Tyra had to say to each other needed to be said in private. But, like everyone else, I stared at Tyra and Hazel. What Hazel had said suggested that both she and Lewis already knew Tyra, and that they hadn't been real glad of the acquaintance.

Tyra looked confused. "Why, Hazel, I'm not sure what you mean. I've only just met you and Lewis since coming here to your quaint little town—which, of course, I only did thanks to dear Josie Toadfern. Do you know her?"

Hazel's eyes flicked to me, took me in.

Everyone else looked at me, too.

Uh oh.

Then Hazel looked back at Tyra. "Get out of here. You are not welcome here. Lewis—Lewis was right to not want you here—Lewis—Lewis . . ." She started sobbing.

Tyra put a hand briefly on her shoulder. "My dear, I can see that you're just too upset to appreciate my condolences. That's okay—by tomorrow morning, I'll have made my announcement, and I'm sure you'll feel differently then."

Hazel moaned. No one moved toward her. No one had ever seen her as anything other than the stony-faced, quiet wife of Lewis, and so seeing her like this, no one was sure what to do.

"Get out of here," Hazel said, her voice a thin, tense whisper. "Get out of here before I kill you."

There were gasps around the room, but Tyra laughed. "Oh, my poor dear, you're so upset you don't know what you're saying."

"Get out!" The voice—firm, strong, commanding—was Vivian's. She'd made her way through the crowd and now, incredibly, her arm was around Hazel's shoulder.

Tyra was finally quiet. All of us were quiet. It had even stopped raining, all of a sudden.

Tyra gave a grand sweeping gesture. "I must be running along anyway—I'm having dinner with some members of the press. Tiresome, really, but I must go freshen up."

Then she turned and left.

Slowly, everyone else started talking, quietly, with extreme politeness—"Ooh, look, Margaret brought her cheese puffs . . ." and "did you see the lovely spray of flowers the Mayor sent?"—and it seemed the strange scene was over.

But, no, not quite.

For suddenly Hazel was in front of me.

And the room went quiet again.

She said, "You brought Tyra Grimes to town. Lewis told me he warned you that blood would flow if she came—but you got her to come here anyway. Now Lewis is dead. And you come here. Disrespectfully wearing a cap with his killer's name on it."

But I'd colored in the tow truck, Elroy's name, all that . . .

and then I realized I must have grabbed a regular black marker, instead of a permanent laundry marker, and the rain must have washed away my efforts to disguise my cap.

I opened my mouth, about to explain and apologize, but I never got the chance to speak.

You see, Hazel yanked my cap off. She grabbed the plate with the lovely lime Jell-O mold and dumped it on my head. Then she stuck my cap back on my head.

With that, she left her parlor and ran up the stairs.

I don't remember getting back to my apartment.

I must have walked home, let myself in, and sat down on the kitchen floor.

Because that's the next thing I remember—hearing a loud bang from Billy's old apartment, and suddenly realizing I was sitting in the middle of my kitchen floor. My cap was on the floor next to me. I had lime Jell-O on my head, and clothes, and I was holding a dishtowel, which also had some lime Jell-O on it. My face was lime Jell-O-free, though, so I figure I'd gotten the towel to wipe the Jell-O out of my face.

Looking back, I think what happened was, I was just so stunned by what had happened at Lewis's house, I had walked home on auto-pilot, my mind trying to sort through everything. Kind of like you might drive somewhere you're used to going, but you've got things on your mind, so you find yourself at the destination, and don't remember driving there at all.

So later, when I had to talk to Chief Worthy, I couldn't really tell him how long I'd been home. Or if I'd relocked the outside door when I came in, or if it'd been unlocked the whole time I was gone, or what. All I could say was that I heard a loud bang in Billy's old apartment.

And that I figured that Tyra had finally come back from wherever she'd been.

And that I must have left the lime Jell-O on my head because finally—finally—my head was no longer itching. The lime Jell-O had cured that problem.

And that I never would have bothered going over to check on her except suddenly, just a few seconds after the loud bang that definitely came from inside the spare apartment, there was the sound of a warning siren going off.

The siren that sounds for a tornado.

We had to get somewhere safe, and that meant down to the laundromat. I figured we only had a few minutes to get down there, into my storeroom, where we'd be a lot safer than in our second story apartments.

So, I ran out of my apartment. A gust of wind knocked me against the wall. The exterior door was open.

I fell to the floor, crawled to Tyra's door. "Tyra, open up! We've got to get downstairs!"

She couldn't hear my voice, of course, not over the terrible roar of the storm. So I pounded on her door. It swung open.

I crawled in, started to holler Tyra's name again, but my voice choked on itself.

There, on the floor before me, was Tyra—head bashed and a long strip of cloth, cut from one of her own red Tyra Grimes T-shirts, tied tightly around her neck.

14

I was in the worst fix of my life: in a second-story apartment with America's favorite home decorating star. Who'd been hit over the head and strangled to death with the cut up pieces of her own designer T-shirt. While a tornado raged outside. And lime Jell-O dripped from my head.

I didn't know what to do.

I wanted to go down to the laundromat, where I'd be safe.

But if I left Tyra's body here, and it got squished by, say, the roof falling in, then the most important evidence in her murder (her corpse) would be destroyed.

And if I tried to take her with me, I'd have to drag her down the stairs—not a possibility I relished—which would surely also be disturbing the most important evidence in her murder . . .

As I was trying to decide what to do, a huge tree limb speared the family room window. Wind and rain and bits of glass came gusting in. The end table's lamp went up like a kite, flying by its cord, then crashed back down.

Now it was too dangerous to take the outside stairs to the

laundromat, even if I wouldn't have had to drag Tyra's corpse along. So I did the only thing that popped into my lime-Jell-O-covered head.

I grabbed Tyra from behind, under the arms, tried not to gag at the sight of her head bouncing on my knees, and drug her to the closet in the bedroom. I propped Tyra in one corner. I shut the closet door and settled into the other corner.

Then I closed my eyes and prayed.

When it got quiet again, I opened my eyes.

I looked over at Tyra.

She was still there. I could just make her out from the tiny bit of light that slid in under the closet door.

I knew she would still be there, of course, but my fervent prayer that I'd survive the tornado had lapsed into a desperate hope that somehow, maybe due to lime-Jell-O-hair-tornado-shock-syndrome, I had only imagined Tyra being murdered.

But there she was. Real as ever. Dead as ever.

I looked away from Tyra and counted to one hundred. It was still quiet outside of the closet. But to be sure, I counted backward to one. Still quiet outside. The tornado was over.

I opened the closet door, crawled out. Then I stood up and looked around. The bedroom was fine. I went out into the family room—a different story there. The big tree limb—half of it inside, half of it outside—was jammed through the window at an angle. Wind and rain had gusted through, knocking over end tables, tossing papers and magazines around. But the roof was still on. The walls were still in place.

I ran over, then, to my apartment. Everything was okay. It seemed the only tornado damage was the tree limb spearing the spare apartment's window. I wanted to go downstairs—check on my laundromat—but I figured I'd better call for help as soon as possible, so I picked up my phone—and of course there was no dial tone. Phone lines were down. I could go back to Billy's old apartment, find Tyra's cell phone. But I just couldn't bring myself to go back near Tyra's corpse.

So I ran outside, down the stairs, around to the front of my building, thinking I'd get help at Sandy's Restaurant.

Across the street, at Sandy's Restaurant, people were starting to come out, looking around, warily, as if the tornado might suddenly pop out again from around a corner and holler "ha!" before sucking them all up. The big pole that held up the Sandy's Restaurant sign had bent over and crashed into the corner of the roof. A few wires were freed from the pole and were sparking, like those little sparklers kids like to use on the Fourth of July. There was enough light from the sign—and the sparks—that I could make out some of the faces.

One of them was Chief John Worthy.

So I ran across the street, circling clear of the Sandy's Restaurant sign, and went up to Chief Worthy, who was telling the already quiet crowd to stay calm.

I tugged on his sleeve.

He whirled around, saw me, and sighed. "What is it, Josie? Can't you see we have a situation here?"

"Is anyone hurt?"

"No, but I have to maintain crowd control, get everyone out of the restaurant before mass panic sets in."

I watched everyone filing out quietly. The only one who might need help getting under control was Sandy, who stood outside her restaurant, pointing up at the sign, and sobbing. She was entitled, considering. Everyone else seemed to be getting out of the restaurant just fine, on their own.

So I said, "Chief Worthy, you need to come with me. I've got a, uh, major problem at my spare apartment—"

"Can't it wait?"

"No."

He whipped out a notepad. "Give me a quick description—"

I stood on tiptoe and whispered, "Tyra Grimes is in my spare apartment. Dead. And not from the tornado."

Chief John Worthy was none too pleased with me for moving Tyra's body, even after I explained about the tree coming in through the window.

But he took my statement, while other officers—from Paradise as well as from the county sheriff's department—took pictures and notes and finally removed Tyra from the closet.

He was also none too pleased that I couldn't really remember if I'd left the side door locked or not.

He only lifted his eyebrows when he asked what had happened to my hair, and I told him.

One of the paramedics was real nice and checked me for shock. She told me that the tornado had touched down only briefly in a field outside of town, so Paradise had gotten off lucky. No one had been seriously hurt, although a few cars and buildings had been damaged.

Finally, when everyone—including Chief Worthy and Tyra—was gone, I went downstairs to see how my laundromat had fared. It was dark by now, so it was hard to be sure, but the biggest damage I had (besides the tree limb through the window upstairs) was that the big flowerpots on either side of my laundromat door had been knocked over and broken.

The electricity over at Sandy's Restaurant must have been turned off, because the broken sign had stopped buzzing and sparking.

Without the glow of Sandy's sign, Main Street in Paradise was dark and quiet and eerie.

Suddenly, I felt an urge to start hollering: "It's not my

fault! The tornado's not my fault! All that's been happened . . . it's not my fault!"

And at the same time, I felt like whispering . . . "I'm sorry."

But I didn't. I went back to my apartment. I showered for
a long time (washing Jell-O from one's hair takes awhile),
then got into my most comfortable pajamas—the Tweety
Bird ones—then tried my phone again. Finally, thankfully, a
dial tone.

I called Owen—no answer.

I called Winnie—no answer.

I called my insurance company's 24-hour hotline. I had to
press 1 (file a claim), then 3 (act of God), then 4 (tornado),
then 2 (business policy) . . . and I finally got a recorded
voice, asking me to leave a message, and assuring me someone would call me back soon. So I left my message.

It was good to know someone was still willing to talk to me.

By 7 A.M. the next morning, I wished no one would ever want
to talk with me again.

The first phone call came at five that morning.

It seemed awfully early for the insurance company to call
me back, but I picked up the receiver with my eyes still shut
and, still lying down, mumbled hello.

"Is this Josie Toadfern?"

"Uh huh."

"This is Trudi Hackman from the *Star Reporter*."

That got me to sitting up, eyes wide open. I'd been seeing
the *Star Reporter* right by the checkout stand of the A&P all
my life. I'd even read a few copies—although I want to make
it clear I much prefer really good books from the bookmobile.

"Is it true you found Tyra Grimes murdered in your apartment?" Trudi asked. She sounded extra-caffeinated—no
cream.

"Uh, in my spare apartment." I felt awkward answering

that question. After all, Tyra's murder was being investigated. And I wasn't sure how much to answer. Chief Worthy hadn't given me any instructions on that.

"Is it true she was staying there because she was having financial problems?"

"Uh—I don't think so—"

"Is it true she was eviscerated?"

"What?"

"That her stomach was sliced open and her guts were—"

"I know what the word means," I snapped. "Who told you that?"

"So it's true, but the authorities want to keep it hidden—"

"Now wait a minute . . . I didn't say . . ."

"Did you find any evidence of satanic cult rituals? They can include sacrifices, you know . . ."

I hung up.

I lay back down.

The phone rang again.

I put my pillow over my head.

The phone kept ringing.

So I answered it. "Look, Ms. Hackman, I'm not answering any of your crazy questions—"

"Oh, man, did she get to you already?" A man's voice.

I sighed. "Who is this?"

"Trent Riteway. From the news show *Vision*."

At least that was a respectable mainstream show.

"What did you tell Hackman?" Riteway wanted to know.

"Nothing," I said.

"Great! I was hoping for an exclusive! Now, I have it on good authority that Ms. Grimes was consorting with Prince Rakashan Abudi, who's an expatriate from . . ."

I hung up.

After three more such calls, all from different reporters, all with equally nutty ideas, I unplugged my telephone. The insurance company would just have to deal with me having a busy signal.

But I couldn't get back to sleep. I kept seeing Tyra, murdered, on my spare apartment's floor. Her death added more questions to the ones already unanswered. Like who would kill her . . . and then I remembered Hazel Rothchild, threatening to kill Tyra. I shook my head—no, no, Hazel had just been speaking under great emotional strain. She'd have no real reason to kill Tyra. Would she?

Or what about Paige? After all, I already suspected her of killing Lewis. Maybe she and Tyra had met, had a fight over the content of the letter I'd delivered to Tyra on Paige's behalf. After all, I knew from having found a previous ripped-up letter in Paige's motel room trash can that Paige had long held misgivings about her boss. Yes, maybe they'd had a fight, and it had gotten out of hand . . .

Then there was Aguila and Ramon. Maybe the plan they'd cooked up to get Paige to make Tyra help them and the little girl Selena had backfired . . . maybe they tried a second time to kill her, but this time succeeded . . .

I worried about Billy. Was he okay? Or had he been an innocent bystander, too, just like Lewis . . . ?

I shook my head. Trying to sort through all these possibilities was giving me a headache. I needed aspirin.

I got out of bed, went into my bathroom, turned on the light, started to reach to open the medicine chest, but then stopped as I saw my image in the mirror. I stared in shock.

Lime Jell-O had worked well to relieve my itchy scalp.

But apparently lime Jell-O, hair perm and coloring chemicals, stress, and my personal hair chemistry don't work well together.

Because my hair had gone frizzy . . . and orange.

* * *

I'm not talking a few waves and an auburn glow.

I'm talking tight frizzy curls and bright orange. As in detour-sign orange. Road-construction-barrel orange. Prison jump suit orange. Bozo the Clown orange. The orange thread in my great-grandmother's quilt that Tyra had hated, orange.

I stood before my mirror, my jaw hanging open as I stared at my hair. Even Tweety Bird, on my pajama top, looked shocked, about to chirp—I think I saw a big orange-haired oaf . . . I did, I did, I really, really did . . .

Then the pounding at my door started.

I went to the front door and looked through the peephole. There were at least six people outside my door. I didn't know any of them. But I could guess who they were. More reporters.

So I went back to my bedroom. Put on my jeans, aqua T-shirt, socks, tennis shoes, and cap—this one white, with a big pink ice cream cone and the words "Dairy Dreeme." I tucked all my orange hair up under my ball cap, stopped back into my bathroom, took two aspirin, and went back to my front door, on which the people outside were still pounding.

I took a deep breath, opened the door, and stepped out.

"Ms. Toadfern—could you—"

"Is it true that—"

I had learned a few things from Tyra. I held up my hand for silence, using the same gesture Tyra had used in the laundromat. When the crowd of reporters quieted down, I said—in my best fake French accent (which I could do thanks to Pépé Le Pew cartoons on cable's Cartoon Network)—"I am *not* Josie Toadfern!"

Henry Romar from the *Paradise Advertiser Gazette* hollered, "She is too Josie Toadfern! Josie, what are you trying to pull?"

I glared at him—indignantly, of course. "I repeat, I am not

Josie Toadfern. I am her distant cousin—" I pronounced that word *"coo-zeen"*—"Jezebel Toadfern, visiting on a break from my American tour with the Great Circus de France-ay."

With that, I pulled off my Dairy Dreeme hat with a flourish, letting my frizzy orange hair spring loose.

The crowd fell silent, staring at me. Tyra would have been proud. I'd never have figured out how to work a crowd like this without her example.

"If you are looking for Josie," I went on, pronouncing my own name *"Jo-say,"* "she left early this morning to go to the Woodlawn Cemetery for the burial of Mr. Rothchild." I hated to send a bunch of reporters to interrupt Lewis's burial, but I figured there were probably already other reporters there. "However, if you would like to interview me about my chief clown role in the Great Circus de France-ay . . ."

"Woodlawn Cemetery? Where's that?" someone hollered.

Henry said, "I know, I know where it is!" He was so eager to be a hero that he'd fallen for my ruse, too.

I was tempted to follow after the stream of reporters, shouting, "Wait, wait," in my best Pépé style, but I thought I'd better not push my luck, since my trick was working.

I waited until they were all gone. Then I made sure my apartment was locked up, and I tucked my hair back up under my ball cap. I went out to my car and took off in the opposite direction from the Woodlawn Cemetery. It was another hour before I was to meet Winnie at the bookmobile, but I didn't want to be here when the reporters figured out Josie wasn't at Woodlawn . . . and that Jezebel was really Josie.

So I took off to the place I like to go when I need to be alone and think—the old orphanage.

I sat at the top of the rise overlooking the orphanage, stared past it out into a sky that even in this early hour was already startlingly blue, a perfect backdrop to a few fluffy clouds that lazily drifted along. Hard to believe, staring into this sky, that a violent storm had blown through in this area the night before. On my drive over, I'd only seen a few signs of it—stray tree limbs, a cracked tree, the door blown off the barn over at the Crowley farm. Of course the tree limb was still sticking through my spare apartment's window, awaiting my insurance company's inspection. And my behind was getting damp, sitting on the grass, but I didn't care.

As I gazed into the sky, my thoughts started off being about how we'd gotten off lucky in that storm. Then my thoughts started drifting off like the clouds, to things much less pleasant than the sky . . . like Tyra's murder. What Tyra had been up to with Stillwater. What her connection had been to Lewis. How it all fit together—or if any of it fit together at all.

And Guy . . . I wondered how he, and the others, were doing at Stillwater. Of course I knew Don Richmond had done his best to keep the reporters off the grounds, but Guy would have noticed all those new people outside the gates. And he'd have noticed the gates being locked. At the very least, I realized with a pang, this change would be unsettling to Guy.

Somehow, even with Tyra's revelation that she'd have come to Paradise even without my letter, I felt responsible for what was happening at Stillwater. To make it up to at least Guy, I decided that as soon as things got back to semi-normal, I'd make a picnic lunch and bring him here. For some reason, Guy always loved to come here with me, sit up on this hill, stare down at the old building. I didn't think he understood I'd lived here for a bit, but maybe at some level he did.

Or maybe there was some other reason—maybe something as simple as the shape of the building, or the view of looking down at a building, that appealed to him. Whatever the reason, the two places he did best on visits away from

Stillwater were here, overlooking the old orphanage, and at ball games, where he counted all the pitches, tallying them on a little notepad.

So I sat there awhile and thought about Guy, and felt all tender and protective and mushy about him, the way I might about a little brother, although Guy, of course, was my much older cousin. Funny how, bloodline-wise, he was the same relationship to me as Billy, but how, heartwise, our relationship was a lot different. Guy was, in a lot of ways, like the brother I'd always wanted. Billy was like the nutty older uncle you never want, but are stuck with, and like anyway.

But Billy—ever since those T-shirts arrived in town and he hooked up with Aguila and Ramon—had been changing. He was almost respectable. Admirable. Good changes. I just wasn't sure how to come to grips with the new Billy.

And that brought my thoughts full circle.

I glanced at my watch. It was 9:30 already. I needed to get a move on if I was to meet Winnie on time. What in the world did she have to reveal to me that she had to treat it so top-secret, hush-hush? I walked slowly down the hill, back to my car parked by the berry bushes, more reluctant than curious to find out. It had been nice, sitting all quiet and peaceful. But I had a feeling that—with whatever Winnie had to tell me—my quiet moments alone had just been the calm in the eye of the storm.

15

Ten minutes later, as I drove to my appointment with Winnie, I heard this thucka-thucka-thucka sound. It sounded just like a tire going flat.

But, no, I told myself, it was probably just moisture from last night's storm in my carburetor, making that funny sound, making my car suddenly drive all jerky.

Denial is a powerful mental force, causing us to do all kinds of things, like keep driving at 35 miles per hour. On just a rim.

But the odor of burning rubber broke through even my fervent denial. So I eased my car off to the edge of the road, turned off my car, then got out to have a look.

My right front tire was shredded. It'd been losing air for a month now, and I kept taking it to Elroy's station and adding air, meaning to get a new tire, but time and money were tight.

I ran around to the back of my Chevy, popped open the hatchback, pulled up the cover to the well that holds the spare tire. I had a spare and a wrench, but no functioning jack.

I got my purse and keys, shut up the car, and started trotting down the road. I figured I was about a mile from where I was supposed to meet Winnie. I hoped—I prayed—she'd wait for me.

By the time Winnie's bookmobile came into view, I was panting for breath. The door to the bookmobile was open—which surprised me. I went up the steps—and stopped at what I saw.

No Winnie. Keys still in the ignition. Winnie's "So Many Books, So Little Time" go cup (which I'd gotten her last Christmas) sat in the cup holder, by the dash, still holding coffee. Several books were knocked to the floor, and the magazine rack had been pulled out of the wall, so magazines were scattered around too.

I swallowed, hard. I was worried about Winnie. She'd never leave her bookmobile—not unless she was forced to.

I heard a car pulling up outside. Banging doors. Then voices—at first too distant to hear, then clear.

". . . Hurry up, will you? What if someone sees us?"

"In this godforsaken place?"

My stomach lurched. I knew those voices. They belonged to Steve and Linda Crooks. And they didn't sound so friendly anymore.

I looked around desperately. There aren't too many hiding spots in a bookmobile, but Winnie had a little desk and chair— both bolted down—in the back corner. I trotted back there, crouched behind the desk, and forced my breathing to slow.

There was the sound of the Crookses' struggling into the bookmobile, dragging something that was thumping up the steps.

"Where should we put her?" That was Steve.

"How about we just dump her on the floor. Why'd you have to use so much ether on her, anyway?"

"Because she was hollering and struggling too much. What if someone drove by, noticed, called the cops?"

"In this godforsaken place?"

"You said that already—and didn't we pass a car a mile back?"

Linda gave a snorting laugh. "That broken down old heap? It's probably been there for years."

That was my car she was talking about. I almost came out from under the desk to defend my Chevy's virtue. But I made myself stay put.

"Here, let's prop her in the passenger seat," Steve said.

There was the sound of them struggling with Winnie—then a thwacking sound that made me wince, just hearing it. I hoped it wasn't Winnie's head. Winnie's prone to headaches.

"God, this woman weighs a ton." Linda was panting.

Now that was downright unfair. Winnie had been struggling for 20 years to lose about that many pounds—hardly a ton, and a struggle I could surely relate to.

"There," Steve said. "The information we got out of her was hardly worth the trouble."

Linda gave another laugh. "Yeah, but at least we got out of her where we have to go next to—"

I didn't hear the rest of what she had to say. They'd left the bookmobile.

I started breathing again. Well, I'd been breathing all along, but barely. Then I got up on my knees, peeked over the top of the desk. The top of Winnie's head was just visible above the passenger seat. I crawled from behind the desk, down the aisle, up to Winnie. She was breathing, raggedly, but breathing.

Then I peeked out the windshield. Steve and Linda had just gotten into their car—a little red sports coupe—started it up, and were pulling out onto the road.

I swallowed hard.

Here I was again, in another fix. I couldn't let them go. I

wanted to know who Steve and Linda Crooks really were—what they were really up to—where they were going that Winnie had told them about. Billy had said they were FBI agents. I wasn't sure if I believed that. But they sure weren't writers out to do a biography of Tyra Grimes.

Still, the notion of driving something big enough to need miniblinds in the side windows made my stomach turn inside out.

I gave Winnie a little shake. She moaned. She wasn't going to wake up any time soon.

I looked back out the windshield. Steve and Linda Crooks were driving down the road.

So I did the only thing I could think of to do.

I quickly pulled the seat belt over Winnie.

Then I sat down in the driver's seat. Turned the ignition key. And pulled out after the Crookses' car.

I grinned.

It was, after all, my first car chase—even even if it was with a bookmobile.

The bookmobile was easier to navigate than I thought it would be, although it did make my stomach careen a little, every time the rear of the bus fishtailed.

Steve and Linda quickly figured out that they were being followed. It's hard not to notice a bookmobile on your tail. I stayed right on them, right up until they sped up past 60 miles per hour.

Then I heard sirens. I glanced—very quickly—in the bookmobile's side view mirror. A police car was following me. Somehow I just knew it was Chief Worthy. I didn't want to think about the fine for hijacking a bookmobile, even with cause.

So I did my best to ignore him while I kept up in Winnie's bookmobile with Steve and Linda in their sporty red coupe.

Suddenly, then, Steve and Linda slowed enough to turn off on another country road—and then they floored it. I slowed the bookmobile, made the turn with the rear of the vehicle swaying wildly, and by the time I got more or less back in my lane, they were out of sight.

I kept driving, my heart sinking. Now what? I glanced around the countryside, as if the trees flashing by held an answer.

And—truth be told—they did. Because I realized exactly what route we were taking. I'd driven it a hundred times before, only in my little car. What with the up-high view from the bookmobile—and with everything else that was distracting me, like Winnie out of it in the seat next to me and the siren blaring behind me—I'd taken awhile to recognize it. We were driving the route I always took to Owen's house.

Pretty soon, Steve and Linda Crooks were out of sight.

So I slowed down—which was a relief—figuring I'd go on to Owen's house and see if my hunch was right. Besides, I didn't trust myself to pull the bookmobile over to the side of the road without getting stuck in the ditch. Or pulling in with too much tilt, and rolling the whole thing over.

Chief Worthy wasn't giving up on me. He stayed right on my tail, all the way to Owen's house, his siren blaring.

At Owen's, parked in front of the fourth garage over from the house, was the car Steve and Linda had been driving, parked right next to Paige's SUV. They weren't in the car any longer.

I stopped the bookmobile and turned off its engine, leaving the keys in the ignition. I checked on Winnie. She was snoring. I stood up and almost crumpled to my knees, my legs felt so weak. Now that my bookmobile heist, tailing, and car chase were all over, I was shaking. But I pulled my hat firmly down on my head, straightened my shoulders, opened the bookmobile door, and walked down the steps and out the door, as tall and proud as my five-feet-three and three/eighths inches—and tufts of orange Bozo hair sticking out from under my hat—would allow.

Chief John Worthy was right by me, angrier than I'd ever seen him. He was breathing hard in an effort to keep his voice under control—but his voice shook anyway.

"Josie Toadfern, that beats all you've ever done in the past! Why, I'm going to arrest you for hijacking a bookmobile, operating a commercial vehicle without a license, fleeing while in pursuit—"

I pulled my arm from his grasp, kept going toward Owen's house. "Then you'd better add resisting arrest," I said. "Because I'm not going anywhere with you until I know what's going on here—and why it's going on at my boyfriend's house."

I was all set to stalk off dramatically to Owen's front door—but suddenly Steve Crooks came around the corner, waving a gun at both of us.

Chief Worthy started for his holster—all set for a shoot-out, I guess—but then Steve waved something else at us. A shiny badge. Even Chief Worthy looked stunned.

"FBI," said Steve. "You'd both better come with me."

Chief Worthy and I followed Steve around to the side of the garage, then through a door into the garage.

The normally empty garage held several boxes. I recognized the boxes—they held the hot Tyra Grimes T-shirts.

Billy leaned against one of the stacks of boxes, his arms crossed, a bemused expression on his face. Owen stood in the middle of the garage, looking so tense I thought he might shatter into a thousand little Owen-bits any second. Paige sat in a lawn chair, legs crossed at the ankles, hands in her lap, as if she might be served tea any moment. She gave me a little nod. Billy moved to her, put a protective hand on her shoulder. Which made Linda—who stood facing the Billy, Owen, and Paige lineup with a gun—frown.

Owen started hopping from one foot to another, as if he were doing a little kid's I-gotta-pee-now dance. "I'm sorry, Josie, I wanted to call you, but after Billy got me to agree to hide the T-shirts here, after he told me everything, I just knew if I talked to you, I'd end up telling you what was going on, and Billy didn't want me to—"

"Just what in the blazes is going on here? I'm a sworn officer of the law—"

"Shut up, Worthy," said Steve Crooks.

Linda looked at Chief Worthy and gave him a little smile. "Pardon my partner's crankiness. We're FBI agents—we can't tell you our real names—"

"Or you'd have to shoot us?" That was Billy, smirking.

"Precisely," said Linda. "And these boxes contain important evidence in a federal investigation against Tyra Grimes. They're stolen property. We've tracked them here to get them back—and to find the people who took them, who are also important witnesses. We were about to confiscate them from an abandoned building, but they disappeared. So we posed as writers to try to discover where the boxes could be—and also to learn as much as possible about why Tyra Grimes was here. We figured she must be up to something to counter the case we have against her."

"Well, just hold on a minute, what does Winnie have to do with this—and why is Paige here—and—and—" I was so confused, I was hollering.

"Actually," Steve said, "Winnie tracked us down at the Red Horse yesterday, thinking we were writers. She said she wanted to meet with us because she had some really shocking information about Tyra's background, and she wanted to see if we wanted to use it in our book."

That sounded like Winnie. She wouldn't be able to resist helping with a book.

Linda went on, "But, she told us she couldn't reveal the information until she talked with you in private. We followed her this morning. Whatever she knew, we wanted to find out before you—God only knows what you'd do with it. We confronted her, took her off for a little—ah—drive—but she can be very—ah—stubborn. We finally did get the information from her, though."

We all stared at them, waiting.

Finally, Chief Worthy snapped, "Well? Is she fine? And what did she tell you?"

"She is fine. And she can tell you what she told us when she comes to. What she learned about Tyra's past doesn't have any bearing on our investigation. The important thing was that once she got scared and started talking—she kept on talking—and told us about the T-shirts here, and—"

I did something then I'd wanted to do ever since we'd been marched in here. I hauled off and slapped Steve Crooks, good and hard. He looked stunned. "Hey—" he said, waving his gun in my face.

"Don't wave that thing at me, you bully! You scared my friend! You used strong-arm tactics on her . . . gave her ether, kidnapped her from her own bookmobile! You're in big trouble, mister, because you violated a whole bunch of rights set down in the Constitution and . . . and in the State of Ohio and in the town of Paradise—"

"Don't talk to me about the Constitution! I work for the government and I—I—I—"

Steve Crooks sputtered to a stop, looked at Linda for help. She just sighed. "Well, I'm afraid Josie here is right, Steve.

We haven't behaved properly. But we did find the evidence here, and of course, by harboring stolen property, which is also evidence in a federal investigation, Josie's other friends are also potentially in big trouble, so if Josie wants to insist on any of them pressing charges against us, then—"

"Enough!" Paige stood up. "I don't know why Tyra wanted to come here to Paradise. She was very guarded about that. All she would tell me is that she had a plan for damage control once it became common knowledge that she was using illegal labor to create her T-shirts. A plan, she said, that would put a whole new spin on the illegal labor practices." Paige patted the big handbag that hung over her shoulder. "In here, I have enough documentation to give you what you need to shut down Tyra Grimes's operation—permanently. Although, with her dead, it would have closed anyway."

So Paige had really taken Tyra's papers—not Steve and Linda. I was taken aback by how matter-of-factly Paige spoke about Tyra's being dead. But she was in a negotiating mode, and wasn't about to be ruffled. She looked evenly at Linda Crooks, then at Steve.

"I would suggest that—if you want the documents I can show you—documents Tyra kept with her at all times, at least until I took them from the apartment—then you will not be pressing any charges against anybody in this room for anything. Nor will you pursue the people who transported the T-shirts here."

Linda smiled, showing just the edges of her teeth. "We could just forcibly take the documents from you."

Paige smiled right back, showing even less of her teeth, which somehow made the smile more ferocious. "You could. But then you'd have lots of witnesses who I'm sure would be willing to testify for me that you violated all those rights

Josie just referred to. Not too good for your FBI careers, I don't think."

Linda dropped her smile, sighed, and stuck her gun back in her belt. "All right. Fine. We'll need you to come with us, though." She shot a look at Billy and Owen. "But these T-shirts better not move again, got it?"

Paige took a step, but Billy put a hand on her shoulder. She looked at him, smiled, this time for real. "I'll be fine."

He nodded.

Paige left with Steve and Linda.

Billy moved over to Chief Worthy. "I'll be going with you."

"What?" Chief Worthy frowned. "Why—"

"Because you need to arrest me," Billy said. "For the murder of Tyra Grimes."

"Billy, what are you trying to do—"

"It's okay, Josie," Billy said. "I know what I'm doing."

"No, you don't." Chief Worthy said. "I've got Hazel Rothchild locked up for that. I have more than a few witnesses who say she was heard threatening Tyra at the gathering over at her house, following Lewis's viewing."

"Now, Chief, you know poor Hazel was just upset," I said.

"And now you've got a confessed killer," Billy said. "I killed her because I was so upset about how she was using people to further her own commerce." He grinned. "It's my new cause. Striking out against what amounts to slavery for the sake of commercialism."

Chief Worthy stared at Billy. Then he said, grimly—but with some satisfaction—"I always knew you'd turn out on the wrong side of the law." He slid a glance at me. "You Toadferns always do. All right, Billy. Turn around. I'm going to handcuff you. You have the right to remain silent. You—"

"Wait! Stop! Billy, why are you doing this?"

He gave me that long, deep look that had become his ever since he'd taken up with Ramon and Aguila. "Because I want to help, Josie. And the only person I can help right now is Hazel. No one in charge in this case wants to question what's easiest to believe."

"But what about—" I dropped my voice to a whisper— "Ramon and Aguila and their daughter? Shouldn't you be trying to help them?"

Billy smiled. "They're long gone. Tyra did respond to Paige's letter, making arrangements for Ramon and Aguila to get home and for Selena to get the help she needs."

"But I thought maybe Ramon and Aguila were Lewis's killers. If they're long gone . . ."

Billy shook his head. "Josie, they're not guilty of anything like that. And neither is Paige."

I thought about his gesture earlier, putting his hand on Paige's arm. Somehow, I knew he'd know if Paige had killed Tyra. And he wouldn't cover up something like that.

"Then Elroy really did . . ."

"I don't know. I still find that hard to believe—but my instinct tells me that Lewis's and Tyra's murders are connected."

"Would you two hush? I'm trying to make an arrest . . ."

"Shut up!" I hollered at Chief Worthy, which shocked him into silence. I didn't want to see Billy dragged off, locked up for a crime he didn't commit.

And that is precisely what Billy understood. He smiled at me. "Josie, it's up to you now. Find out why Tyra really came to Paradise. It's the only way you're going to find out who really killed her—and Lewis."

Chief Worthy finished reciting Billy his rights. Then he escorted him out of the garage.

That left in the garage just a few boxes of Tyra Grimes T-shirts—and me and Owen. I turned away from them and faced Owen.

* * *

"You had these T-shirts here. You had Billy and Paige here. And you didn't call me? And Winnie was involved, too?"

Owen looked miserable. "We love you, Josie . . . but we know how you are. Billy told me later that he and the Cruezes had seen you out at the old orphanage."

Ah. Guess I hadn't been as stealthy as I thought.

"They got worried that you might say something to Tyra, and so started moving the T-shirts here on the night of Tyra's party, without telling me, thinking I never come out here to the garages."

Ah. The "deer" I thought I'd heard by Owen's garage that night.

"But then the Cruezes' truck broke down on one of their runs. The Cruezes hiked on back to the Red Horse, while Billy went back to your apartment, hoping to borrow your car. Instead, he encountered Paige. This was after everyone left. He confronted her about Tyra's T-shirts and the working conditions, without yet mentioning the Cruez couple. This was after everyone had left and Paige was cleaning up.

"Not wanting Tyra to encounter Billy again—knowing how upset the first encounter had made her—Paige convinced Billy to let her drive him back to the Red Horse. I guess on the way there, he made a pretty convincing argument against Tyra's business practices."

Ah. The "cocoa" stain on Paige's sweater. Billy would have been muddy from all that work, and she could have easily brushed against him as they argued or in the SUV. And she'd thoroughly cleaned my apartment before my return—that's why I hadn't seen any mud there. But she could have easily missed the smear of mud on her sweater sleeve—and she wouldn't have wanted to tell me about her encounter with Billy if she was already starting to think of turning away from Tyra.

"Later that night, Billy met Paige at the Red Horse again, and this time she met the Cruezes and finally decided to help them. They used Paige's SUV to transport them here in the middle of the night. But I had a restless night, thinking about you, and discovered what was going on. I agreed to let them use my garage and to stay here with me after they left the Red Horse, but Billy insisted I not tell you."

Ah. That's why Owen had been avoiding me.

"If you knew Billy and Paige were here, you'd come out and start asking questions, and then those agents would have followed you—"

Ah. The old Nosy Josie thing again . . . "You could have told me to stay away. You could have told me on the phone—"

"Josie," Owen said in his quiet, smooth voice that makes him irresistible to me. "You would not have stayed away."

I thought about that for a second. I knew he was right. "They found Billy and Paige and the T-shirts, anyway," I muttered. "And now Billy—" I stopped, my voice catching. I hate it when I don't want to cry, but I do anyway.

Owen brought me to him in an awkward hug. I didn't hug back—I was still sore at him. But I didn't resist, either. "Billy did what he thought was right," Owen said.

Yeah. Just like Billy. But now it was up to me to get him out of jail. And the only way to do that was to figure out who really killed Tyra—and while I was at it, Lewis. The only thing I could think of to do next was to fetch Winnie from the bookmobile and see if what she had learned about Tyra's past might help.

So we went out to the bookmobile. Winnie wasn't awake yet. I picked her up at the top end, while Owen got her at the foot end, and we hauled her into Owen's house, then put her down on his couch in the library. I was getting pretty good at moving bodies. At least this one—though dead weight—was alive.

I sat down on a chair, pulled off my hat, wiped my brow. "Whew," I said. "Do you have any lemonade, maybe, Owen, or—"

I stopped. Owen was staring at me—with a look of horror.

My hair. I'd forgotten that my hair had turned Bozo orange. Oh, great. Just what I wanted the (potential) love of my life to see.

"Uh, Josie, uh, what happened, what—"

Owen was stuttering. Owen never stutters.

Then, this incredible idea—this impossible, wonderful idea—popped into my head.

I grinned at Owen.

"Owen," I said. "Did Billy happen to bring his Cut-N-Suck with him?"

16

"You sure you want to go through with this?" Owen asked.

I looked at Billy's Cut-N-Suck, now hooked up to Owen's old Hoover canister vacuum on the kitchen table. Of course I wasn't sure. What woman is ever sure that going bald is the right decision?

Still, the other option was Bozo hair.

Even if my own tatty, dishwater blond hair never grew back, bald was a better choice than Bozo.

But there was more to it than that.

Truth be told, I had gotten Tyra to come to Paradise. And as soon as word got out that she was coming, the whole town had started going nuts. Even I'd gone and tried to change myself, to be better, but not to *really* be better. Just better to be good enough in someone else's judgment.

In the end, all of Paradise was a mess. Two people were murdered. And I had Bozo hair.

So now I had to put things right.

And I was starting with my hair. Maybe, in a funny way, like a reverse sort of Samson and Delilah thing, Owen cutting off all my hair would give me the strength to put everything else right, too.

So, I looked at Owen, and with a voice as pointed as the scissors he held, said, "Yes. I'm sure."

There's something very strange and intimate about having your hair cut, then shaved, by the man you care about.

Owen was organized and neat.

He set the cutting station up at his kitchen table—scissors, mirror, Cut-N-Suck attached to his vacuum, trash can.

Owen was gentle.

First he cut my hair close to the scalp, putting each tuft in the trash can. Then he gently used the clipping tool, which comes with every Cut-N-Suck, giving me an orange burr, while the vacuum chugged down the tattered ends of my hair. Then Owen went over my head one more time—this time with the shaving tool, and cleaned off the last bits of my hair. He didn't nick me once.

Owen was kind.

When he was all done, he gave me the mirror without saying a word. I looked into it. Yes, it was me—Josie Toadfern—but with a totally bald scalp. I started to tear up, then fought against the sudden strong urge to cry.

Owen leaned over, kissed me atop my head. It felt strange—the feeling of skin brushing skin at the top of my head. Then he said, "You're beautiful."

I went ahead and cried.

And didn't stop, until Winnie staggered into the kitchen, blinking, saying, with a thick voice, "What's all the racket . . . and how'd I get here . . . and—"

She stopped when she saw me, her mouth hanging open.

We had to get Winnie a cool cloth, and some iced tea, then spend some time explaining things to her—like how she (and her bookmobile) came to be here at Owen's, how Paige had gone off with Steve and Linda Crooks, how Billy had confessed to Tyra's murder and gone off with Chief John Worthy, and how I came to be bald. She kept looking worriedly at me—well, really, at my bald head, jumping in with things like, "you know, the top of your head will freeze in the winter," and "you know, the top of your head will steam if you get too hot in the summer."

Finally, it was her turn to talk. We gathered around Owen's kitchen table, Owen and me politely quiet, waiting for Winnie to start. Winnie looked even more worried than ever.

"As you know, Josie, you tasked me with finding out all I could about Tyra Grimes's background," she said, finally looking me in the eyes, instead of at my head.

I nodded.

"So, all I'm reporting here are the facts. You can't blame me for what I found out."

"Right."

She sighed deeply, took a long sip of iced tea, and patted her forehead with the damp cloth.

"Well, you know Stringtown."

Stringtown . . . sure I knew Stringtown. I'd just been there a few days before. I felt a chill, wondering what connection Tyra had to the tiny village.

"Well, it turns out that Tyra Grimes is actually from Stringtown. She was born there. And she grew up there. Until she left, when she was sixteen, for New York."

I shook my head. "That can't be. Everyone knows Tyra Grimes's bio. She grew up an only child, in middle-class suburbia outside of Chicago, then decided to become a designer to help people have a sense of proper style, and ended up with a TV show first on a local station, then went to New York—"

"That's all spin," Winnie said. "The story we've all heard. The truth is I did my research thoroughly—and lots of it—

and believe me, thirty years ago, Tyra was an only child living in Stringtown. I searched everything I could find on Tyra Grimes, going back as far as I could, and I finally found an article, in the *National Insight*—"

I rolled my eyes, thinking of the wave of reporters I'd fended off earlier with my Jezebel-the-clown-from-France act. "That rag? They're still reporting Elvis sightings at 7-11's in Michigan—"

Winnie looked over the top of her glasses at me with her best librarian look. "While I'm glad to know your ability to discern good reading from trash is improving, Josie, please bear with me."

I shrank back in my chair at that. She knew that, while I was more than glad to read good books, I also couldn't resist rags like *National Insight* and *Sweet Love's Salty Confessions*—especially if I was feeling blue. And had a box of salty chips handy. Plus Big Fizz diet cola. And a super sized bar of chocolate, of course.

"Go on," Owen urged.

"Well, the *National Insight* had a little article, about ten years ago, that Tyra Grimes had really grown up in Stringtown, and that Tyra was not her real name. Seems a widow from Stringtown claimed Tyra was really her long-lost daughter, and especially now that her husband was dead, she wanted in on Tyra's fame and success—preferably in the form of cash. When Tyra denied her claims, the woman went to the *National Insight* with her sob story."

"Ah—a classic case of fame and fortune suddenly drawing friends and family out of every nook and cranny," said Owen, warming to the story Winnie was weaving. "A theme covered by all the classicists—Aristotle, Shakespeare . . . why, in one play—"

I jumped in, anxious to hear Winnie's story. "So what happened then?"

"Tyra, of course, denied the story again, in articles published in Chicago newspapers—and the *National Insight* printed a retraction with an apology to Tyra. Then the whole story disappeared from the press."

My eyebrows went up—and my skepticism kicked into red alert mode. "They retracted the story? They never do that."

Winnie gave a little satisfied smile. "Exactly. Made me suspicious right off. If they had kept on with the story, I'd have probably dismissed it out of hand. But instead, I did some more digging. And I found out that the woman really was from Stringtown, and had had a daughter, who suddenly left Stringtown at sixteen. I checked at Mason County South High School, where the daughter would have gone, and found out the girl had actually missed most of her sophomore year. No one really remembered her—I talked to a few teachers and the principal, all retired now.

"But I did find one clipping in an old school newspaper about how this girl had won a home ec contest on how she'd decorate a house, and the article talked about how she always wanted to be a decorator—and she was determined to become a very famous and rich one, too. And that she wanted to go to New York to live."

A sudden wash of tingles came over me. I shook my head. "But that could just be coincidence. I mean, there must be thousands of young girls who have dreams like that . . . and plenty of people who'd try to take advantage of someone as famous as Tyra Grimes."

"True," Winnie said. "So I called Samantha." Samantha is Winnie's oldest daughter, a financial planner who lives in New York. "And she got in touch with a private detective she knows for me, who checked out motor vehicle records. And what the detective discovered was that the girl had gone to

New York, gotten a driver's license, and an apartment. Then the girl's name just disappeared from all such records. So he checked the records by address, instead. And discovered, at the same address, a year later, someone with the same license number but another name—Tyra Grimes."

Owen hopped up, started pacing. "So Tyra came back here out of sentimentality, perhaps to reunite with her dear old mother, after all. Perhaps under the pressure of the investigation into her company's activities, she needed the comfort—"

"No," Winnie said. "The woman claiming to be Tyra Grimes's mother is long gone from Stringtown. She just up and disappeared not long after the retraction about Tyra. Eventually their house—which was mostly a shack anyway—fell in on itself. Not a trace of it now—"

"Okay, this is all interesting," I jumped in. "But there's something you've been avoiding telling us."

Winnie cast her eyes down, took another sip of tea, her hand shaking so that she sloshed some out on her chin. Owen looked at me. "Actually, Winnie's been quite impressive in her thoroughness—"

"Yes, except she hasn't told us one thing—Tyra's real name when she was growing up in Stringtown."

"Why, that's true," Owen exclaimed. "Do tell us, Winnie. What was Tyra's birth name?"

Winnie looked up at me, a look of apology in her eyes. She took a deep breath. "Tyra was born Henrietta Toadfern. The only child of Myrtle and Henry Toadfern—the son of your great-grandfather's brother, Clitus Toadfern."

I felt myself go light-headed.

"Josie," said Winnie. Her voice suddenly sounded very far away. "Do you understand what this means? You and Tyra Grimes . . . why, you're second cousins, once removed . . ."

And at that, I took a deep breath—and passed out.

* * *

Mrs. Oglevee was waiting for me in the white fogginess. She had on a hot pink leather pantsuit, white spike-heeled boots, and her auburn Tyra Grimes-style wig.

She held an extra Tyra Grimes-style wig in her hand—and held it out to me. "Here," she said, her throat all croaky, as if she'd been up all night, partying. "You'll be needing this."

I crossed my arms, stuck out my chin. "No thanks. I'm fine the way I am, and—"

Mrs. Oglevee rolled her eyes. "Suit yourself, baldy." She tossed the wig over her shoulder, into the fog. The wig disappeared. "So, why'd you call me up, then?"

I gaped at that. "Me? Call you? Why would I do that?"

She shrugged. "Beats me. But sure as shootin', I don't keep making these trips out to see you because I'm dying for your company." She paused, laughed herself into a fit of coughing, then laughed some more. "Ooh—that was a good one, referring to myself dying for something, when I'm already—"

She stopped when she saw I wasn't laughing. "Okay, I see you're not in a mood for hilarity, not that I blame you. So what is it you want? I'm a busy woman and I'm expecting some high-falutin' company."

I frowned at that. "I don't think Tyra Grimes is going to think you look very sophisticated, or—"

Mrs. Oglevee laughed again. She sure was in a cheery mood. "The look I'm going for isn't sophisticated. And I'm not waiting for Tyra—I'm waiting for Lewis Rothchild." She waggled her eyebrows, gave me an evil grin, which made me unsure of where she'd ended up in the afterlife—although I'm pretty sure pink leather is flammable. "We were friends, you know. Soon as he's through processing, we've got a lot of catching up to do."

I didn't want to know what their earthly friendship had been.

She suddenly looked concerned. "Although . . . once Tyra gets here—assuming she does, which I hear is kind of iffy—things could get pretty tense . . ."

"Because of her and Lewis being around each other?"

Mrs. Oglevee rolled her eyes. "Du-u-u-h," she said. "You don't think bad karma goes away just because you die, do you?"

I didn't think the Mrs. Oglevee I knew would have worn pink leather and talked about karma. But pointing that out was liable to make her disappear, and she seemed to know a few things I didn't, which I was sorely in need of understanding. "So Tyra and Lewis knew each other when they were, um, back here on earth? A long time ago?"

"What do you think?"

"It would make sense," I said. "Plus, I just found out Tyra really grew up around here—"

"And you're her second cousin, once removed!" Mrs. Oglevee laughed so hard that she snorted, slapping her pink thighs at the same time.

When she finally finished laughing, I said, "Look, I'm glad you're tickled, uh, pink. But I've got a serious problem here. I've found out a lot. Like about Tyra's company and its illegal—and immoral—use of illegal aliens to do her manufacturing. And about Tyra's real background—or some of it, anyway. But I still don't know why she came to Paradise in the first place. Or what she was planning to do at Stillwater. Or who killed her—and why. I just know I've got to find out, because otherwise Billy—"

Mrs. Oglevee rolled her eyes again as she said, "Oh yes, dear Billy. He was a lot more fun when he wasn't being a martyr. Look—"

She stopped. I waited. Then I said, "Look—what?"

"Just—look. You pretty much have all the answers. You just need to look a little closer at what you already know."

"But—but—but—"

"Oh, for pity's sake. Do I still have to spoonfeed you the answers, just like back in school?" She sighed—her old teacher's sigh. "Let's try this approach. Lewis was upset about Tyra coming to town. Right?"

"Right."

"And you've already figured out that Lewis and Tyra are connected somehow in the past—and that they knew each other way back."

"Right."

"Okay—who else was really upset about Tyra coming?"

"Billy."

"No, no, no. Not him. He was only upset after she came. Think, please!"

So I thought. Then, slowly, an idea coming to my head, I said, "Vivian. She was real upset about Verbenia wearing the Tyra T-shirt. And about Tyra coming. And about Lewis dying. And I hadn't even known she knew him. And . . . and . . . and . . ."

"Come on, put the pieces together. I haven't got all day."

"Vivian knew Lewis . . . and Lewis knew Tyra . . . and . . ." I hesitated, then blurted out what seemed too incredible to be true. "Tyra and Vivian already knew each other, too. The three of them are connected, somehow."

"Bingo! You're coming along, after all. All right, now, why did Tyra say she was here?"

"Something about an announcement at Stillwater."

"And why is Stillwater so important to Vivian?"

"Well, because Verbenia's there, of course, and Verbenia matters more to Vivian than—" I stopped, swallowed hard. "They're all four connected, somehow. Tyra. And Vivian and Verbenia. And Lewis. So the real reason Tyra came here had nothing to do with her company—"

Mrs. Oglevee waggled a finger at me. "Careful. Don't

jump to conclusions, dear." She sounded almost kind and encouraging—which was scarier than seeing her in pink leather.

"She was here because of her company . . . and something to do with Stillwater. Somehow, that's connected, too . . ." I stomped my foot—a very unsatisfying thing to do when you're mad and you're standing adrift in fog. "But how—besides just wanting to make a donation to Stillwater?"

Mrs. Oglevee sighed. "I'm not giving you the answers. You have to find out the rest of it for yourself."

"And just how am I supposed to do that?"

Mrs. Oglevee smiled. "You find out answers by asking questions of the people you haven't asked yet—of course."

And with that, she turned and sashayed off, disappearing into the fog.

Vivian, I thought. I needed to talk to Vivian . . .

Suddenly, a sharp odor spiked in my nose. I started coughing, and sputtering.

Owen kept sticking the bottle of smelling salts to my nose even after my eyes had fluttered open.

I pushed his hand away. I tried to sit up, but it made my head dizzy, so I flopped back down, which wasn't the best choice, since in passing out at the news of my family ties to Tyra, I'd slid off the kitchen chair and onto the kitchen floor.

I moaned.

"Josie—Josie are you okay?" That was Owen, sounding very anxious.

"Yes—my head just hurts." I pushed up on my elbows. I felt a little dizzy, so I paused. Then I sat the rest of the way up. I rubbed my head—was surprised by the feel of smooth skin. The happenings of the whole day came rushing back at me—the reporters, Winnie on the side of the road, the bookmobile car chase, Billy turning himself in as Tyra's killer, getting my head shaved, finding out about Tyra's past (and her relation to me), passing out and seeing Mrs. Oglevee again. And the most normal of all these events seemed the talk with Mrs. Oglevee. That made me moan again.

I grabbed the smelling salts from Owen and took a big whiff. I needed to be alert for what was coming next. I started to stand, and Owen helped me on up.

"Josie, I'm so sorry, I didn't mean to—"

I held up my hand, stopping Winnie. "It's okay," I said. "Finding out about Tyra's true past—or at least some of it—gives me an idea about what I need to do next to find out the rest of the truth."

"About Tyra's reason for coming here?" Winnie asked.

"That. And about who killed her. And Lewis." I went over to the phone, mounted on the wall by the fridge. I dialed the number for Stillwater. After a few rings, Susan, the secretary, answered, giving the usual greeting.

"Susan," I jumped in, "this is Josie Toadfern, I need to talk to Don Richmond as soon as possible. It's urgent."

I needed to find out how to contact Vivian. I'd been seeing her out at Stillwater for years—but I'd never swapped phone numbers with her, or had lunch with her, as I did with some of the other residents' family members. In fact, I had never really spent any time talking with Vivian until after Lewis died. And I couldn't remember ever seeing anyone else talk with Vivian much—which was strange. The rest of us had formed a casual sort of support group—except Vivian. She was a loner, definitely.

"Susan?" I said again, since she hadn't responded. "I need to—"

"How—how did you hear? My God, Josie, I'm so sorry . . . We tried calling you and calling you, but there's been no answer, at your home or at the laundromat—"

"Uh, Susan? What are you talking about?"

There was another long silence.

"Susan?"

"Josie—you'd better get over here. Don wants to talk to you. You see—somehow—Guy and Verbenia have been missing since breakfast. We think they may have taken off together in the middle of the night, and—"

I hung up, whirled around. "Owen." My voice was tight, thin. "I need to get to Stillwater—now."

17

Owen loaned me his car. He offered to drive me to Stillwater, but I wanted to be alone, to have a little time to think. I told him to go with Winnie instead in her bookmobile, make sure she didn't suffer any aftereffects from the ether. He didn't look happy at the idea, but he said he would go with her.

So Owen and Winnie saw me off, waving at me from the end of Owen's massive driveway, while I backed out Owen's car, an old red Volvo.

Looking back, I'm not sure going by myself was the best decision. It ended up putting me and other people in danger. But if Owen had gone with me, maybe I'd never have found out the whole story behind Tyra's and Lewis's murders—and a killer might have gone free.

As I drove, I tried to pep myself up, telling myself that by the time I got to Stillwater, of course Guy and Verbenia would have turned up. They'd probably just wandered off to look at Guy's beloved pumpkin plants, instead of keeping to their regular schedule.

But I didn't do a good job of making myself believe it.

Guy had never, in all his years at Stillwater, gone missing. He loved his routine, his schedule. Verbenia, I was guessing, was the same way. Most of the residents were. So for them to go missing like that had to mean that they were upset—very, very upset—about something.

And what was worse, I couldn't shake the feeling that their disappearance had to have something to do with the Tyra-Lewis-Vivian-Verbenia connection I'd just put together. Something to do with why Tyra had come to Paradise. Something to do with why Lewis—and Tyra—had been killed. Which meant if my hunch was correct about who had really killed Lewis and Tyra, then Guy and Verbenia were in trouble, too. None of us are very well equipped to deal with the dangers of the world. Guy and Verbenia, I feared, would be even less so.

I got to Stillwater and found the front gate open, with no one nearby. I guessed that since Tyra wouldn't be giving her press conference here today, the reporters' attention was turned elsewhere—probably to bugging law enforcement agents about what they'd figured out about Tyra's murder.

I parked in visitor parking, near the main building, and rushed on in. Susan was waiting for me.

"Don is anxious to see you," she said. Susan gave a long, hard stare at my head, which was covered in a cap, but it didn't take more than a glance around the edges to figure out that it wasn't covering anything other than skin. She gave her head a little shake, as if to remind herself that she had more important things to deal with than my radical change in looks. "Vivian Denlinger is already in with him. I don't know how this happened—I'm so sorry—"

We started walking toward Don's office.

"Have you called the police?" I asked "Started a search?"

"We've contacted the sheriff," Susan said. "And we've been assured they'll start a search soon. But with Tyra Grimes's murder—" her voice trailed off.

I nodded. "They're too busy, helping to work on that, aren't they?"

Her "yes" was tiny and miserable. We were now outside Don's door. Susan knocked, opened the door, looked in. "Josie's here," she said.

I went into Don's office. Vivian sat in one of the two visitor chairs across from Don. She was speaking quietly, but tears were streaming down her face. And she was shredding a tissue. "I don't understand. One of the reasons I chose this facility for Verbenia was it seems so secure—"

"Secure, yes," Don said, nervously straightening an already straightened stack of papers on an overly neat desk. I slipped into the other visitor chair. "But not a prison, of course. The sense of living freely is one of Stillwater's features. We've never had anything like this happen before—"

Vivian thumped her fists on the desk, making the papers jump. "I don't need to hear your sales pitch! I already know the supposed features of this place!" Her voice was still low, but sharp, too tight, like it was about to break—like she was about to break. "And I don't care whether this has ever happened before or not! My sister is missing, and—"

"So is Josie's cousin," Don said, giving me a nod, hesitating as he stared at my ball cap. Vivian didn't even look my way. "I called you both here not just to assure you we're doing everything possible—"

"Oh, really?" Vivian asked. "Then where are the police?"

"They are occupied with another urgent matter, but assure us—"

"The murder of Tyra Grimes," Vivian said, her face drawing into a frightening sneer. "It's been all over TV this morning."

"Yes," said Don. "But I can assure you—"

"Stop assuring me!" Vivian hollered, her voice finally going up a notch. I could see her point on this one. I didn't want to be assured either. I wanted to find Guy.

Don sighed. "Look, I have as many of my people as I can spare canvasing the grounds, looking for Guy and Verbenia. It's what we can do until the police get back to us—later this afternoon, I've been told. What I need to know from each of you is if you can think of anything—anything at all that would have motivated Guy and Verbenia to take off like this." He looked at me. "Josie?"

I thought. The last time I'd visited Guy, he'd been fine. "I can't think of anything."

"He wasn't upset about anything, as far as you know?"

"No," I said. "I'm sure the storm upset him, though." I felt guilty, remembering with a pang that Guy is terrified of storms—and I hadn't even thought of him during last night's tornado.

"We're guessing they left sometime after the storm," Don said. "Their beds haven't been slept in. We had everyone in our tornado shelter area until the storm passed. Then everyone had a snack, and went on back to their rooms."

"How did they seem then?" I asked.

"Everyone was jittery because of the storm. Guy was especially upset, but calmed down after we got him some pistachio ice cream." Tears pricked my eyes. Pistachio is Guy's favorite ice cream flavor. "He kept asking if the storm would come back out during the night, and we told him no. Verbenia didn't seem bothered by the storm at all. Eventually, everyone went on back to their rooms."

"Susan said they've been missing since breakfast," I said. "Were they at breakfast, or—"

"No, they weren't, so we went to check on them—"

"He took her!" Vivian stared at me with horror. "Somewhere in the middle of the night, he took her—"

"No, Vivian, Guy wouldn't do that," I said. "If they left together it was because they chose to do so together."

"Can you think of any reason Verbenia would have wanted to leave?" Don asked.

"No," Vivian snapped. "You yourself said she was calm, even after yesterday's storm."

"Last night she was calm," Don said. "But right after your visit yesterday afternoon, she was agitated. I'm wondering if—"

"What are you trying to imply? It's not my fault my sister is missing!"

"No, of course not, Vivian, but you've come to see her twice this week on days you normally don't visit," Don said. "You spent a lot of time with her yesterday. Was there anything during your visit with her that might help us figure out why she'd leave with Guy? Did she seem upset? Say anything?"

"She barely talks at all, you know that," Vivian said, suddenly crossing her arms, and pressing back into her chair. "And she wasn't upset when she was with me. She was glad to see me—very glad, as always."

"Verbenia was upset after you left," Don said quietly. "She started scratching her arms at dinner, pulling at her hair, shrieking repeatedly. We couldn't get her to calm down, or figure out what was upsetting her. We finally had to restrain her for a time."

Vivian burst out sobbing. "I don't—I don't know what was upsetting her—I just want her back! And you can go over theories all you want, but while you're just sitting here, and the police are worried about some dead media star, I'm going to look for my sister!"

She stood up, shoved past me, fled from the room.

Don sighed again, then looked at me. "Josie—are you sure you can't think of why Guy would leave with Verbenia?"

"I think that Guy might want to leave if Verbenia were

leaving. They're—" I didn't want to say friends, exactly. People with autism don't connect with other people in the way that people without it do. But Guy and Verbenia were always together when they could be. They rarely talked. They'd just rather be together than not. And people with autism like order. Maybe Verbenia leaving seemed like too much of a change at Stillwater for Guy, and so he followed her. Or went with her. I shook my head. "I don't know. It's next to impossible to guess why either of them would do this."

"Can you think of anywhere Guy would go? Any favorite places you take him on your outings away from here? I wanted to ask Vivian that question too, but—"

Just like Vivian, I jumped up. There was only one place Guy would go. I wasn't sure if he'd know how to get there on his own. And I didn't know if he was following Verbenia, or if she'd followed him, or if they'd actually left together. But one of Guy's favorite places was the old orphanage.

"There's something I want to check out," I said. "I'll be back in touch as soon as possible, okay?"

I, too, left Don's office.

I left the building and started in a trot toward the visitor's lot. And then I stopped.

For one thing, it struck me that if Guy and Verbenia really were at the orphanage, they were probably okay there. And that if they weren't there now, me rushing over there wasn't going to help find them.

For another thing, I saw Vivian, heading across the front grounds toward the residential wing. And I had lots of questions for her. Plus, with my idea about where Guy and Verbenia might be, I had a little carrot to dangle before her to get her to talk to me.

Not real nice, I know, thinking of using emotional blackmail to get Vivian to talk. But I had to find out about her connection to Lewis and Tyra.

I followed her. She went into the residents' building, and I went in too, right behind her. It was totally quiet. I glanced at my watch. Nearly noon. Everyone was at lunch.

She turned left down a hall, opened a door that was locked at night but not in the day. I followed and opened the door a wee crack, peeking down the hall at her. This was the women's wing, smaller than the men's, since there were always more men that lived here than women. Autism happens more often in men.

I watched Vivian, working at a door. Verbenia's room, I guessed. But Vivian wasn't using a key to open it. She was picking the lock—which meant for whatever reason she hadn't wanted to get Don's permission and the key to go to Verbenia's room.

I waited until Vivian got Verbenia's door open, glanced around, went inside. Then I opened the women's wing door, slipped through, and shut the door behind me very quietly.

I went on down to the door Vivian had just picked open. I didn't bother to knock. I just opened it, and stepped in.

Verbenia's room, like Guy's and all the other residents' rooms here, was small, but comfortable. It had a desk with some drawing paper, and a box of colored pencils, neatly on the desk's center. On a bulletin board over the desk were drawings—perfect still life copies of vegetables and flowers and fruits. The drawings were signed with a childish "V" that didn't match the sophistication of the art.

There were a few simple light fixtures, attached to the walls rather than freestanding. A private bathroom and a nicely sized closet. And a twin bed, made up with a cream crocheted coverlet and an assortment of pastel pillows.

Sitting on the end of the bed was Vivian, staring at me, her hands in her sweater pockets.

The way she stared at me should have been a warning—turn and run, Josie. But I'd come for some answers. So I started to speak—found instead my voice was suddenly gone and my mouth was hanging open.

So Vivian spoke first, in a very flat, very quiet voice, "You followed me. Why did you follow me, Josie?"

"I have a few questions, and I think I can help us both find our loved ones, and—"

Her right hand moved around in her sweater pocket. Then, suddenly, it emerged, holding a gun. Which was pointed right at me.

Oops. I'd identified my suspect, cornered her to ask questions, and managed to get myself cornered instead by being—I admit it—stupid in my overeagerness. That seems to happen to me a lot, and I get myself into messy jams. This was the messiest, though, I'd ever gotten into, seeing as how it involved a gun being pointed at me. Never follow your murder suspect into a closed room, especially if you have no weapon and if it stands to reason that she (being a murder suspect) might.

I swallowed, hard. "Don't you, um, don't you even want to know what my questions are?"

Vivian smirked. "You brought her here."

"Tyra?"

"Of course, Tyra. And she's why Verbenia's missing."

"Tyra's dead, Vivian. I don't think she could make Verbenia disappear after she's already dead. People don't just pop up again after they're dead and kidnap people." I thought, for an uncomfortable moment, of Mrs. Oglevee, who did seem to keep popping up and bugging me. But only in my dreams.

"No. But if Tyra Grimes hadn't come back to town, then I wouldn't have had to—" Vivian stopped, shook her head.

"Never mind. Her coming to town led to Verbenia leaving, and you're the one who got her to town. For that, you're going to die. I figured it could wait until I found Verbenia and carried out my plans for her, but today will do just as well."

I crossed my arms, trying to look unconcerned by that last comment. Truth be told, I was about to pee my pants, and crossing my arms was an instinctive self-protection gesture.

"Just like you killed Tyra—and Lewis?" I said.

Vivian gasped. Her gun wavered. "I—I didn't kill Lewis. I would never have killed Lewis."

That surprised me. Hole number one in my theory. "Okay—but you killed Tyra?"

"Yes." She sighed as if she was bored. "You're really annoying, you know that? All I wanted to do was check whether Verbenia had taken the bag I'd packed for her with her, before I go out searching for her. Then you come in here, with all your questions, and I've got to deal with you now instead of later."

"You didn't have to pull the gun on me now if you wanted to give me another day or so to live," I said, starting to feel a bit annoyed myself. "And what bag are you talking about? Wait—did you have something to do with Guy and Verbenia disappearing?"

"No, you idiot!" Vivian snapped. "I was planning on moving her from here today! I had packed a bag of her essentials yesterday. It's still here. I wanted us to leave without anyone knowing ahead of time that we were going. I was going to take her with me, to move out west—" She stopped, shook her head. "Enough of this. We're going to walk out slowly because I obviously can't kill you here, but I will if I have to, so don't try anything funny—"

"No," I said.

"No?" Vivian echoed, clearly disbelieving. She was standing now, waving the gun in my face. "You're saying no when I have this gun pointed right at your nose?"

"Yes," I said. "I mean yes, I'm saying no. No. No. No. I'm not going to be pushed around by you."

"I killed Tyra. I'll kill you—"

"No, you won't. Because I know where Verbenia and Guy are." I looked as confident as I could, considering I didn't really know for sure—I just had a pretty good theory—and considering the gun in my face.

"Then—you'd—better—tell—me—"

"No."

"No?"

"That's right. No, I won't tell you. Not until you answer a few questions for me."

For a long minute, Vivian and I just stared at each other, neither of us budging.

Finally, she sighed. "All right. We're going to my car. You're going to drive me to wherever they are, and I'll answer your questions—"

"Is it a stick shift?"

"What?"

"Your car—is it a stick shift?"

"Yes."

"Then we'll have to take mine—actually my boyfriend's, since mine has a flat tire out on Sweet Potato Ridge, because I don't drive stick shifts, although I did manage to drive a bookmobile earlier in a high-speed car chase, and—"

"All right, all right. We'll take your boyfriend's car." I think that's what Vivian said. Her teeth were gritted so hard, it was tough to be sure.

We got out to Owen's car without anyone noticing us, although Vivian stayed right behind me, gun in my back, sweater draped over her hand to hide the gun.

I was sweating and trembling and needing to pee and throw up, all at once.

I had Tyra's killer—well, she really had me—and she was going to answer questions for me, but then what? Then she'd probably kill me. Because I had no intention of taking her to the orphanage. If Verbenia and Guy were there, I'd be putting them at risk.

I got in the car, crawling over from the passenger's side, at Vivian's insistence, with Vivian right behind me. I got to the driver's side, strapped in, and waited for Vivian to do the same. She kept her sweater-wrapped hand pointed right at me.

Maybe, I thought, maybe after I got my answers I could drive us to Owen's. Owen wasn't there, so I wouldn't be putting him at risk. Maybe once I got there, I'd think of a way out of this. Or maybe I'd just get shot.

"Start driving," Vivian said.

I put the car in gear, pulled out of Stillwater. I waited until we were out on the road to ask my first question.

"You and Lewis and Verbenia and Tyra—you're all connected somehow, aren't you?"

To my surprise, Vivian gave a sharp laugh. "That's not what I expected you to ask. I thought you'd want to know why I'd killed your poor dear hero, Tyra."

"Well, I figure you're connected somehow, and so is Lewis, and that the connection is why you killed them both. Although you say you didn't kill Lewis—"

"Of course I didn't!" She sighed. "All right—here's the explanation. You figure we're all connected? Well, you're only too right. Verbenia and I—we're Tyra's daughters."

I did a double take that made the car sway. Vivian laughed harshly. "Yes—dear Tyra was our mother. She's actually from around here. She got pregnant, years ago, by Lewis's father. Had us, dumped us literally on Lewis's father's doorstep, around the time Lewis was fourteen. About two years later, after Lewis's father—our father—died, Lewis's mother had us put off in an orphanage. It was terrible—especially after people began to be aware that Verbenia was—different.

"Then, for a long time, we were apart, Verbenia put in an institution, me going from foster home to foster home. Lewis, somehow, kept track of us. When his mother died, when he was in his early twenties, he tracked us down. Finally found a decent foster home for me, a decent place for Verbenia. Eventually, he got Verbenia into Stillwater, and I made a life up in Columbus. He has been a true brother to us. And everything was pretty good—until Tyra came to town."

My hands tightened around the steering wheel. I resisted the temptation to look at Vivian—I knew she was crying just from how her voice sounded. I focused on the road—going just under the speed limit, taking a few back-country road detours to Owen's. She didn't live down here and wouldn't know the difference until we'd been driving for a while, when she might get suspicious about why it was taking us so long to get anywhere. I just listened to Vivian's story, which, now that we were on the road, she'd settled into telling. Maybe she needed to tell someone the whole story—even if she was planning to kill that someone (me) as soon as she could.

"Then you got Tyra to come to town. I didn't know, of course, that she was my mother. I never wanted to know who our mother was—she'd abandoned us, knowing we wouldn't have much of a life. It was only thanks to Lewis that we each have decent lives at all. All I ever knew was that we'd been abandoned, and Lewis had rescued us."

Vivian fell silent. Maybe she was thinking about Lewis, what he had meant to her and Verbenia. After a bit, I said softly, "So you haven't known all along about Tyra Grimes being your mother?"

Vivian stayed silent, and I thought maybe she wasn't going to answer my question. Finally she said, "No. Until a few weeks ago, all Lewis had ever told me was that our mother had left us with his father, that he was our half-brother, and that he wanted to make things right by us. Maybe it was because he and Hazel couldn't have kids. Or maybe just because he was a good man. Anyway, Lewis came to me shortly after you sent your letter to Tyra. He said Tyra had grown up here with a different name. That's when he told me about her being our mother.

"Then, after she got here, he came to her party at your apartment." He must have come after I left, I thought. "He got her aside, told her they needed to talk privately. She told him to pick her up on the edge of town, after the party. She thought she could charm him—maybe pay him—into going along with her plan. You see, Tyra was having troubles with her company—and damaging news about her use of illegal labor to create her stupid T-shirts was about to break.

"So her plan was to donate a whole bunch of money to Stillwater, then have a press conference, announcing Verbenia and me as her long lost daughters. She was going to play on the sympathy factor—give her story a good spin, by presenting herself as poor Tyra Grimes, wanting to make things right for her daughters, that was the only reason she'd tried to make more money. Hah!"

Vivian was silent again, and I thought about what she'd said, as I turned down yet another country lane. "How did she know what had become of you and Verbenia?"

"She'd hired a private eye a few years back to find out whatever had become of us," Vivian said, as if the fact meant nothing. I wondered, though. I thought about how Tyra had talked about relationships on the way to Stillwater. I thought about the pictures she had in her purse—especially the one of two young girls torn from a magazine.

Maybe she'd dreamed of having a family . . . or of the daughters she'd left behind. Maybe there'd been just a bit of her that wanted to know what became of the children she'd abandoned so long ago—before she even became Tyra Grimes. Maybe.

"Are we ever going to get to wherever we're going?" Vivian asked suddenly.

"Yes," I said. "It's just, it's this place, out in the country that Guy likes to go to every time we have an outing away from Stillwater. So I'm sure he's there. With Verbenia. So, go on. Tyra comes to town with this plan—"

"Yes," Vivian said. "And Lewis and Tyra get together. As she's telling him her plan, he drives her to this wooded land he owns. You know where I mean?"

"I know," I said.

"He forced her out into the woods, she told me. His plan was to kill her. But the stress got to him. He started to have a heart attack, dropped his gun. She grabbed it and shot him. How could she? Why didn't she call for help?"

Because, I thought, Tyra was scared and knew she'd gotten into a situation she couldn't charm her way out of. Yes, she should have called for help when she saw Lewis was helpless. Instead, she'd panicked.

"Tyra threw the gun into the woods," Vivian went on. "When she heard someone coming, she went back by Lewis and pretended to be knocked out until you found her." Vivian gave a little sob.

Vivian's story made more sense than Elroy killing Lewis, though. Elroy must have found Lewis's gun, picked it up without thinking about what he was doing. And of course Chief Worthy had never bothered to check to be sure that the gun was Elroy's because it just seemed so obvious that Elroy had killed Lewis. And Tyra . . . Tyra had pretended to be knocked out the whole time I'd searched through her purse and used her cell phone to call 9-1-1.

"How do you know all this?" I asked.

"She told me! After Lewis's funeral, after she had the nerve to show up and act that way, I followed her back to the apartment. I told her who I was, and she just stared at me a long minute, then laughed. I begged her not to do this to Verbenia. Not to get all this media attention pointed at her. I'd already told Verbenia we would be leaving today to go out west, that I'd find us someplace nice to live, and she was really upset. But without Lewis to protect us, I wanted to get us away, somewhere that Tyra could never find us. I told her that I was taking Verbenia away, and she got angry. She slapped me!

"I grabbed a lamp, threw it at her. It knocked her out. One of her T-shirts was lying on the couch. I grabbed some scissors laying out on the desk, cut up the T-shirt. And I strangled her. I thought it was a fitting end for her. I figured someone might find out the truth later. So I decided I had to take Verbenia as soon as possible and get away. I've gotten all the money we'll need—and this gun, in case someone tries to stop us."

It struck me then, with Tyra being Vivian's mother and my second-cousin-once-removed, Vivian and I (and Verbenia and I) were third cousins, which made Lewis my half-third-cousin . . .

Suddenly, Vivian moved the gun from its cozy spot under her sweater, up to my temple.

"I've told you the story. Now get me to where my sister is. And she'd better be there, or I'm killing you on the spot."

So much for family ties saving me. This woman had killed her mother—granted, a mother in name only . . . a mother who'd abandoned her . . . who only came back in her life to use her and her sister for her own means . . . but still. I had no doubt Vivian Denlinger would kill me.

We pulled into Owen's driveway a few minutes later. The bookmobile was gone. I knew Owen had said he'd go off with

Winnie—and he always keeps his word—but I hoped that for once he hadn't. That he'd charge out, my white knight, to save me. I really did. I was desperate. I was sweating. I was terrified. Being saved by my boyfriend seemed like a great choice over being shot to death. I could show my liberated side later, by picking up the tab for a celebration dinner of turkey hot shots and cherry pie over at Sandy's Restaurant.

I parked in front of the fourth garage over. I looked over at Vivian, offered a wavering smile. "Um, this is it, my um, boyfriend's house. Guy likes to come here."

"To your boyfriend's house?" Vivian did not sound convinced. And she did not look amused.

"My boyfriend has, um, lots of books. Guy likes to count them."

Vivian nodded—satisfied for the moment. It wasn't true, but it was something that, as the sister of an autistic woman, she'd find believable.

Then she thought of something else. "Are you trying to set me up? What if your boyfriend's here?"

"Actually, he told me he's spending the whole day at the library today." Which was kind of true.

We got out of the car. I led the way to the front door, Vivian staying right behind me, gun in my back. I didn't knock or ring the bell. I just took hold of the doorknob, hoping that Owen had left it unlocked, like he usually did—not because of the safety of Paradise, but because he kept forgetting to lock it. In case he was still here, I didn't want Owen coming to the door, face to face with a gun.

I opened the door, but didn't step in. Running was still an option. It would work better if I was outside, I figured, than inside Owen's tiny house.

"Guy," I called cheerfully and loudly. In case Owen was still here, I wanted Owen to realize I was here—and not acting quite myself. Of course Guy wouldn't be here, and Owen would know that. "Yoo-hoo, Guy, it's Josie. You counting the books in there with Verbenia?"

Vivian gave me a shove, making me trip my way into the house. She shut the door behind us. We both stared at the front room, filled with books, but no Guy. And, of course, no Verbenia.

"You said they'd be here. You'd better not be lying, Josie Toadfern, or I swear I'll kill you right here, leave your body for your stupid boyfriend to find." She was shrieking. If Owen were here, he'd have heard her by now. But no, Owen wasn't rushing out to save me. I was alone with Vivian.

"Well, let's just check the kitchen, okay?" I started moving in that direction. "Guy really likes to eat."

I was thinking maybe I could make a dash out of the kitchen door without getting shot, circle around to Owen's car, and speed off.

She followed me into the kitchen. I groaned. I'd forgotten that the kitchen table plus Owen's vacuum—still attached by an extension hose to Billy's Cut-N-Suck on the table— blocked my way to the door.

Vivian's eyes narrowed. She lifted the gun, pointing it right at my face.

And then Owen came in. He was yawning and scratching his head, his eyes still half shut. "Josie, that you? I was taking a nap—"

Vivian whirled around, turning her gun on him. Suddenly, Owen's eyes got wide. His jaw fell slack.

Here was my white knight, frozen in place.

So I did the only thing I could think of to do. I quickly undid the hose from the vacuum, grabbed it by the end, and whirled. Billy's Cut-N-Suck whacked Vivian's head on the first go round, knocking her out, cold.

Epilogue

It's taken awhile, but life in Paradise has pretty much gone back to normal.

That afternoon at Owen's, I had to call the Paradise Police Department a few times before I convinced the dispatcher I wasn't a crank phone caller just pretending to really have Tyra's killer, felled by Billy's Cut-N-Suck, in Owen's kitchen. Sooner or later, the dispatcher believed me, and Chief John Worthy came out. Vivian eventually came to, refusing to speak until Verbenia was found.

And Verbenia was found, along with Guy, out at the old orphanage, just like I'd guessed. No one is sure how they got there, or if Guy followed Verbenia, then led her to the orphanage when she couldn't think of where else to go, or if they planned it together, or why, exactly, they went. Don's theory is that Verbenia probably wanted to leave to hide somewhere until Vivian went out west, so Verbenia could then go back to Stillwater. It's not a theory Vivian would like.

Vivian, though, upon learning her sister was okay, wept gratefully. At first she told Chief John Worthy that she'd killed Tyra because she was an unhappy fan, frustrated by too many fancy napkin folds and window toppers that didn't quite work out. She was trying to protect Verbenia, still.

I could understand that—but I had to tell the whole story to Chief Worthy anyway, because Elroy and Billy were still in jail for murder.

He didn't seem to believe my story.

But Paige came forward, and confessed that she knew of Tyra's plan to make an announcement having to do with Stillwater in order to turn attention away from her business problems, although she hadn't known the specifics. Don verified that Tyra had been about to make a huge donation—she'd just needed a few days for her accountants to pull together the funds—although he didn't know about Vivian and Verbenia being her daughters and wouldn't have accepted the donation if he'd known of her plans. And Hazel confirmed Vivian and Verbenia's relationship to Lewis and Tyra.

So, finally, Vivian confessed the whole story, just as she told it to me. A short version of it got out, and the press had a field day with it, interviewing everyone they could think of about this shocking revelation about Tyra Grimes's real life, including each other. Stillwater hired guards to keep the media away from Verbenia.

And then, all at once, the reporters left. Some of them trailed after Vivian when she was taken to the women's penitentiary to await her trial. The rest just took off—kind of like a flock of starlings that land somewhere, and then suddenly take off again, for no apparent reason. Maybe there was news elsewhere to find. Maybe, with Tyra being dead, the story wasn't as interesting as it would have been if she'd been alive.

In any case, the reporters left. Billy was let out of jail. He and Paige came to see me, the same day I reopened my laundromat, to let me know Billy was going with Paige back to

New York, where together they were going to start a shelter for unwed runaway pregnant teens—kind of a way, for Paige, of making up for what she called "wasted time" working for Tyra. And definitely a cause Billy could believe in.

Guy and Verbenia settled nicely back into Stillwater.

The day Billy and Paige left town was also the day of the grand re-opening of Elroy's Gas Station. Nothing about it has changed, except that Elroy sells tuna fish salad sandwiches again. And he seems to have a new confidence that suits him well, most recently shown when he announced at our last Chamber of Commerce meeting that he'd learned from the state's travel commission that removing Paradise from the official state of Ohio map had been a mistake due to a computer glitch. Paradise is set to reappear in the next edition of the map.

The sign and pole at Sandy's Restaurant got fixed, so Sandy's happy again.

As for me, well, I repainted the front window of my laundromat with a toad sitting happily on a fern, and the name of my business spelled the right way: Toadfern's Laundromat. I gave the cappuccino maker away.

Owen and I are still dating. And I'm liking his kisses more and more.

I see Winnie every Wednesday, on the bookmobile.

My insurance company finally took care of the broken window in Billy's old apartment, which is for rent.

My hair has grown back to a nice little blond fuzz that gets a few stares, but that feels really nice now that it's summer, so I've shucked my baseball cap for the duration of warm weather.

And just the other day, I found right outside my apartment door a package of homemade peanut butter cookies. No note.

The logical thing is to assume they're from Becky, since I did her family's laundry even while my laundromat was closed, and Becky's known for making great cookies and leaving them as thank yous for people.

But logic isn't always what's needed, I find. Sometimes a leap of fancy helps. Or a leap of faith.

Either way, I'm packing up a nice picnic lunch, just for me and Guy, just because it's a nice Sunday afternoon. We'll have tuna salad sandwiches from Elroy's gas station. A few peanut butter cookies. And Big Fizz diet colas. We'll take our picnic out to the old orphanage.

Maybe, while Guy stares at the orphanage, thinking whatever it is he thinks when we're there, I'll think a little too about all that's happened.

But mostly, I'm just going to enjoy this perfectly beautiful, sunny, bright day in Paradise.

PARADISE ADVERTISER–GAZETTE

Josie's Stain Busters

by Josie Toadfern
Stain Expert and Owner of Toadfern's Laundromat
(824 Main Street, Paradise, Ohio)

As most of you already know, I'm writing this month's column right after one of the biggest weeks of mayhem ever in Paradise. But now that the TV news trucks have pulled out of town, it's time to take a deep breath and consider lessons learned (stain-wise) from these events.

Note: A hearty congratulations to Mrs. Beavy, one of my Toadfern Laundromat regulars and our town historian, for her fine interview on WMAS-TV's Masonville Nightly News regarding how recent events are like nothing that's ever happened here before.

I'm sure Hazel Rothchild will do a fine job as the new owner of Rothchild's Funeral Parlor. Already, she's creating several new promotions, including a free gift to all who pre-pay for a casket (installment plans available): *What To Bring When Loved Ones Die: Recipes from Paradise's Finest Wakes and Funerals.*

I for one hope Hazel's cookbook includes her fine recipe for lime Jell-O salad. And I'm sure she won't mind if I share a bit of laundry lessons learned from having done Lewis's shirts for many years:

1. Pre-treat heavily sweat-stained shirts with a mixture of equal parts water, dish washing soap, and ammonia.
2. And pretreat ring-around-the-collar with shampoo—the cheaper the better. (*Note*: Wally's Drug Emporium up in Masonville is having a 50% off promotion on shampoo this week.)

May Lewis rest in peace.

On a brighter note, before all mayhem broke loose I was able to advise Becky Gettlehorn about how to get the mustard stain out of little Haley's new sundress—simply pre-treat mustard stains with a dab of glycerin. Becky tried it, and it made Haley's sundress look so new that Haley wore it to the Gettlehorn family reunion last weekend over at the Second Reformed Church of the Holy Reformation's fellowship hall.

Of course, none of us will ever forget our visitors, Tyra Grimes and her assistant, Paige Morrissey. We'll all miss Tyra's homemaking expertise, but I'm mighty proud I was able to give her good advice about laundering her favorite white blouse when she spilled some Big Fizz diet cola on it during a little tussle at my place.

Cola, tea, and coffee—as I told Tyra—are tannin stains, so don't pre-treat them directly with soap, because that may just set the stains in. Instead, wash as soon as possible in warm water. If a stain remains, re-wash in warm water with all-fabric bleach.

Fortunately, Tyra's favorite blouse was stain-free after she followed my advice. And I hear, from Paige Morrissey, that Tyra looked mighty fine decked out in it for her funeral up in New York. May Tyra also rest in peace.

Speaking of Paige, I'll admit that for a while I suspected her of foul play when she told me her sweater was stained with cocoa . . . but the stain looked a lot like dirt. I tested her claim by soaking her sweater in cold water. The stain didn't budge—as it would have with cocoa—but came right out when I washed it in hot water, because:

1. Cocoa stains fall in the protein category (along with blood, I might add). Presoak in cold water and then wash; if you wash something with a protein stain straight off in warm or hot water, you'll basically cook the stain right into the fabric.
2. On the other hand, soaking dirt-stained items in cold water won't do a bit of good. Instead, wash them in the hottest water the item can handle. (Always check care labels!)

As it turned out, Paige's sweater got dirty when she was helping Billy move some things around. Paige and Billy are doing just fine in New York, and ask me to tell Paradisites one and all "hello." And

Billy says to let everyone know he's still a Cut-N-Suck distributor, just in case anyone has home hair-cutting needs.

Until next month, may your whites never yellow and your colors never fade. But if they do, stop in and see me at Toadfern's Laundromat—Always a Leap Ahead of Dirt!

Want to be in the next
Josie Toadfern Mystery Novel?

Josie knows a lot about stains—but she's always willing to learn more! Send your best stain-fighting tip to Sharon Short, at www.sharonshort.com. She'll select her favorite and use it in the next Josie Toadfern mystery novel, and give you a hearty thank you in the acknowledgments. Deadline: August 15, 2003.